A Pose Before Dying

Books by Alex Erickson

Bookstore Café Mysteries
DEATH BY COFFEE
DEATH BY TEA
DEATH BY PUMPKIN SPICE
DEATH BY VANILLA LATTE
DEATH BY EGGNOG
DEATH BY ESPRESSO
DEATH BY CAFÉ MOCHA
DEATH BY FRENCH ROAST
DEATH BY HOT APPLE CIDER
DEATH BY SPICED CHAI
DEATH BY ICED COFFEE
DEATH BY PEPPERMINT CAPPUCCINO
CHRISTMAS COCOA MURDER
(with Carlene O'Connor and Maddie Day)

Furever Pets Mysteries
THE POMERANIAN ALWAYS BARKS TWICE
DIAL 'M' FOR MAINE COON

Cat Yoga Mysteries
A POSE BEFORE DYING

Published by Kensington Publishing Corp.

A Pose Before Dying

ALEX ERICKSON

Kensington Publishing Corp.
www.kensingtonbooks.com

ISBN: 978-1-4967-4737-2 (ebook)

ISBN: 978-1-4967-4736-5

First Kensington Trade Paperback Printing: June 2024

10 9 8 7 6 5 4 3 2 1

Printed in the United States of America

A Pose Before Dying

CHAPTER 1

A chorus of meows echoed throughout the room. Cat perches, scratching posts, toys, and just about everything a kitty could ever want filled the area. I had to keep a close eye on every step to keep from squashing a tail.

"Look at this one, Ash!" my best friend, Sierra Wahl, said as she scratched the chin of a scrawny tuxedo cat with a black splotch across his nose. "He's so cute! I'd adopt him right this instant if I thought Herman wouldn't eat him."

Herman was her tiger-striped monster of a cat that was the definition of a super chonk.

I flashed Sierra a smile that faded as soon as I turned away. Cats were everywhere, but they were supposed to be. Today was the grand opening of my cat yoga studio, A Purrfect Pose, and I was furiously trying to make sure I was ready.

I so wasn't ready.

"All right, you should have everything," Kiersten Vanhouser, head of the local animal shelter, said as she came in from the office. "Adoption forms are on your desk. They just need to be filled out and then they can be dropped off at the shelter or handed to me directly." She took me by the arm and led me out of the room, into the small hallway at the back of the building. "Are you going to be okay today?"

Was I? I'd been groomed my entire life to take over Branson Designs from my mother, or at least, to have a major share in the business once she finally called it quits. But instead of designing T-shirts and purses and designer masks like most of the rest of the family, I was here, surrounded by cats, waiting for what I hoped would be a full house of yoga enthusiasts.

Concern flashed across Kiersten's face before she all but shoved me into the small office across from the cat room. Sure enough, a stack of cat adoption forms were piled on the desk. "People will come. You'll do great."

"I have three preregistrations," I said, doing my best not to wail it as I sat in my office chair. "Three! And that's spread out through the entire weekend. What if no one shows up? I pushed back the grand opening until today in the hopes that more people would preregister, but . . ."

"Breathe." Kiersten massaged my shoulder. "You're doing a good thing. People will see that."

The panic ebbed as I sucked in deep breaths. This was just another big step in Ashley Cordelia Branson's series of major life changes. I had yet to fall flat on my face over the last few months, and if I kept a level head, I should be able to avoid doing so for the foreseeable future.

"I'm okay," I said. "Just a little overwhelmed."

"Take a minute more. I'll be right out there." She jerked a thumb toward the door, gave me a good once-over, and then Kiersten headed out to join Sierra with the cats.

Breathing easier, I adjusted the applications on my desk. A folded piece of paper sat beside the pile. On it, I'd scrawled the password to the security system because I had a horrible habit of forgetting things like that. I opened the top drawer of the desk and tucked the page inside where I could find it easily if I needed it.

"I've got this," I muttered before joining the others.

"Okay, if that little guy is still here in a week, I'm going to have a chat with Herman about getting him a brother." Sierra rose from her crouch after one last scratch behind the kitty's ears. "I really wish I could stay, but I've got to get to work."

"It's all right," I assured her. "I'll see you later?"

"Of course." Sierra pulled me into a hug. "I'm so happy for you."

"Good luck, Ash." Kiersten took Sierra's place. She gave me an extra squeeze before she released me. "If you need anything at all, I'll be at the shelter. Just give me a ring, okay?"

"Will do." Feeling more centered, I took a deep breath and let it out through my nose. "Thank you both for coming."

Sierra and Kiersten left, leaving me a few precious minutes to myself. Well, to myself and a dozen semi-well-behaved felines. My customers—if I had any—could adopt any of the cats they saw, cats who would be "helping" them with their yoga poses. If no one showed up, I'd be failing not just myself, but these poor kitties as well.

I double-checked to make sure the cats had clean litter and full water dishes before carrying a full trash bag out through the back door. The alley was blessedly quiet as I tossed the trash into the can, and I took a moment to just breathe before heading back inside.

At the front of the studio, I checked the display of yoga mats and water bottles emblazoned with the Purrfect Pose logo— the silhouette of a cat doing the half-moon pose—to make sure everything looked okay. To the back of the studio, shirts with the same logo hung, all available for purchase. It had taken a lot of begging to get my mom to agree to make the shirts for me, and I was glad she'd given in because I thought they'd turned out great.

My phone rang somewhere in the studio, and for a moment, my brain blanked on where I'd left it. I smacked my rear end where I usually kept it in my jeans pocket, but yoga pants didn't *have* pockets. I spun in a circle before I realized I could follow the sound. It led me to the tiny bathroom in the back where the phone sat on the edge of the sink from when I'd splashed water on my face earlier.

A quick glance at the screen caused me to smile.

"Hey, Alexi," I said, answering. "What's up?"

"Did I interrupt you?" my sister asked. "You sound out of breath. I didn't think you started until seven?"

"I don't. I've just been running around like a madwoman for the last twenty minutes, trying to make sure everything's ready."

"I should be there." Alexi—full name, Alexandra Lee Branson—was my older sister by four and a half years, and had succumbed to our mother's pressure to dedicate her life to Branson Designs, which, I assumed, was where she was now. "I can't believe Mom is acting like this."

"I can." I sighed as I walked to the large plate glass window that fronted the studio. I had to lean forward a little so I could look toward Branson Designs.

A large fountain dominated the square where many of the businesses of Cardinal Lake, Ohio, were located. Downtown was sleepy at this time of morning, but sure enough, I could see Alexi standing outside the family business, which was directly across the square and a little to my right from my studio. She was holding her phone to her ear and gnawing on her thumbnail.

"I see you." I waved, though she wasn't looking.

Alexi's head jerked up and she leaned to see past the fountain before she returned the wave. "It's all hands on deck here. Mom has turned into a dictator. She insisted everyone come in today and we're required to remain until noon. No breaks outside the building. No early lunches."

"Convenient."

"I swear she's going to do everything in her power to make sure you fail." Alexi sounded as annoyed by it as I felt. Cecilia Branson cared about one thing and one thing only.

No, make that two, actually: Cecilia Branson and money. It's the only reason she'd given in on the shirts.

"It's probably better that you're not here," I said, stepping away from the window before our conversation somehow conjured Mom. "I'm already nervous enough without an audience."

"Yeah, well, it still sucks. Mom needs to grow up." There was a rustle and then, faintly, "I'm coming." Another rustle. "I've been summoned."

"Usually, it's the demon who gets summoned, not the other way around."

Alexi chuckled. "Maybe I'll tell her you said that and see where it gets me. It's not like things can get much worse."

"Don't tempt fate," I said. "You're just asking for trouble now."

"Yeah, I know. Good luck today, Ash."

"Thanks." I was about to click off when I remembered something. "What are you doing tonight? About sevenish? The gang's getting together at Snoot's to celebrate." Whether we were going to be celebrating my success or failure had yet to be determined.

"Tonight? I've already got plans with Fiona, but we can stop by. Evan's going to be home with the kids, so I'm free to do what I want, and I plan on taking full advantage of it." Evan was her husband and often remained home while Alexi was running around town with her best friend.

"Sounds great. Hopefully Mom doesn't catch wind of it or she'll force you to work overtime, just so you can't have any fun."

"Ugh. Don't even say that. Talk to you tonight."

"Later."

We clicked off just as someone stepped up to the locked front door and tugged. Checking my Fitbit, I noted it was ten 'til seven, which meant it was time to start letting people in.

"Welcome to A Purrfect Pose!" I said as I unlocked and

opened the door. "Thank you so much for coming. I'm Ash Branson."

The woman appeared to be in her mid-forties with reddish-brown hair speckled with a heathy dose of gray at her temples. It was being held back by a yellow headband, which she adjusted as she walked through the door.

"Lulu," she said. "Lulu O'Brien. I hope I'm dressed properly for this." She eyed my yoga pants and tank top. She was wearing neck-to-ankle spandex, with a loose-fitting tee on top. She looked as if she belonged in an '80s workout video.

"You look great," I said. "You can come to class in anything you feel comfortable in."

"I want to do this right," Lulu said, patting herself down nervously. "I've been promising Cal that I'd start exercising more for the last two years and I don't want to mess it up."

The door opened and two more people entered. The man appeared to be in his mid-fifties while the woman looked a little bit younger. They were quickly followed by a pair of college-aged boys who looked dissimilar enough that I knew they weren't related, despite my first thought that it was a family coming through.

I showed Lulu the cats and told her she could go in and pet them if she'd like before I went over to the newcomers for introductions.

"Professor Valentine!" one of the younger guys, a good-looking, athletically built blond wearing a Def Leppard shirt that looked well-worn said as I approached. "I didn't expect to see you here."

The man turned with a faint scowl. He looked the two boys up and down, brow furrowing as he did, clearly not recognizing them.

"It's Topher, right?" the woman with Professor Valentine said. I placed her between forty, forty-five. "Topher . . . Newman?"

The boy beamed. "It is. I'm happy you remembered me."

The woman looked to the professor. "He was in my class last semester, Jonas." She turned to Topher. "English Lit, I believe?" "It was. And I had chemistry with Professor Valentine that same semester. We both did." He motioned toward his black-haired companion, who had yet to say a word.

A brief uncomfortable silence followed. It was apparent Jonas Valentine wasn't too keen on talking to students outside of class. Based on the Cardinal Lake University tee the dark-haired kid was wearing, I assumed they were all from the local college.

After a moment, Jonas turned away and muttered, "Let's go, Fay," to the woman next to him. He urged her away from the boys.

"Welcome to A Purrfect Pose," I said, stepping in. "Thank you so much for coming!"

"Are those the cats we're going to be using?" Topher asked, nodding toward a large window where you could look in on the kitties before bringing them out. It also gave the cats a view of the room so they could get used to all of the people.

"They are. Feel free to go in and pet them."

"Cool. Let's check them out, Chad."

Chad of the dark hair nodded to me, and then followed Topher over to the window.

I spent the next few minutes greeting newcomers and showing everyone around. Then, once I had everyone together in the same room, I explained the cost and adoption policies. It wasn't something I planned on doing every day, but figured it would be a good idea on my first-ever session.

"Individual classes are twenty dollars each, but you can pay monthly if you'd prefer, which would get you a discount." I pointed to the sign that listed the various options, including a yearly plan I expected no one would take. "If you adopt one of our cats, you get a forty-dollar voucher you can use on your own classes or give to a friend."

A man with the cherubic face of a middle-schooler and the thinning hair of a middle-aged man raised his hand. He'd introduced himself as George Wilkins when he'd arrived.

"Yes, George?"

"What if I pay for the three-classes-per-week monthly plan and then decide to come to a few extra classes?"

"You can pay for individual sessions if you wish," I said, excitement thrumming through me. My first early morning class was nearly full, which was far better than I'd anticipated. There were three younger women who'd come in together soon after the Valentines and the two male students, along with an older couple I feared might struggle with the more demanding poses, bringing the total up to eleven. I had room for fifteen.

Well, technically, I could fit more than that, but I didn't want to cause the cats too much stress by packing the place full of people.

Once everyone was settled on the pricing, and had chosen their spots on the floor, I released the felines. It wasn't a flood of fur and tails like you might expect, but the cats did come, albeit slowly.

This was the part that worried me. Yoga mats and cat claws didn't mix all that well. And with nearly a dozen strangers in the room, I wasn't sure how the cats would react.

I shouldn't have worried. As soon as the first cat stepped into the room and found someone to rub up against, the rest followed. Before I knew it, I was in front of the class, in command of a room full of fluffy tails and cooing students. Even the stern Professor Valentine softened when a chubby kitten batted at his ankles.

"Okay, let's start off with some stretches," I said once the initial excitement died down. Light, calming music played over speakers strategically placed at the front of the room as I demonstrated a few easy stretches to get everyone warmed up.

The morning session was meant to be a sort of wake-me-up, and was less demanding than the following classes. I figured that since I was the only instructor, I could use the slower pace so I didn't wear myself out before the last class of the day. Once the stretches were out of the way, it was time to get into the actual poses. I straightened, rolled my head on my neck once more, and then said, "Now, let's start with the crescent moon pose."

"You mean the *erd have a hasta la sauna?*" George said as he raised his arms above his head.

I hesitated before asking, "What was that?" I wasn't sure I'd heard him right.

"The *erd have a hasta la sauna.* It's the official term for the pose."

I opened my mouth, but snapped it closed again when I realized what he was trying to say. *The urdhva hastasana.*

I was debating how to respond when Lulu spoke up. "I'm sure she wants to make it easy on the rest of us." Sweat beaded her brow, despite only having gone through a couple of stretches. She wavered as she tried to hold the rather simple pose. "I'd never remember those *official* names, not when I have to put my full concentration on not falling over."

George grunted at that, but otherwise didn't comment as we flowed into the next pose.

A shriek caused me—and half the class—to jump. It was followed by a laugh.

"Sorry!" one of the younger women—a lithe girl named Kelly—said. "His tail tickled my nose." The cat, which happened to be the tuxedo Sierra had been so fond of earlier that morning, proceeded to butt his head against Kelly's supporting arm. She wavered, and then giggled in response.

We were working into more difficult poses when a bang from the back caused me to stagger and nearly fall. It took me a moment to realize the sound was the back door—the supposedly auto-locking back door—slamming closed.

"Excuse me a moment," I said, straightening. "Take a few minutes with the cats while I check on that."

"Whew," Lulu said, wiping her brow. Her hair was plastered to her face where it had come free from her headband. "Thank goodness! My legs feel like jelly."

I hurried past her, into the back, fearing that I'd find the back door hanging open and cats pouring out into the alley. What I found instead was my brother, Hunter, sitting on the floor, back against one of the shelving units there, with his head in his hands.

My stomach dropped. "What's happened now?" I asked him.

Hunter—or, if you talked to my mother, Reginald Hunter Daniels—looked up. "It's good to see you too, Sis."

I sighed. "Hunter."

He pushed his way to his feet. I was glad to note he didn't look rumpled, as he often did when he came to me for help.

And that's exactly what this was. I could tell by the way he wouldn't meet my eye, the way he ducked his head as soon as he was on his feet, that he wanted something from me.

"You know today is important," I told him. "It's my first-ever class here at A Purrfect Pose and I can't mess it up."

"I'm not here to mess anything up," Hunter said. "I just needed somewhere to sit for a few minutes."

"So you broke in through my back door?"

Hunter snorted. "I didn't break in. It was unlocked."

"No, it wasn't. The door locks as soon as it's closed." My eyes flickered past him, to the door, which was indeed firmly shut now that he was inside.

"Uh, yeah, it was." He rolled his eyes. "Whatever."

A part of me wanted to scream in frustration, but it was often like this with Hunter. He hadn't had it easy ever since Mom and Dad had split. Petty crimes. Not knowing where he fit in with the family. That didn't mean we didn't try to help him. I did whatever I could, as did Alexi, but Hunter was Hunter, and he did things his own way.

"Hunter," I said, fighting back a sigh. "Why are you here?" I peeked back out front. Most everyone seemed content to play with the cats, but Jonas was scowling at where his wife, Fay, and Topher were petting a Maine Coon who had rolled over onto his back to absorb the attention. Jonas checked his watch and then looked to the door as if thinking about leaving. "I really need to get back out there."

"Go ahead," Hunter said, waving a dismissive hand. "We can talk after. I'm in no rush."

And from the sound of it, I wasn't going to like this little chat. I rarely did.

I returned to the main room. Before I could resume the session, the front door opened and a harsh series of barks filled the space, causing nearly all the cats to flee to the back in a flurry of scrabbling claws and poofing tails.

"I told you it would be like this," a short, white-haired man with a high-pitched, whiny voice said. He was carrying a yippy Pomeranian under one arm. "Didn't I say that there were cats everywhere? Cats *meowing* and causing absolute mayhem. It's going to ruin me if it keeps up."

Behind him, a police officer entered. She was Black, short, and annoyed.

And I knew her extremely well.

"Mr. Leslie," Officer Olivia Chase said. "No one is meowing in here."

"But they were! I heard it." He shifted the Pomeranian from one arm to the other. "The dogs were having fits. How am I supposed to groom them when they're so riled up? You've got to do something."

Officer Chase rubbed at the bridge of her nose, and then turned to me. "Hello, Ash. I'm sorry about this, but Mr. Leslie has concerns."

Mr. Leslie's eyes widened at the familiar tone. "Wait. You *know* each other?"

Olivia answered before I could. "Her sister married my older brother, but that doesn't stop me from doing my job."

"That's not fair." Mr. Leslie stomped like an angry toddler, causing the Pomeranian to start barking again. "I want another officer to come down here and take care of this problem at once!"

"Mr. Leslie, there's nothing we can do. Ash isn't bothering anyone, nor are her cats. In fact, it's only *your* dog that's causing anyone distress as far as I can tell."

Mr. Leslie stepped back as if Olivia had struck him. "You *dare?* I called you to help me, and this is how I'm treated?" He turned on me and jabbed a finger at my face. "I will get you to close this place before the end of the month, mark my words. I won't let this stand." He spun on his heel. "Let's go, Ginger. These people aren't worth your breath."

Stunned silence filled the room as Mr. Leslie stormed out of the building. He paused outside, peered in through the plate glass window that fronted the studio, and, to my shock, he stuck his tongue out at me before he marched away.

"I . . . I . . ." Was flabbergasted. Stunned.

"Don't worry about him," Olivia said. "You should get back to work." She nodded toward the unsettled group of people waiting on me.

I caught Jonas Valentine glancing at his watch again, and this time, he made a point to make sure I noticed him doing it.

"Yeah," I said to Olivia, not sure if I should thank her or apologize to her. I settled on "I'll talk to you later?"

"Of course." She glanced around the room. "I think I might have to give this a try." And then she tipped her officer's cap and left.

I hurried across the room. "Give me one more second," I said to the group. "I'm sorry. I need to check on the cats."

"Take your time," one of the elderly women said. I'd completely forgotten her name in the chaos, which made me feel even worse.

I entered the back, but not to check on the cats like I'd said. Instead, I was looking for my brother. "Hunter?" I called, keeping my voice pitched low enough not to carry. "Please tell me you're not hiding from Olivia." I poked my head into the cat room. "Hunter?"

There was no answer because Hunter was no longer there. "Great. Just great," I muttered as I headed back out front. Thankfully, some of the younger cats followed me and resumed looking for attention. A vast majority had decided to stick to the back for now, and honestly, I didn't blame them.

"Is everything okay?" Lulu asked.

"Of course. Just a misunderstanding. Shall we continue?"

I was glad to note the Valentines were still there and they fell into their poses like everyone else.

With a worried glance toward where I'd last seen my brother, I resumed class.

CHAPTER 2

Glasses clinked from around the table at Snoot's on the Lake, a popular local pub that sat on the large man-made lake that the town was named for. A pop punk song I didn't know played over the speakers at a volume that was close to too loud, but no one minded. You didn't come to Snoot's to have serious conversations. You came to have fun.

And that's exactly what I planned on doing.

We were seated outside at one of the tables on the deck over the lake. The air was cool, crisp, and smelled of the water. Lights dotted the shoreline. Expensive houses were interspersed with rental cabins. Nearly every house and business had a dock. A small beach stretched across the western shore across from where we sat.

I swallowed a large gulp of a local brew and slammed my glass down onto the table. I wasn't tipsy, and I didn't plan on getting there, but boy did it feel good to relax.

"My legs hurt," I said with a grin.

"That's a good thing," Henna Korhonen said. She was blond, of Finnish heritage, with startling blue eyes. She leaned into her boyfriend, and member of our little gang, Aaron Kipp, who'd inherited a slightly darker skin tone from his Shawnee mother.

It made a compelling contrast to Henna's pale tones. "Was every session like ours?"

Henna and Aaron had come to the eleven-to-noon session, the last of the day on Fridays and Saturdays. The room had been so full, I'd had to turn away a few prospective customers, which was both bad *and* good.

"Pretty much," I said. "I have a dozen monthly commits already. If it keeps up like this every day, I might be able to afford to hire someone to run a few of the classes, giving me a break."

"I'm happy for you," Aaron said. His long, dark hair was pulled back in a loose ponytail that Henna played with like it was her own. "We all knew you would succeed."

"And I plan on showing up tomorrow. With friends." Sierra pointed at me. She'd changed out of her Snoot's uniform, having worked during the morning shift. It was a pub, but Snoot's opened early to serve coffee and breakfast before closing again until four. "You'd better not turn *us* away."

I laughed. "I'll try not to."

"What about you, Bri?" Aaron asked. "Want to join Henna and me tomorrow? You should see how bendy Ash can be." He waggled his eyebrows, which earned him a good-natured smack from Henna.

The last member of our group, and our most reclusive, antisocial member, Brianna Green, shrugged. The bangs of her brown hair hung low enough to nearly conceal her matching brown eyes and thick-rimmed glasses. "I'll think about it." After a moment, she burst into a wide smile. "Of course I'll go!"

"I'll make sure you get a corner spot," I said. "And the fluffiest kitty."

Bri shot me a thumbs-up.

"Speaking of kitties," I said, turning to Sierra, "your tuxedo has already been claimed. Herman will have to wait on getting a brother."

"Oh no." Sierra paused. "Well, I mean, I'm happy for the kitty, but I was really thinking about adopting him."

"Maybe if Herman had a friend, he wouldn't be so rotund," Aaron said.

"Maybe if you didn't open your mouth, you wouldn't say something so mean." Sierra shot out a lower lip in a fake pout.

"Did you see that guy glaring at us?" Henna asked. "He watched us all the way into A Purrfect Pose, and was still standing there afterward."

"The short guy? The one with the snowcap hairdo?" Aaron asked. "He was kind of creepy, if you ask me."

"That was Mr. Leslie," I said. "He owns Bark and Style, the dog grooming place beside my studio."

"He didn't seem very happy to have you there."

"He's not." I leaned forward. "He called the cops on me. Said the cats were meowing too loud."

"He didn't!" Sierra said. "Jordan called the cops?"

I gave her a blank look.

"Jordan Allen Leslie, though don't call him that to his face," she said. "It's either Mr. Leslie or J. Allen. My parents used to take Jasper to him, but stopped when he blew up at them after Jasper got into some briars and they asked Jordan to clean him up. He said they should have brushed him clean before bringing him."

"Isn't that his job as a groomer?" I asked.

"You'd think." Sierra shrugged. "From what I hear, he's good at what he does, but isn't the nicest guy around. I'm not surprised you had trouble with him, but to call the police?" She shook her head in wonder.

"Thankfully, Olivia was the one who showed up," I said. "Can you imagine what Chief Higgins would have done if he'd taken the call?"

"You wouldn't be sitting here right now, that's for sure," Aaron said.

I wish I could say Aaron's assessment was an exaggeration, but it wasn't. Chief Dan Higgins wasn't a fan of anyone on my father's side of the family. And Hunter . . . well, Hunter's constant run-ins with the law only made things worse.

Speaking of . . .

"Have any of you seen Hunter lately?" I asked. "He came into the studio today like he had something to say, but left before he said it."

Heads shook from around the table.

I finished off my beer and considered the empty glass. I was worried about Hunter, but then again, I was always worried about Hunter. Should I let his strange behavior ruin my day? I didn't think so, yet I couldn't stop wondering about him.

Why had he left so suddenly?

A new couple approached the table, arm in arm.

"Fiona!" Henna popped to her feet, nearly toppling Aaron over as she did. She threw her arms around the petite woman. "It's so good to see you."

"You too." Fiona accepted the hug and winked at me from past Henna's shoulder, though she had to stand on her tiptoes to do so.

Alexi gave them a bemused smile before turning to me. "How did it go today?"

"Great. You?"

"Mom was a tyrant. More so than usual." Alexi eyed Aaron's partially full beer. "I've spent the last hour recovering."

"That bad?" I asked.

"It's not your fault, though I'm sure Mom doesn't think so. She spent half the day pacing in front of the window, shooting glares across the street. Every time someone even hesitated outside your door, she'd fume."

"She wants me to fail that badly?" I asked. I could have been hurt, but with Mom, it was expected.

"She ranted at me that Branson Designs is her legacy, and that you should appreciate all she's done for you. She acted like yelling at me would somehow make you come back."

I could have pointed out that Mom hadn't started the business—her parents, Linda and Sterling Branson, had—but Alexi already knew that. And when Mom had first taken over after they'd retired, she'd struggled to make ends meet. It was the pandemic that had changed her fortunes. Online sales of her designer masks had gone through the roof, and before we knew what was happening, Branson Designs was a household name in Cardinal Lake and beyond.

I wish I could say that Mom's self-centered behavior was new, brought on by her sudden success, and that it would eventually wear off, but nope. It was a family trait, passed down through generations of Bransons, that had somehow missed her children, much to her infinite dismay.

Fiona and Henna were deep in conversation, so I sidled up closer to Alexi while I had the chance.

"Have you seen Hunter today?" I asked her.

"No." She frowned. "Why?"

"I'm not sure. He came to me today and was acting funny. When Olivia showed up in full uniform, he beat a hasty retreat."

"You think he's in some sort of trouble?" Before I could answer she held up a hand. "Honestly, I don't think I want to know. Hunter will do Hunter and Olivia will bail him out of trouble like always."

"But if he's avoiding her . . ."

"Then I doubt you want to get involved." She paused. "But I'll talk to Evan tonight and see if he's talked to his sister lately. Maybe he can fill me in."

"Thanks."

Fiona bussed Henna's cheek and then rejoined Alexi. "Hi, Ash. Congrats on your place. I can't wait to see it."

"We are going to join you on Monday night," Alexi said. "The class starts at six, right?"

"Seven," I corrected her. "Seven until eight."

"We'll be there," Alexi said with a firm nod. "Evan has already said he's fine with making sure the kids get their homework done without me." Alexi and Evan's children, Lily Rose and Philip, were five and six, respectively. I couldn't imagine they had much homework at that age, but what did I know? I didn't have kids of my own, and didn't plan to for a very long time. Being in my mid-twenties, I felt I was too young for them.

And busy.

"You don't have to if you don't want to," I said. "Mom won't like it if you show more support for me than you already have."

"Which makes it all the more important that I do." Alexi winked at me. "We're going to run. I'll see you Monday if I don't talk to you before."

"I'll be waiting," I said.

Fiona took Alexi's arm, and together, they headed for the door that led back into the pub proper, heads nearly touching as they spoke.

As soon as they were gone, I picked up my empty glass. "I'm going to get something to drink." I considered. "Something nonalcoholic. I've got to get up early tomorrow."

"Bring me a coffee?" Henna asked as she plopped back down next to Aaron. He immediately put his arm around her.

I nodded, and after making sure no one else wanted anything, I went inside and headed for the bar.

Snoot's was packed near wall to wall, so the going was slow. The place was busy most of the time, but the local college caused the numbers to swell whenever class was in session. It was why I thought A Purrfect Pose was a good idea. A constant flow of students, along with vacationers come to see the lake, as well as the locals, could equal a never-ending supply of yoga enthusiasts and dabblers.

Yes, that meant I would have occasional lulls, especially during winter break when the beach was closed. And yes, that meant I had to hope that each new batch of incoming college students would contain a few who would want to do yoga with cats tickling their noses and ruining their mats. I thought it would work, and so far, after one day, it seemed as if I'd been right.

I waved to one such person, a girl named Brittany, who'd come for the cats more than the yoga, and had paid up front for the monthly, three-classes-a-week plan. She hesitated, as if not recognizing me, before returning the wave.

I reached the bar and ordered a pair of coffees, both black, though I normally preferred sugar and creamer in mine. I figured I could use the extra kick so I didn't fall asleep on the way home.

"Ashley?"

I turned at my name to find two people I knew approaching.

"Drew." I accepted a hug from my ex-boyfriend before I turned to his current girlfriend. "Ginny. It's good to see you."

Ginny Riese made a face like she might be sick as she muttered something that might have been, "You too," or could easily have been a word that started with an *F*.

To say Drew Hinton and I had a complicated relationship would be an understatement. We'd met in kindergarten, and had been inseparable for years afterward. Friendship turned into something deeper, more meaningful, and by high school, we'd already been considered a couple for a year. We graduated still a couple, and within a month, we'd moved in together with plans to get married, have the requisite two kids, and so on and so forth.

And then I made a series of life-changing decisions, which included breaking it off with Drew.

It wasn't that I just up and decided to leave him one day; it had been brewing for years. I'd been doing exactly what my mother had wanted me to do without thinking about what it was that *I* wanted. It wasn't Drew's fault. He'd been my best friend before we'd started dating, and we were still friends to this day. He understood that I wanted a fresh start, and that staying with him would keep me from doing that. He was hurt, sure, but he did what a true friend would do and stuck by my side, even when it was hard.

Ginny had swooped in almost immediately. She'd wanted to date Drew since we were freshmen, and had made it abundantly clear throughout high school that she thought I wasn't good enough for him. I suppose, in some ways, I'd proved her right.

"I heard about your studio opening. The one with the cats," Drew said. "Congratulations."

"Thank you. It's only been a day, but it's been a success so far."

"That's great to hear." He hugged me again, causing old memories to resurface. I leaned into him briefly, relishing his closeness before stepping back. "Ginny and I were thinking of taking a class sometime."

"Really?" I asked, looking to Ginny. She didn't appear as if she wanted anything to do with A Purrfect Pose, but when Drew's eyes landed on her, her grimace turned into a dopey smile.

"Really," Drew said. "I want to support you. I know how hard you've worked for this."

"You don't need to do that," I said. "Not if you don't want to."

"Of course I do," Drew said as the bartender, who tonight was the owner himself, Snoot, set my two black coffees on the bar. "That reminds me." He put a hand to his stomach. "I'm about to swim away. Wait here?" he asked Ginny.

I picked up my coffees. "It was good to see you, but I've got to get these back to the table." I raised the mugs in salute. "Drew. Ginny."

"I'll see you soon," Drew said before he leaned forward and gave me a quick kiss on the cheek. "And good luck with the yoga!" He hurried toward the bathroom.

I started to return toward the deck and my table, but Ginny stepped in front of me, her eyes hard.

"I know what you're trying to do."

I blinked at her. "Carry these coffees back to my friends?"

"No." She ground her teeth. "Drew is *mine*. You can't have him back."

"I don't want him back." I tried to step around her, but Ginny mirrored my movement and glided into my path.

"Don't lie to me. I know you do. Everyone wants him." She glanced around the room like she expected to find a bunch of salivating women following Drew back to the bathroom. "I will do everything in my power to ruin you if that's what it takes to make you go away."

"Ginny," I said with a sigh. "I have no interest in Drew. He's my friend, a good one, and I don't want to lose him as a friend, but as a boyfriend? No. I don't want that."

"You do." She said it like she knew it as a fact. "You'd better watch yourself, Ash." She spun on her heel and marched away.

The petty part of me wanted to shout something after her, but it would be like shouting at a wall. Ginny would believe what she wanted to believe. Antagonizing her would only make her that much more unbearable. Trust me; I knew from experience.

I turned away from her, took one blind step, and ran directly into a brick wall made of denim, flannel, and muscle.

Hot coffee sloshed out of the mugs, onto my hands. I yelped and jumped back, causing more coffee to spill, some of which landed on the aforementioned denim.

"I'm so sorry!" I said, somehow managing not to drop the mugs. "I didn't see you there."

The wall—or more accurately, the square-jawed, well-built Greek god in cowboy attire—had his arms spread outward, and was looking down at the wet stain on his jeans. There was a moment when I thought he might pick me up and chuck me across the room like a bale of hay before he smiled.

"It's quite all right," he said. His voice was strong, but kind, with no hint of a country-boy accent. "I wasn't watching where I was going either."

I set the mugs down on the bar and shook the coffee from my hands. Snoot appeared, as if by magic, and handed me a damp washcloth. I immediately offered it to the hunky stranger.

"Thank you." He wiped at his jeans, and then shrugged. "It'll come out in the wash."

"Are you okay?" I asked him. "You're not burned, are you?"

"No, I'm fine." He took one of my slightly scalded, red hands and looked it over. "You?"

"I'm good." I let him hold on to my hand for a heartbeat longer than I probably should have before extracting it from his grip. "Do you want me to get you anything? A beer, maybe? I feel bad."

"Don't. It was an accident, and accidents happen." He paused, frowned. "Don't I know you from somewhere?"

I looked him up and down, eyes most definitely lingering where they shouldn't, before I shook my head. "I don't think so."

He considered it, and then snapped his fingers. "You're the woman who opened the yoga studio. The one with the cats."

"I am." This time, I offered my hand, longing for him to take it once more. "Ash Branson."

We shook. His grip was strong, but not too strong. "Walker Hawk."

I raised my eyebrows at him.

He laughed. "I know, I know. It sounds like I walked out of one of those romance novels you see at Walmart." He struck a pose, hand on his cowboy hat, head tipped low. He peeked at me out of the corner of his eye. "You'll have to imagine my shirt is hanging open to get the full effect."

Oh boy, did I *not* need to do that right then. I had to fight to keep from fanning myself off. "Impressive," I said, happy that my voice didn't squeak or crack.

He chuckled, righted himself. "My parents didn't think about how the name would follow me all my life. They named me after a character in their favorite show."

"Are they from Texas?"

"Nah, just unaware that I'd have to live life explaining my name to everyone I meet."

I winced. "I know how it feels. My middle name is Cordelia."

"Ouch."

Silence followed where we just stared at one another. Admittedly, Walker Hawk wasn't bad to look at, so staring was warranted. I vaguely noted Snoot stealing the half-spilled coffee mugs away and replacing them with fresh ones.

"I should let you get back to your friends," Walker said, nodding toward the table where said friends were openly staring through the doorway.

"Yeah, I should. It was good to meet you, Walker."

"You too, Ash." He paused. "I might stop in sometime and see what this cat yoga thing is all about." And then he walked away.

I took a moment to admire the retreating view, which vanished into the crowd far too soon, before I scooped up the coffees with a thanks to Snoot, and carried them back to the table.

"Oh. My. God. Ash!" Sierra was just about dancing. "Who was *that?*"

"Walker Hawk," I said, handing Henna her coffee. It was then that it dawned on me to wonder how he'd known that I was there with my friends. I didn't recall saying anything to him.

Then a new thought:

Had he been watching me?

I wasn't sure if I should be flattered or creeped out.

"That sounds . . . manly," Sierra said as Henna nodded. "What did he want?"

"He was just being nice," I said. "I spilled coffee on him."

Bri sucked in a breath. "Not a great first impression."

"You should go for it," Aaron said. Once again, Henna agreed with a nod. "You need to move on, leave your past in the dust." He paused, and then explained. "I saw you talking to Drew."

"And Ginny," Sierra added. "That couldn't have been pleasant."

"It wasn't," I said. "And I *have* moved on from Drew."

My friends shared exaggerated, disbelieving looks.

"I have!" When they didn't relent, I sighed. "Fine. Don't believe me. Walker did say he might stop by A Purrfect Pose sometime. If he does, I'll be sure to talk to him, just to make you all happy."

"And make sure you see if he's available," Henna said.

"You'd better," Sierra agreed. "You could use the distraction."

"Even *I* wouldn't mind a distraction like that," Bri said.

Laughter went around the table. I joined in because, why not? Walker Hawk had a lot of good qualities, at least on first impression. He could have gotten angry when I'd ruined his jeans, could have simply ignored me.

But no, he'd taken the time to talk to me. And if I hadn't missed my guess, he'd noticed me *before* I'd dumped half my coffee on him.

Could he have bumped into me on purpose?

Even as the conversation moved on to other topics, I found myself smiling at the possibilities.

CHAPTER 3

I sipped from a freshly unpacked coffee mug as I stared at the boxes sitting around my apartment. It had been months since I'd moved in and I had yet to begin the process of unpacking outside of the necessities. This was the first time I'd ever lived on my own. I had a deep-rooted fear that if I unpacked too soon, something would go wrong and I'd have to pack everything up again.

I'm sure a psychiatrist somewhere would take one look at my family and tell me my trepidation was to be expected.

I didn't know if my fears were unfounded or not, but here I was, a week later, and A Purrfect Pose was still up and running. In fact, I was feeling darn good about my future prospects, business and personal alike. For the first time since I'd lugged the boxes in, I was seriously considering unpacking them.

But not quite yet.

I polished off my coffee and rinsed out the mug before grabbing my purse. I had just reached the door when my cell phone rang. A glance at the screen and my stomach dropped.

It's too early for this.

A deep breath, and then I answered.

"Hi, Dad."

"Ashley." I could hear the relief in his voice. "I was afraid I wouldn't catch you." The implied *Or you wouldn't answer* was as clear as day.

"You almost didn't."

"Well, I'm glad I did." He cleared his throat and then fell silent.

Even though I had to run a class in less than an hour, I waited him out. Like many of my relationships recently, Dad's and mine was complicated. Wayne Daniels was the sane parent, the one who never pushed any of us kids toward anything we didn't want to do. He was the one who'd convinced Mom to name me Ashley instead of Cordelia, had chosen the middle name Hunter for my brother, Lee for Alexi. He was, in a sense, normal.

And then he married my high school best friend.

In the background, I heard her voice, urging him on. Kara Mullins, now Kara Daniels, swears up and down that she never had any intention of falling for my dad, that they didn't even start talking until after Dad and Mom had split.

I suppose I believe her, and yet, how do you call the girl whose house you slept at, watching movies and commenting on the cute guys, the girl who'd had a massive crush on Benedict Cumberbatch to the point where I was convinced she was going to find him and marry him, Mom?

"I really do need to go," I said when it was clear Dad wasn't going to say anything unprompted. "Was there something you needed?"

"I, uh, yeah." He coughed, sniffed. I imagined him looking around the room as if searching for the right words. "So, I was thinking that it's been a while since we got together and talked."

I closed my eyes. *Here it comes.* "Okay?"

"You wouldn't want to have dinner, would you? Or maybe lunch? Here. At ho—at my place. It'd be just the two of us."

A flurry of emotions shot through me as I considered it. I loved my dad, but it was hard to be in the same room with him. It was more than just Kara. There was a whole family history there, one that was more complicated than the fact that Mom had never taken his last name, had insisted his daughters take hers, while any sons were to be excluded. That was why Alexi and I were Bransons and Hunter was a Daniels.

"You don't have to answer now," Dad said, correctly interpreting my silence as reluctance. "Think about it. Call me anytime. I'll always make time for you." He whispered something to Kara, and then returned. "Congratulations on your yoga thing. I've heard it's going well."

"Thank you," I said. "I'll call you in a day or two and we can talk about that dinner. I have Wednesdays off." And Sundays, but I wasn't ready to commit to anything that soon.

"That'd be great." I could hear the smile in his voice, which softened the shell I'd built around my heart when it came to Dad. "I'll cook your favorite. I'd better let you go."

And before I could change my mind or tell him that I hadn't promised to stop by Wednesday, he clicked off.

"I guess I'll see you then," I muttered.

Just as I was about to pocket my phone, it pinged with a text. Mom. ESP, I supposed. It read simply: **The Hop. 12:30.**

Great. Not only did I get to have dinner with Dad in a few days, I was blessed with lunch with Mom today.

Knowing that she wouldn't take no for an answer, I replied with *OK* before pocketing my phone and stepping out into the hall.

"Ash!" My upstairs neighbor, Pavan Patel, was standing next to Edna Cunningham, my elderly neighbor from across the hall. "I see you're getting an early start."

I tugged my door closed with a grunt. I checked the lock, making sure to push on the door a couple of times to verify it was indeed closed, before turning.

"Hi, Pavan. Edna. I'm heading to work."

"A Purrfect Pose," Pavan said, as if savoring the words. His Indian heritage could be heard in his accent and seen on his features. "If I was more flexible, I might join. As it is . . ." He motioned toward his frame, which was on the stockier side.

"You should call Ian about that," Edna said, nodding toward my door. "The place is falling apart and he's just sitting back and raking in the dollars." She clucked her tongue. "It's not right."

"I will," I said. Ian Banks was the landlord, who was often MIA whenever repairs needed to be done. "I should get going." I checked my Fitbit. I still had time, but I liked to be early.

"Have fun," Edna said, patting her hair, which was stark white and cut short. "And don't forget to call Ian."

"Stop by tonight if you get a chance, Ash," Pavan said with a wave. "Jae will be home. Seo-Jun is making one of her family's best Korean dishes. There'll be enough for everyone." He looked to Edna, who appeared pleased at being invited.

"I'll be there," I said, intrigued. I had yet to meet his daughter, Jae, and Seo-Jun was a bit of an introvert, so we rarely spoke. Pavan and Edna were the only people in my apartment complex I knew, so it would be good to meet Pavan's family.

I left the complex with a skip in my step. I was excited about tonight, and somehow, it made my inevitable dinner with Dad seem more bearable. Perception, I supposed.

There was a chill to the early morning air that was expected to burn off as the day wore on. I had on a light jacket over my yoga outfit as I walked from the apartment complex to A Purrfect Pose. The walk was a relatively short, ten-minute trek that gave me time to settle any nerves I might have about the day. The downside was that I had to walk right past Bark and Style.

As expected, Mr. Leslie was standing just inside, staring out at me with his Pomeranian, Ginger, tucked under one arm. The dog immediately started yapping, which seemed to please Mr. Leslie to no end. He grinned, said something to Ginger, and then turned and walked deeper into Bark and Style.

With a sigh, I entered A Purrfect Pose to prepare for the day.

There really wasn't a lot of prep work that needed to be done before a class. I checked on the kitties, spending an inordinate amount of time with a black-and-white cat with a cute little bob of a tail. She followed me from room to room and would plop down and watch me as I worked. She didn't meow, didn't demand attention. What she *did* do was capture my heart.

"If you're still here in a day or two, I might have to take you home," I told her as I headed for the front door. Lulu and George were waiting outside, ready for the Friday morning session.

"Hi, Ash!" Lulu gave me an enthusiastic hug as she entered. "I'm ready for today. I've been stretching and working on my elasticity every day I'm not here." She paused. "That's what you call it, right? Or is it bendability?"

"It's the same thing," George said, greeting me with a nod instead of a hug. "But if you want to know the technical term . . ." His voice trailed off into a mumble as he and Lulu headed for a spot next to one another on the floor.

Nerves had me peeking up and down the street before closing the door. Week one had been a success, but what about week two? If George and Lulu were the only two repeats, I could be in trouble.

And yes, I admit, I was also looking for a certain Greek cowboy who'd yet to make an appearance after our encounter at Snoot's.

Had he truly been interested in me? Or had his comment about stopping in sometime been just him being polite?

I didn't have time to think about it because as soon as the door swung closed, the floodgates opened and the rest of my Friday crew started pouring in.

"Good morning, everyone," I said, unable to keep the stupid grin off my face. I was so relieved that they'd come back—

all of them—I could have wept. "Find a place on the floor, and if you have a particular kitty you're fond of, please, feel free to take them to your spot."

Jonas Valentine said something that appeared clipped and harsh before Fay headed for the cat room. Topher was quick to follow after her, leaving Jonas alone with Chad. They looked at one another, and then turned away as one, clearly uninterested in pursuing conversation.

I waited at the front of the room while everyone settled in. I noted no one had chosen my bobtail, and wasn't sure if I was happy about it or not. Living alone was hard. A cat would make it a smidge more bearable, but would also be one more responsibility for me to deal with.

Still, I noted how she sat in the room, watching me through the large window as content as could be. At this point, there was zero chance I could let her go, even if someone were to ask about adopting her.

"Okay, everyone," I said once the group was in place. "We're going to start with some simple stretches. Does everyone remember the routine?"

A meow from a long-haired ball of floof had everyone but Jonas chuckling. He looked like he'd rather be anywhere else in the world but here. I had a feeling he was only in class for Fay's benefit, and if he were to get his way, he'd stop coming entirely once she was suitably settled.

We went about our warm-ups, and started in on some easy poses. Lulu was muttering under her breath as we flowed from one pose to the next. She was struggling, but doing her best not to let it show. Beside her, George grumbled every time I called a pose by its common name. At least he didn't call me out on it. This time, anyway.

"Oh!" Fay wobbled and her foot dropped during tree pose. Topher, who'd taken up the spot on her left, steadied her, and then kept his hand on her arm as she righted herself. On her right, Jonas muttered something that caused Fay to blush and Topher to remove his hand. An insult or a warning, I didn't know.

I tried not to let my displeasure show. So far, I liked everyone in all my classes, but Jonas had rubbed me the wrong way from the start. He always treated Fay like property that he wasn't entirely sure he wanted, but felt responsible for.

Maybe he wasn't a morning person and he lightened up as the day went on. Since he only came to the early, weekend classes, this was all I ever saw of him.

"Okay, let's move on to—" The words caught in my throat as the door opened and Walker Hawk strode through, sans cowboy hat. He was wearing shorts that clung to him in an extraordinarily appealing way, and a tank top that exposed arms corded with muscle.

"I'm sorry I'm late," he said, eyes finding me where I stood in front of the room, mouth hanging open. "Is there room for one more?"

Eyes shifted from Walker to me.

"Uh." My mind blanked briefly. "Yes! Do you have a cat? I mean mat." I could have slapped myself. "You need a yoga mat."

Walker, whose hands were empty, looked around as if one might materialize around him before patting his thighs and shrugging. "I suppose I don't."

"Let me get you one. I have them for sale. If you want one." Why was I babbling? I bit my lower lip as I crossed the room to the display. "Do you have a preference on color?"

"How about blue?"

"Perfect." I snatched up a blue mat and handed it to him. "Find a spot anywhere. There are cats."

As if he couldn't see them meandering throughout the class.

Walker was kind enough not to laugh at my sputtering as he turned to the rest of the class. I noted Kelly, Lulu, and even Fay were watching him with something akin to lust, which, if I was being honest, I couldn't blame them for. He *was* nice to look at, especially dressed as he was.

He paused as his eyes passed over the Valentines and then he pointedly moved to the far end of the room to place his mat. A gray short-haired kitten trotted over to him and butted her head against his shin as he stepped atop the mat. He patted her on the head, almost awkwardly, and then he gently shooed her away, as if afraid he might break her.

I forced myself to stop watching him and turned to the rest of the class. Lulu was staring at me with a grin and as soon as I looked at her, she winked.

Am I that *obvious?* I cleared my throat. "Where was I?" I said, fighting down a blush.

Before I could regain my balance, there was a pounding on the front door. It was followed by an all too familiar yap.

I closed my eyes, cursed quietly under my breath, and then said, "Let's all take five. I'll be right back."

"Hey, you have a restroom, right?" Topher asked as I made for the door where Mr. Leslie and Ginger were glaring in at me.

"It's in the back, past the office on the left. Go right ahead."

"Thanks." Topher hurried away as I went outside to see what Mr. Leslie wanted.

"You've got to do something about the yowling," he demanded the moment I opened the door to join him. "It's sending Ginger into a frenzy!"

Ginger's tongue lolled out of her mouth as she panted.

"No one is yowling," I said, pausing to listen and prove it. "See. No meows or yowls or hisses to be heard."

"Not now, but what about when you're not around? The dogs can't take it. I'm surprised animal control hasn't been here to deal with you. Something *has* to be done."

Go back inside, Ash. Ignore him.

"Mr. Leslie, the cats aren't hurting anyone and they barely

make any noise. Could something else be bothering Ginger and the other dogs?"

"No, it's you." He held up a hand to stop my protests. "When you're not here, all I can hear is banging and screeching, like the cats are having a party."

"No one is making noise," I said. "I have a security system set up. If the cats got out, or if they started knocking things over, it would set off the system and it would ping my phone."

Mr. Leslie's jaw quivered. "You . . . I . . ." For once he appeared speechless, though it didn't last long. He leveled a finger at me. "I will find a way to get you to leave." His gaze flickered toward the front of A Purrfect Pose, and then he spun on his heel and marched back into Bark and Style, muttering to Ginger the entire way.

I heaved a sigh and took another couple of minutes to calm myself before heading back inside. I didn't need the class to see me flustered—the class or Walker. If this kept happening, I might have to look at moving my studio, though there was nowhere else on the square I could have it. The lake might be more serene than here downtown, but the cost of opening a business there was ridiculously prohibitive.

Once I was back inside, I headed to the front of the room. Everyone was in their place, including Topher. "All right," I said with a wide smile I hoped didn't betray my frustration. "Let's get back to it."

Class resumed, and I'd like to think I did a good job of not making too much of a fool out of myself. It was almost a relief to see that Walker wasn't great at yoga and struggled with some of the simpler poses because I was most definitely not at my best.

Maybe I could offer him some private lessons. The thought had me stumbling over a word and nearly falling, which earned me a correction from George, and another wink from Lulu.

Class ended with little other fanfare. I kept one eye on

Walker, hoping I could talk to him before he left, and the other eye on the rest of the class. To my dismay, and, I suppose, delight, Lulu approached me as soon as we were done, her yoga mat loosely rolled under her arm.

"You know, I think I'd like to take that gray kitten home with me. Cal will hate it, but I can't help it. He's just too cute!"

My eyes were on Walker when she said it, and for an instant, I thought she was talking about him instead of a cat. Thankfully, I caught myself before I said something embarrassing.

"You'll have to fill out the adoption form," I said, turning my focus on Lulu. "I have them in the back."

"That would be great. Do I need to fill it out here, or can I do it at home?"

Lulu followed me back into the office where I got out the form and handed it to her. "If you fill it out here, I can take it to Kiersten at the shelter for you. Or you can take it home and give it to her yourself." I tore off an *Adopted!* sticker that would go on the gray kitten's name card to let others know he was already claimed. "After that, it might take a day or two and then you can take your kitty home."

Lulu considered and then picked up a pen from my desk. "I'll do it here. If I ask Cal, he'll wax on about missing Sammy. That will make me feel guilty, and then I'll end up changing my mind. Cal's more of a dog man, though we haven't had one since Sammy passed."

I waited while she filled out the application. Every few seconds, I'd peek out into the main room to check on the class. Normally, everyone took a little extra time to play with the cats—everyone but the Valentines—and that appeared to be the case now, though I couldn't see the entire room from the doorway.

"There," Lulu said. "This is so exciting! I can't wait to see the look on Cal's face when I bring him home. He's going to be so surprised!"

Hopefully in a good way. Surprise pets didn't always go over well.

I walked Lulu back out into the main room and was pleased to find Walker still there, though his face was red and his chest was heaving as if he'd just run a marathon. When he saw me, he tried on a smile, but I could tell it was forced.

The rest of the class was straggling out the door, so it was just the three of us. Lulu patted me on the arm, whispered "Good luck," and then she hurried out the door, leaving me alone with Walker.

"So," I said, not sure where to begin. "Enjoy the class?"

"It was fun," he said. "Though I'm not sure yoga is my thing."

"Too many muscles." I almost slapped myself, but thankfully, Walker didn't leap at the opening I'd left him.

"Perhaps. Or it's that I've never been great with my balance. I've been known to fall *up* a flight of stairs or two."

"Up?" I asked with a laugh, imagining it. "I don't think I've done that."

"I don't recommend it. It's hard on the shins. Though, I do suppose it's better than falling down them."

"I bet."

Walker checked his watch, which I noticed was a real timepiece with moving parts, not digital. "I have to run now, but I am available for lunch." His eyes rose, met mine. "If you're interested."

The oxygen vanished from the room, leaving me standing there, unable to breathe for a trio of long, thudding heartbeats. Was he asking me out for lunch? As in a date? With him?

I wasn't dying, but a certain element of my life flashed before my eyes. My years with Drew, of living with him, spending nearly every waking moment with him.

An odd sense of guilt washed over me, and I very nearly declined for that reason alone. I'm not sure where it had come from, considering Drew was dating Ginny now and I had no intention of ever going back to him, even if they were to split.

Yet, all those years, having dated no one else in all my life, and I couldn't help myself. Drew was the only boyfriend I'd ever known. He was the only person I'd ever gone on a date with. It felt strange to even *consider* going out with someone else.

But, oh boy, did I ever want to.

"I can't," I said, heart sinking. "I already have lunch plans."

Walker nodded, as if this was exactly what he'd expected me to say. "I get it," he said. "Boyfriend."

"What? No!" Out of reflex, I grabbed his arm as if I feared he might walk away before I could explain. "It's lunch with my mom. I can't get out of it." If I tried, she'd send someone to drag me there, kicking and screaming.

Walker's eyebrows rose. "So, no boyfriend?"

"None."

"But lunch is out?"

"Unfortunately." I considered. "I *am* available for dinner. If you'd want to, that is."

A pained expression crossed his face. "I can't. I have something I have to do tonight." He frowned, looked away. "What about tomorrow night?"

A zip of adrenaline shot through me. "I'm free if you are."

"Great." Walker's smile caused the room to brighten. "I'll pick you up Saturday night at seven?"

"Sounds perfect."

He waited. I stared.

And then it hit me. "Oh! You need to know where to pick me up."

He merely smiled.

We did the number exchange thing and I sent him a text with my address. I had a fleeting thought that I should have had him pick me up at A Purrfect Pose, that he was still a stranger and that telling him where I lived could be dangerous, but it was too late now. Besides, Edna always kept an eye on the complex, so if Walker turned out to be a psycho killer, she'd be able to intervene.

"Saturday it is," Walker said, pocketing his phone in his too-tight shorts.

"I can't wait." I walked him to the door and then we stood facing one another, neither of us quite sure what to do next.

He looked at me. I looked at him. There was definitely a spark there, an attraction that went beyond the physical.

What the hell? I thought as I stepped forward and pulled him into a brief hug. I only lived once, and if Walker and I were going to hit it off, I couldn't be afraid to show I cared.

He squeezed and then stepped back, grinning like I'd just made his day. "I'll see you tomorrow then. Seven sharp." And then he turned and walked away.

I watched until he was gone, before melting back into A Purrfect Pose to cool off for my next class, though I doubted my mind would be on yoga—or anything other than Walker Hawk—for the foreseeable future.

CHAPTER 4

"See you next week, Ms. Branson."

"See you then, Dylan." I paused, and nope, my skin didn't stop crawling. "And please call me Ash." Mom was Ms. Branson and there was no way I could handle being compared to her, even this indirectly.

Dylan laughed as if he thought I was joking before he waved and left A Purrfect Pose, leaving me alone with the cats. I heaved a sigh, wiped sweat from my brow, and then began herding the kitties back into the cat room where they could be fed and watered and kept safe while I was gone.

The bobtail watched me as I got everything ready for her companions. Her eyes were bright and happy. If my heart hadn't already been captured, it would have been then.

Each cat had a name card, though the names were temporary in most cases. Many had been named by whoever had rescued them, which meant they weren't always the best. There were a few named after *Star Wars* characters. Another group after characters out of *The Hunger Games*. I checked the bobtail's card and was disappointed to see she'd been given about as generic a name as you could get for a short-tailed cat.

"Bobbie?" I asked, sticking my tongue out. "If you come home with me, that'll have to change."

Not that I was amazing at naming anything, cats or otherwise. But Bobbie was a smidge too on the nose for me.

I finished cleaning up and promised Bobbie I'd be back after my dreaded lunch with Mom, before I headed to the office for my things. I left Lulu's adoption application on my desk, next to a blank one I planned on filling out for Bobbie later, and then left the office.

"See you all later," I called to the cats.

I was so preoccupied with thoughts of Mom and her inevitable criticism she'd be leveling at me during lunch that I didn't notice someone was standing outside A Purrfect Pose until we nearly collided.

"I'm sorry," I said, just barely missing running into her. "I was lost in my head and didn't see you. Are you interested in yoga classes?"

The woman appeared to be in her twenties with short, coal-black hair, and a square jaw that looked as if it could take a punch or two. She was standing so close to the door, it was a wonder that I hadn't plowed her over.

"I don't think so," she snapped, eyeing me up and down. "You're Ashley Branson."

Clearly a comment and not a question, but I answered anyway. "Ash, yes."

"You run this place." Once again, not spoken like it was a question, but more like an insult.

"I do." Already, this was feeling a lot like a conversation I didn't want to have.

"You cage the animals."

This time, I didn't bother to respond, other than to ask, "Who are you?"

"Zaria Williams." Spoken as if I should know her.

I didn't. "And you're outside my studio because . . . ?"

"Because this place is a prison. You need to release the cats to where they belong. They are meant to be free, not caged."

"They aren't *caged*," I said. "They are in a room to keep

them safe, but are otherwise free. They have food, water, litter boxes, toys."

"They are prisoners." She planted her hands on her hips and squared her shoulders. She was a rather large, muscular woman, made larger by her posturing.

"They are homeless," I said, mirroring her stance. If it came down to a fight, I was going to lose, no question, but I wasn't about to let her talk down to me without standing up for myself. I'd dealt with Mom for years, and this was nothing compared to her. "I am helping them find homes."

"By exploiting them in your business."

I ground my teeth and was about to respond when I caught movement through the window next door. Mr. Leslie was standing inside Bark and Style, grinning ear to ear. There was a knowing twinkle to his eye that told me that this encounter wasn't random.

"Ah. I get it," I said. "I don't know what Mr. Leslie told you, but I do not harm the cats. They are well cared for. They're provided by Kiersten Vanhouser at the animal shelter, if you want to check on it. The cats all have their shots and they are happy and healthy."

"They are pris—"

I cut her off. "I don't have time to debate with you about this. I have a lunch date I can't miss. If you'd like to see the inside of A Purrfect Pose sometime and verify that I'm not sticking the cats in tiny little cages or whatever it is you think I'm doing, then please come during normal operating hours. The days and times are printed on the window. Have a nice day."

I spun and strode quickly away, leaving Zaria sputtering after me. Mr. Leslie's voice followed a moment later, questioning what happened, which confirmed my suspicion. He'd sent her, and I had a feeling that, like Jordan Allen Leslie before her, Zaria Williams wouldn't give up easily.

I paused at the square. Cars zoomed past in an unorderly fashion with many of the drivers not bothering to heed the yield signs. A few horns blared when a truck nearly collided with a car that had plowed straight through. Oh, the joys of having a square instead of a roundabout.

Once the way was clear, I crossed the street, and then walked the short distance to The Hop where Mom waited.

The diner, both in design and name, was meant to evoke memories of classic sock hops. Vinyl records hung on the walls, and a sign on the door cheekily proclaimed that shoes were *not* required, but socks were. Old-school rock played over the speakers, kept at a volume that wouldn't bother the lunch crowd. I knew from experience that they would be turned up during the post-dinner hours, especially on nights when they held dances.

It was the perfect place for a college town, even one with a smaller university such as this one.

Mom was sitting outside on the patio at one of the small, round metal tables, sipping a latte and nibbling on a salad. Leave it to her to not wait for me even though I wasn't late. In fact, despite Zaria stopping me, I was five minutes early.

A woman in her early fifties, Mom—better known to the world as Cecilia Branson—looked half her age. Her hair was lightened to near blond, her every blemish hidden by carefully applied makeup. She didn't look up when I approached, but I could tell she knew I was there by the way her shoulders bunched and she subtly shifted in her seat, as if bracing for a blow.

I took the seat across from her without a word. The waiter appeared almost instantly. He had an awkwardness about him that told me he was new. Most of the staff at The Hop were college students, which meant there was a constant rotation of waiters and waitresses that never quite settled into being comfortable before they moved on.

"I'll just have a water and a house salad," I said before he could ask.

Mom sniffed as if she disapproved.

The waiter mumbled something, and then scurried off.

I knew the drill and just sat there. Mom wouldn't want to talk until we both had our food in front of us. Any attempts to do so beforehand would be met with a stern look and a lecture about etiquette afterward.

It took less than five minutes for the salad and water to arrive. My stomach was in knots, but I took a bite anyway. As soon as I'd chewed and swallowed, Mom set her fork aside and leveled her no-nonsense stare at me.

"Have you had enough?"

"Enough of what?"

"Your frivolous exercise." She fluttered her fingers in the air, vaguely in the direction of A Purrfect Pose. "Your rebellion."

"Mom, I'm not rebelling."

"You're like your father, you know?"

I took a bite of salad to keep from rolling my eyes at her. *Here we go,* I thought.

"He only thought about himself from the moment we met. He pretended to care deeply for me, but it was his emotions he catered to."

"You're the one who left him," I pointed out. "Because he didn't want to have anything to do with the Branson legacy."

"And look at where he's at now." Mom sipped her coffee, set it aside. "We are civil to one another, but it's clear he regrets his decisions. I don't wish for you to follow in his path."

"Like Hunter?"

A twitch of an eye was as close to a flinch as Mom came to showing emotion. "Reginald made his choice, just as you have, Ashley Cordelia."

I deserved that, I knew. Mom knew I hated my given middle

name, just as Hunter hated his first, though she insisted on using them both. Calling Hunter by the name he preferred only provoked her, something I knew all too well.

"You have Alexi." At her narrowed eyes, I amended it to "Alexandra."

"Branson Designs is a family business," Mom said. "It is stable, profitable, and where you belong. Your sister understands this. I don't understand why you can't do the same."

"Because this is what I want to do," I said, meaning the studio. "I want to help animals, do my own thing without feeling like I'm being held back."

"We could run special events that would benefit animals, if that's what it would take for you to see reason."

I sighed, ate more of my salad.

"I'm only saying this for your benefit, Ashley. That place of yours won't last. Even with this moderate success you've obtained, it's not sustainable. It's a fad for most of the people you call clients, and I'd hate to see you hurt when it falls apart."

While her words stung, I understood what she was trying to say. Mom could be difficult. She could be—and often was—hurtful and insensitive. But it wasn't because she didn't care. She did. She just had an odd way of showing it sometimes.

"I'm happy, Mom," I said. "This is what I want to do."

"And when people stop coming and you are forced to close?"

"If that happens, then . . ." I stabbed a tomato, waved it around in the air before shoving it into my mouth and speaking over it. "I suppose I'll have to consider coming back."

That seemed to satisfy her. Mom resumed eating her salad, a faint smile on her face.

"Dad called this morning," I said, feeling the need to knock her down a peg. Petty, yes, but Mom did that to me. "He wants me to stop by for dinner."

"Will your friend be there?"

I cringed. "Kara's not my friend anymore."

Mom shrugged. "I don't see why not. Nothing's changed between you."

I couldn't help it, I laughed. "Nothing's changed? She married *Dad.*"

"And?"

"And?" I sputtered. "She's over twenty years younger than him! Almost thirty!"

Mom sighed, set down her fork, and pushed her salad away. "Not everything works out as we choose, Ashley. There are times when something that may seem strange to us in the moment, turns out to be the best for everyone involved."

"And you think Dad marrying my best friend is a good thing?"

Mom shrugged one delicate shoulder. "If you give it a chance, you may find that, indeed, it is."

I opened and closed my mouth a few times before giving up. It still messed with my head to think that Mom could be okay with Dad marrying someone so young, and that she almost seemed to respect it.

Then again, I barely understood why Mom thought the way she did about much of anything. The same went for Dad, my brother, and pretty much everyone in the Branson family.

Maybe I really am the oddball here.

Still, it wasn't easy. Mom and Dad were a bad fit from the start. I honestly have no idea how they even ended up together in the first place. He didn't fit the Branson ideology. He didn't want to work for them. It was natural that they eventually split. It was hard to deal with at first, but it made sense after I thought about it some.

And then Dad had ended up with Kara.

My Branson side came out then. I hate to admit it, but I'd thrown my own little petty fits, had acted like it was all about me. Never mind that Dad was happy. Never mind that Mom didn't care. It felt like a slap in my face, in hers, and I made sure they all knew about it.

Thinking about it now made me feel like a fool, yet I couldn't bring myself to let it go.

"I suppose I should get back," Mom said, dabbing at her lips with her napkin before tossing it onto the table. "Think about what I've said."

I nodded, but kept my eyes on my salad. What I really wanted was a beer and a burger. The unhealthier the better.

Mom rounded the table and rested a hand on my shoulder. She gave a brief squeeze and then left.

I stewed over my salad a few minutes longer, but couldn't eat it. As much as I hated to admit it, her words had gotten to me. About A Purrfect Pose. About Dad and Kara. Was I fooling myself? Was I the bad guy here?

Mom meant well. That last squeeze told me as much. She cared, but had no real idea how to show it. She wanted what was best for me and did whatever she could so that I could get it.

Of course, our opinions on what that might be were often light-years apart, but hey, it's the thought that counts.

The waiter returned and when I went to pay, his smile was apologetic.

"It's already been taken care of. The woman you dined with paid before you arrived."

I was annoyed to see she'd predicted my salad and water purchase. Maybe I *was* becoming too predictable. Did that mean she was right about my life choices too?

No, I decided. I refused to let her get to me. Mom wasn't psychic any more than I was. The only way to know whether I was making a mistake was to *make* that mistake and learn from it.

If that meant I'd end up back at Branson Designs, then so be it. But until that happened, I was going to make the most of my freedom, and to start, that meant making room in my life for others.

And I knew exactly where to start.

"And here's your new home!" I said, opening the carrier and letting the soon to be renamed Bobbie out. "Complete with a full suite of entertainment for a discerning kitty, such as yourself."

The bobtail wandered my apartment, which at this point looked as if only a cat lived there since most of my own stuff was still in boxes. As soon as I'd left The Hop, I'd gone shopping for cat supplies, including a couple of scratching posts and a large cat tree that would allow my new companion the opportunity to look out the window.

I had yet to fill out the adoption papers, but I *had* stopped by the shelter to talk to Kiersten. She enthusiastically told me to take Bobbie home, see how it went, and that we could fill everything out later. I'm sure she wasn't supposed to do that, but hey, I'd take it. If the kitty was unhappy here, then I could take her back to A Purrfect Pose and hope that someone found her just as irresistible as I did.

I watched her wander and sniff everything in sight for a few minutes before I snatched up my phone. Pets were welcome in the complex, but I thought I should give Ian a heads-up.

And talk to him about the sticky door.

He answered on the first ring, sounding out of breath. "Yeah?"

"Mr. Banks," I said. "It's Ashley Branson in apartment 201."

"Uh-huh."

"I wanted to let you know I just got a cat. She's young, but litter trained."

"Good for you." There was a clatter, then a curse. "That all?"

"My door," I said, speaking quickly out of fear he might hang up on me. He sounded more than just distracted; he sounded annoyed that I'd even called. "It's sticking to the point it doesn't close right and I sometimes struggle to open it."

A pause. "And?"

"And I was hoping you might be able to fix it."

"A sticking door?"

"Yes."

He gave a put-upon sigh. "I'm rather busy."

"It doesn't have to be now. I understand you have a lot to do."

"I do. In fact, why don't you fix the door yourself?"

"Me?"

"Why not? Just don't break it. I'd hate to have to charge you for repairs."

"But—"

"Sorry, gotta go."

And then I was listening to dead air.

"Jerk," I muttered, before tossing my phone onto the table. I glanced at the door, but it was already getting dark. There was no way I was going to look at it tonight. Not that I even knew what I was looking for.

Instead of wasting my time on it, I spent the next couple of hours with Bobbie, trying out new names with her to no avail. Nothing seemed to fit, and that included her temporary name.

"So, what do you think?" I asked her as she settled in on the top of the cat tree by the window. Her eyes were wide as she watched the birds. "Do you like it?"

She eased down, never taking her eyes from the window. I took that as a yes.

Checking my Fitbit, I decided it was time to head up to the third floor for dinner with the Patels. I made sure Bobbie had everything she needed, promised her I'd be back, and then left her to her birdwatching.

Pavan opened the door with a wide smile and a hug. "I'm glad you made it, Ash," he said, escorting me inside. "Edna had to cancel. Her gastro-something or other was acting up, so she couldn't stick around for dinner. She stopped by about ten minutes ago to say hi."

Seo-Jun was seated at the table, head slightly bowed as if embarrassed when I entered the dining room. She had high cheekbones and beautiful dark brown hair that matched her eyes.

Next to her sat their daughter, Jae. She had many of the same features as Seo-Jun, though unlike her mother, who had long hair, Jae's was cut short, and she wore no makeup.

Not that she needed it. She was stunning as she was, something I wished I could pull off.

"Jae, this is my downstairs neighbor, Ash."

"Hey," Jae said with a crooked smile. "Dad roped you into dinner too, huh?"

"Hey, now," Pavan said. "No one roped anyone into anything."

Jae mocked tugging on a rope and made a face before both she and her father burst into laughter. I had a sudden flash of longing, of feeling as if I'd missed out on this sort of family banter, but it quickly dissipated. We might not express it in the same way, but my family members *did* care for one another.

"It's a pleasure meeting you," I said, before turning to Pavan's wife. "Seo-Jun."

"Ash."

Pavan motioned toward a chair before moving to take a seat at the head of the table. I was about to sit when my phone buzzed in my pocket. Hoping it might be Ian calling back after reconsidering his comments about fixing my door, I quickly pulled it out to check.

It wasn't Ian or a call.

It was an alert.

Door ajar.

"One second," I said, turning my back to the table. I clicked on the security app and brought up the cameras.

Or, at least, I tried to.

"Is something wrong?" Pavan asked.

"I'm not sure." I tried the cameras again, to the same result. A third try and they steadfastly refused to come on. "I need to check on something at A Purrfect Pose," I said, pocketing my phone, nerves jumping. "I'm sorry."

"No, no. Go." Pavan rose. "Do you want me to come with you?"

"No, you stay with your family." I reached for the door, but paused before opening it. "It was good to meet you, Jae. I'm sorry I can't stay."

"Nah, it's fine. Go check on your thing."

And with her blessing, I did.

I have a car, but I didn't even think about it as I left the apartment complex. I was so used to walking to A Purrfect Pose, it seemed only natural, despite my worry. Still, I did one of those fast, almost-run types of walks. I kept checking the cameras, but they weren't working, though I was positive they were earlier that day.

Power outage? I wondered. No one else on the block appeared to have lost power, so I doubted it. And why would it tell me the door was ajar if the power was out?

I wasn't panicked yet, but I was getting there. I couldn't help but think of Mr. Leslie and Zaria Williams. Could they have done something? And what if I'd made a mistake and left the door to the cat room open. They could escape through the ajar door and if one of them were to somehow get into Bark and Style . . .

A Purrfect Pose came into view. It was now dark, but the streetlights were on, lighting up the entire square. Someone was standing out front of the yoga studio, peering inside. They wore a Cardinal Lake University hoodie with the hood pulled up, concealing their head and face.

"Hey!" I called as I approached, which was a mistake. As soon as the person heard me shout, they bolted. "Hey!"

Already winded, I took about two running steps before realizing I wasn't going to catch them. Instead, I hurried to the front of A Purrfect Pose and tugged on the door, thinking I'd find the lock broken, but it wasn't. In fact, the door didn't budge at all.

It wasn't the front door that was ajar.

Chest heaving, I scanned the area, but nothing was out of place. I tried the door once more, just to be sure, but it was firmly locked. Inside, the lights were off, just like they should be. The only glow came from the kitty room, where I'd installed a night-light, just so the cats wouldn't be left in the dark overnight.

The back door. I mentally cursed myself. Of course it would be the back door. I'd been so distracted by Mom, and then gathering up Bobbie and making sure the cats themselves were settled, I didn't even think to double-check the back door's questionable lock.

I hurried down the street until I reached the alley access. I headed back toward A Purrfect Pose, shivering against the darkness that swelled around me. There were no lights in the alley, not now that most of the shops on this end of town were closed.

A bottle clattered as I kicked it in my haste. It caused all the hairs on my neck to rise. I sprinted the last few yards to the back door of A Purrfect Pose, positive someone was going to jump out at me at any moment.

But no one did. When I reached the back, I immediately grabbed for the door and pulled. Sure enough, the door swung outward, but it hadn't been open enough for a cat to get out. I stepped inside quickly and closed the door behind me, flipping on the lights as I did.

Something bumped up against my leg. I let out a scream and nearly bolted out the back again before I saw the cute little tiger-striped face looking up at me.

The cat jumped at my scream and then he darted into the cat room.

The *open* cat room.

"Hello?" I called, not daring to move. Unsurprisingly, there was no answer. I had my phone in hand and was halfway to dialing the police, but I wasn't sure something bad had actually happened yet. I *thought* I remembered closing the cat room door, but could I have forgotten in my excitement to bring Bobbie home?

I crept into the cat room and peered inside. Some of the cats were asleep, while a few were milling about, playing like they always did. Most of them, however, were wandering the rest of the studio and would need to be corralled.

Like prisoners at a jail. The voice in my head was not my own, but that of Zaria Williams.

Anger started building. Had that woman broken in and let my cats out? For what purpose, other than to cause trouble and risk getting one of them lost or hurt?

I dialed, hands shaking as I closed the cat room door so more kitties wouldn't get out.

"You've reached the Cardinal Lake police department," the woman who answered said. "How may I help you?"

"Yes," I said, moving toward the front room so I could retrieve more cats—and make sure nothing was stolen or broken. "I'd like to report a break-in." I flipped on the light and then let out a bloodcurdling scream that had all the wandering cats fleeing as fast as their little feet could take them.

A tiny voice in my ear rose. "Ma'am? Ma'am? Are you all right?"

I couldn't answer. I could only stare straight ahead at what lay on the floor in the middle of my yoga studio.

A single yoga mat had been rolled open in the center of the room. Stretched out in child's pose atop it was Jonas Valentine. He wasn't moving.

"Jonas?" I whispered, but he didn't answer. He couldn't.

Considering the knife that was sticking out of his back, I was pretty sure that Jonas Valentine was dead.

CHAPTER 5

I chewed on my thumbnail as I watched what was happening inside A Purrfect Pose from the sidewalk. The police and paramedics were swarming the place, shunting me outside to stand in a cascading glow of swirling red and blue lights.

It was a relief when the first officer to show was Officer Olivia Chase, but before she could ask me much more than "What happened?" Chief Dan Higgins had arrived and had taken over with a harsh command that I wasn't to move from my spot on the sidewalk until he'd had a look inside.

That was almost twenty minutes ago.

Anxiety gnawed at me as I waited. Who would want to kill Jonas Valentine? And why would they do it in *my* yoga studio of all places?

To ruin me, of course.

The thought had me glancing toward Bark and Style, which was dark and empty. What if Jonas wasn't the target, but *I* was? Mr. Leslie had wished me ill will. That activist, Zaria, had shown up on his command. And what about Ginny? She'd threatened me and the studio because she thought I was trying to steal Drew back. Heck, even my mom wanted me to fail so I'd come back to Branson Designs.

But would any of them kill an innocent man just to get me to do what they wanted? It didn't make sense.

By the time Olivia came outside to join me, I was jumping at every shadow, convinced someone was out to get me.

"You doing okay?" she asked before raising a hand and shaking her head. "Don't answer that. Of course you're not."

"Why here?" I asked her, voicing the one question that repeated nonstop in my head. "Why kill him at A Purrfect Pose?"

"We were hoping you might have some idea about that." Olivia put an arm around me, squeezed, and then released me. It was likely the only compassion she'd be allowed to show since she was on duty. "Do you have any idea why Mr. Valentine was here at this time of night?"

"No, I don't."

Olivia frowned. "That won't fly with Chief Higgins."

"I wish I had an answer," I said, raising my thumb to my mouth before catching myself. If I kept at it, I wouldn't have a nail left by morning. "I was at dinner with my neighbor when I got an alert about the door being ajar. I came right away and found him like that." I pointed toward the window, though Olivia didn't need to look to know who I was talking about.

"The front door was open?"

"No, it was the back. It has a habit of not locking right and I haven't had a chance to get anyone to look at it. The cats were also out of their room, but I closed that door, so Jonas or the killer must have gone inside." Tears threatened. "I closed it. I know I did."

Olivia turned and studied the front of A Purrfect Pose. "Are all the cats accounted for?"

"You don't think someone came here to steal a cat, do you?" Dumb question, but I couldn't help myself.

"No, but if one was taken, then it's something to go on. If someone has one of your cats roaming their house, it would make them an awfully intriguing suspect."

That, it would. "The cats are all there. I checked before you got here."

Olivia sighed. "So, you have no idea why Mr. Valentine was here? You're sure?"

"I'm positive. He came to the morning session with his wife like they always do. I assumed they both went home or to class at the university afterward."

Olivia nodded and then stepped closer. "I called Evan when I learned that it was your place we were called to. He'll let the family know."

"Thank you." Though, the thought of what Mom would say when she found out about it was almost as bad as dealing with the murder itself.

The door opened and Chief Dan Higgins stormed out into the night. He was a tall, muscular man in his fifties. A high school football standout, Higgins swore he would have gone pro if not for a freak wall-climbing accident. Looking at him now, even at his age, I wouldn't have bet against him.

As soon as he saw Olivia with me, he jerked a thumb back over his shoulder, a clear sign she was to beat it.

"Just tell him the truth and everything will be fine," she said under her breath before heading back inside A Purrfect Pose.

Higgins strode over to me, running a hand over his bald pate. I could see the distrust in his eyes as he looked me over.

"You found him?" he asked.

"I did." I explained the alert and how the security cameras didn't work when I'd tried to access them and how it led to me finding Jonas.

"Who knows about your security system?" he asked when I was done. "I don't see a sticker anywhere."

"A sticker?"

"Or a sign. Like those, 'this place is protected by such and such security' stickers. You know what I'm talking about?"

"I guess."

Chief Higgins glared at me.

"I don't have stickers or signs because my system isn't run by a big company or anything like that. It's just a couple of apps, a do-it-yourself sort of thing."

"Apps?"

"You know, on your phone? I have one for the cameras and another for the door."

"I see." Higgins chewed over that for a moment before he asked, "So, who would know about these apps since you don't advertise them?"

I tried not to take offense to his less than cordial tone as I considered it. "Kiersten Vanhouser from the shelter knows. Me, obviously."

Higgins scowled at that, motioned at me to hurry it up.

"Jordan Leslie, my neighbor here knows. I said something about it to him earlier today when he was complaining about the cats making too much noise. I probably mentioned it to Alexi at some point."

"And to Hunter?"

My heart hiccupped. "I'm not sure."

Chief Higgins took a step closer to me, putting him well into my too close for comfort radius. "If you're protecting him . . ."

"I'm not!" I said, taking a slight step backward. "I can't remember if I mentioned anything to Hunter about the cameras." Though he *did* know about the faulty lock on the back door.

It couldn't have been Hunter. My brother wouldn't kill someone, especially not at my place of business. Right?

Higgins eyed me a moment before asking, "Did you recognize the weapon?"

"The knife?"

He scowled at me and didn't respond. Of course he'd meant the knife.

"No. It's not mine."

"You're sure?"

"As sure as I can be. I didn't inspect it too closely, and I definitely didn't bring it with me and stab him with it."

That earned me another scowl.

A car drifted by slowly. The driver's side window was down and the woman was just about hanging out of it as she went past, gawping at the scene. I watched until she rounded the square and was gone.

"What aren't you telling me?" Higgins asked, drawing my attention back to him.

"What do you mean?"

"You've left something out. I can tell. If it's about your brother, I'm not going to be happy."

"I'm not—" I cut off as a detail popped into my head. "Someone was outside A Purrfect Pose when I got here. They took off running when I called out to them."

"Was it your brother?"

"I couldn't tell. I don't think so. It could have been a woman."

"You don't know the difference between a man and a woman?"

"They were wearing a loose CLU hoodie with the hood pulled up." It came out as defensive, especially since my brain wanted to add that the person was about the same height and build as Hunter. He also had that exact same hoodie and had been acting strange for a week now. "Could Mr. Leslie have done it?" I asked, trying to turn the focus on someone else. "He called the police on me last week."

"For?"

"He doesn't like the cats. Like I said, he complained and I told him about the system earlier today. He could have decided to kill Jonas once he figured out he could sneak in. He's been trying to force me to close ever since I opened."

Chief Higgins didn't appear to buy it. Admittedly, I was

having a hard time seeing it as well. The person I saw didn't have the same build as Mr. Leslie. Even Zaria didn't quite fit. Hunter, on the other hand, was the right size. It was like some messed-up fairy tale where I was looking for a person who fit their CLU hoodie just right.

"Do you know where your brother is now?" Higgins asked, veering the conversation back to where I didn't want it.

I shook my head.

"Have you spoken to him recently?"

"Once. Last week." I crossed my arms. "Hunter didn't do this."

Higgins ignored me. "If you see him, tell him to contact me. Don't make me come find him." He sighed, seemed to deflate. "You and I both know your brother is trouble."

"He's not." It came out flat.

"He is. Maybe he didn't mean for this to happen, but it did. If Hunter is involved, he needs to tell us his side of the story. If he takes too long to come forward, we won't be able to protect the Branson name."

Anger flared through me then. "Protect the Branson name? A man *died!*"

"Yes, and while his death is a tragedy, there's no reason for it to ruin innocent lives either."

Innocent lives? Really?

I knew Branson Designs was an important staple of the town, that Mom donated money to events and restoration projects when it suited her, but this was ridiculous.

"You can't pin this on Hunter," I said. "He had no reason to kill Jonas Valentine. I don't think they knew one another. And even if they did, he wouldn't have killed him in A Purrfect Pose."

"Are you sure about that?" Higgins asked.

Was I? I wanted to be, but there were far too many coincidences that tied Hunter to the crime. He'd been acting strange lately. He'd known about the back door, likely knew about the security systems, if not from me, then possibly Alexi. The CLU hoodie. The way he'd vanished a week ago when Olivia had come in.

If my brother was involved in this, I was so going to kill him.

"Does Fay know?" I asked, desperate to change the subject before I started to believe in my brother's guilt. "Fay Valentine. She's Jonas's wife."

"Someone will contact her," Higgins said, just as the door opened and another officer called for him. He waved the officer back inside. "Here's the deal," he told me once we were alone again. "You're closed until further notice. I don't want anyone trampling all over my scene."

"But—"

"No." He cut me off. "I don't care. As you said, a man is dead. We're going to do this right."

"How is ruining my business doing this right?" I asked. I could feel tears coming on. "If I don't hold classes this weekend, I might lose my students, and then I won't be able to pay rent." For this place *or* my apartment.

"You might want to strap in for a rough ride," Higgins said. "This could drag on for weeks, maybe months. Unless . . ." He spread his hands. He didn't need to finish.

Unless Hunter comes clean.

He started to turn away, hesitated. "You should think about upgrading your security system." And then Chief Higgins returned to A Purrfect Pose, leaving me sagging against Olivia's cruiser.

What was I going to do? I didn't want Hunter to get into trouble, but I didn't want to lose my yoga studio either. Everything had been going great, and now it looked like I might lose it all.

"Ash? What's going on?"

I turned to find Alexi approaching. She was alone, but her

outfit told me she'd had another night out on the town, likely with Fiona. Her heels clacked on the pavement as she made her way from her car, which was parked behind the police cruisers, over to me.

"Evan called me," she said, "but he didn't know the details."

I opened my mouth to speak, but instead, the tears won out and I started bawling. I didn't know Jonas Valentine well, but he'd been one of mine. He wasn't great at yoga, didn't really want to be there as far as I could tell, yet he was a human being. I liked his wife. His former students appeared to respect him.

And now he was dead.

Alexi wrapped me in a hug, pulling me in close. "Hey, it's all right." I could feel her head moving as she scanned the front of my place. By now, Jonas was covered and the police were searching for clues, so there wasn't much to see. That meant I'd have to explain it to her, something I wasn't sure I could get through.

So, I cried it out, hating that I was getting her dress wet, and really not caring at the same time. I needed to let it all out now so it didn't rear up and slap me upside the head down the line. I'd learned at a young age that holding my emotions back was a good way to let them pile up, so best to just roll with them when they hit so I could move forward afterward.

"You okay?" Alexi asked as my sobs petered out to mere sniffles. "What happened?"

I stepped back, wiped my eyes dry. "Someone was killed," I said. "In A Purrfect Pose."

"Oh no!" Her hand went to her mouth. "Who was it? Someone you knew?"

I nodded, took a shuddering breath. "He was one of my students; Jonas Valentine."

Alexi gave me a blank look. She didn't know him.

"Chief Higgins thinks Hunter might have done it."

That got a reaction out of her.

Say one thing about Alexi Branson: she didn't let anyone bad-mouth her siblings. She was the eldest, so I suppose it was natural that she wanted to protect us, but it went beyond that. She knew Hunter messed up a lot. Everyone knew. She also knew him better than Chief Dan Higgins ever would.

Alexi jerked straight and spun as if she might march right into A Purrfect Pose to give Chief Higgins a piece of her mind. Loudly. She *was* her mother's daughter, and could scald with her tongue with the best of them.

But I didn't want that. Not yet anyway.

I took Alexi by the arm and steered her away before she could make things worse.

"Hunter knew about the back door," I told her. "He was here last week and found out it didn't lock right. I'm pretty sure the killer came in through the back door because the front was still locked when I got here." I gave her a meaningful look.

"The back door leads into the alley, right?" At my nod, her face hardened. "Anyone could have gone in that way. They could have tested all the doors on the street and yours was the first that opened."

I considered it. Could the altercation have happened in the alley and Jonas was killed there, and *not* in A Purrfect Pose? There wasn't a sign of a struggle inside as far as I could tell. No blood trail. Nothing was knocked over.

It was entirely possible that someone had killed Jonas, found my door unlocked, and then brought him inside and posed him to make it look like it was connected to my yoga studio. But why release the cats? Had they been looking for something to help mask their identity? To clean up?

"We need to find Hunter," I said.

"You don't think he did it, do you?"

"No, but what if he knows who did?" I thought it through.

"When he came to see me last week, it was during the Friday morning session, and he seemed upset by something. Jonas was there. Hunter took off before he could tell me what was bothering him, and I thought it was because Olivia showed up."

"Like, he'd done something illegal and was worried that she was looking for him?"

"Something like that." And it wouldn't have been the first time. "But what if it wasn't Olivia he was scared of, but Jonas?" I didn't recall him saying anything about it, but I'd had a lot on my plate since it was opening day. "If he knew Jonas, there's a chance Hunter might know who would have wanted to kill him."

Alexi was nodding. "And if he knows, he might be afraid he could be next."

"Which is why we haven't seen him."

Alexi and I looked toward A Purrfect Pose at the same time, as if we expected Hunter to pop out the door like a jack-in-the-box. He didn't. No one did.

She pulled out her phone, pressed a button, and then waited as it rang. She frowned as she clicked off. "Hunter isn't answering."

"What are we going to do?"

Alexi didn't think about it long. She took me by the arm and led me to her car. "Let's go find our brother and make him tell us everything he knows."

I threw myself down into a dining room chair with a huff. "That was a colossal waste of time."

Alexi sat across from me, sluicing water from her face. About fifteen minutes into our search, the skies had opened up and it had started pouring. It wouldn't have been so bad if we'd stayed in her car during our search, but we hadn't. We'd hit up just about every spot where Hunter might be, including his small apartment on the far end of town, to no avail.

"Did he say anything about leaving town when you talked to him last?" Alexi asked.

"No. He didn't say much of anything before he took off."

Bobbie poked her head into the room, saw Alexi and then vanished back down the hall on silent kitten paws.

"Do you think he could be with Dad?"

I gave her a flat look.

"Yeah. Right. Never mind."

Hunter had once had a crush on Kara so big, I could hardly bring her home without him lurking around every corner and flirting with her. Then, after Dad married her, it became even weirder, to the point where Hunter made himself scarce anytime Dad was around, just in case Kara happened to be there as well.

"What about Mom?" I asked. "She can be difficult, but she wouldn't turn him away if he were to come to her."

"I doubt it," Alexi said. "Hunter might be desperate, but not *that* desperate."

I buried my face in my hands, elbows planted on my knees. "This is such a mess."

Alexi reached across the table to pat me on my damp back. "It'll all work out, Ash. It has to."

I knew she was trying to be supportive, but I wasn't feeling it. "How can you say that?" I asked, sitting back. "Hunter is missing, possibly in trouble. A man I knew is dead. He was found in A Purrfect Pose and now I have to close for a few days, maybe weeks, and I don't know if I'm ever going to be allowed to open again. Or if I should. What am I going to do with the cats?"

"I'll help if you need me to," Alexi said.

"Thanks." I sighed. "I should probably cancel my date with Walker, too."

Alexi perked up at that. "Date? You have a date?"

"Dinner tomorrow night with a guy I met at Snoot's."

She leaned forward. "Tell me more."

"There's not much to tell, honestly. We met, he came to yoga, and then he asked if I might want to grab lunch with him, but I had plans with Mom, and you know what that's like."

"Oh yeah. Can't cancel on her if you don't want to end up miserable for the rest of your life."

"So, I asked him about dinner tonight and . . ." My breath caught. *No way.*

"And?"

"And he said he had something he had to do."

"Come on, Ash, you can't think he had anything to do with that man's death, can you?"

"It's better than thinking Hunter did." But not by much. "I definitely have to cancel now."

"Don't," Alexi said, raising a hand to forestall any arguments I might have. "Think about it. If he *is* the killer, then canceling on him might tip him off that you suspect him."

I stared at her. "So?"

"So, if he realizes you're onto him, he might flee town. Or worse." She gave me a meaningful look.

I sagged in my seat, feeling thoroughly defeated. "And going out with a guy who might be a serial killer is better?" I asked. "Oh hey, instead of making him work for it, I'll just go ahead and go out with him so he can take me home to dissect me for his collection without fuss."

"You wouldn't let it get that far."

If I even had a choice. "I think it's a bad idea."

"Think of it this way," Alexi said. "If you go out with him and talk to him, you'll have an opportunity to question him."

"Oh yeah, that sounds like a plan. 'Hey, you didn't happen to kill Jonas Valentine in A Purrfect Pose, did you?' I'm sure that'd go over well."

Alexi chuckled. "You wouldn't have to put it like that. You could simply ask him what he was doing last night, if he knew anyone from class. Basic stuff. If he gets all evasive on you, then you know you should suspect something. If he answers freely and honestly, then . . ."

"Then he might be a good liar."

"Perhaps. You can text me your location throughout the night if it'll make you feel better. I can stick near the area and if he tries anything . . . Pow!" She punched a fist into her hand.

It was so ridiculous, I managed to laugh. "Right. Wouldn't it be better to call Olivia and let her know?"

"She would stand out a whole lot more than I would. I could call Fiona and we could eat at the same place you do, keep an eye out for you and make sure he doesn't try to put anything into your drink. You know, stuff like that."

I thought about it, but shook my head. "No, that'd be too weird. But I suppose I could text you and keep you in the loop."

"You do that." Alexi stood. "I think the rain's stopped. I'm going to go before it starts up again. Evan's probably wondering where I am."

"Thanks, Alexi. I don't know what I would have done if you hadn't shown up."

We hugged and she made for the door.

"Call me if you learn anything more," she said. "Or if you hear from Hunter."

"I will. You do the same."

Alexi stepped out into the hall, pulled out her phone. "Talk to you later, Ash," she said, tapping the screen as she walked away. "Hey, Evan, I'm on the way home. I was with Ash. I'll tell you all about it when I get there. Did you get the kids to bed?"

I closed the door, locked it, and then tugged a few times to make sure it was secure.

Just like I should have done at A Purrfect Pose.

Maybe if I'd double-checked the door and made sure it had actually locked, Jonas would still be alive.

No, I couldn't think like that. None of this was my fault.

I went to my room and changed into my PJs, desperate to get out of my damp clothing, before I sat down on the couch.

A moment after my butt hit the cushion, a black-and-white fuzzball landed in my lap and immediately curled up. I laid a hand on her, eyes drifting to the window where the moon could just be seen peeking between the curtains.

"Luna," I said. "How does that sound for a name?" It might not be overly creative, but it felt right, and was a whole lot better than Bobbie.

Beneath my hand, she started to purr.

If that wasn't an answer, I didn't know what was.

CHAPTER 6

Pro tip: never fall asleep sitting up on the couch with a cat in your lap.

I woke early the next morning with a stiff neck and with my left leg buzzing from lack of circulation. Luna had jumped down sometime in the night, but I'd remained locked in the same upright position as I'd dozed off in, and for the first few minutes after waking, I wasn't so sure I'd ever move again.

As the pins and needles subsided, I went about my morning routine, mind churning over what little I knew about Jonas Valentine and his death. Conclusions were few and far between, but I did know Hunter had nothing to do with the murder. Despite the fact he always seemed to be getting himself into one scrape or another, he simply didn't have killing someone in him.

And Walker Hawk? I was pretty sure he was innocent too, but that might just be wishful thinking.

Once both Luna and I were fed, I called Olivia on her cell. With the murder, she was likely hard at work on the case, but I hoped she'd have a minute or two to answer a few questions.

"Please tell me you didn't find any more bodies," she said by way of answer.

"Not yet," I said. "But the day is young."

"Ha-ha." Deadpan.

"I *am* calling because of the one body I did find and was wondering—"

"Let me stop you right there, Ash," Olivia said, cutting me off. "I was given a lecture last night by Chief Higgins about making sure I don't bend the rules for you. He wants your place closed, and nothing you say will change his mind. Believe me, I tried on your behalf."

"It's not that." Though I'd hoped Olivia might be able to put a little pressure on him so I could open by Monday. Apparently, that wasn't going to happen. "But I do need to get into A Purrfect Pose."

"What did I just say? Higgins will have my hide if I let you hold your classes and people trample all over his scene."

"Not for yoga," I said. "It's the cats. I need to make sure they're fed and watered. And I'll likely need to get in so I can move them back to the shelter until I can open again." *If* I open again.

There was a tapping sound I assumed was Olivia drumming her nails on the back of her phone as she thought about it. I held my breath as I waited for her reply.

After a long five seconds that felt like an eternity, she heaved a sigh. "If you go in there, I don't want you to go anywhere near that front room, all right? Stick to the cats."

"Of course."

"I mean it, Ash. Higgins will flay me if he finds out you were in there. Check on them. Feed them if you have to, and then get out."

"I will. And if I need to move them, I'll take them out through the back alley. No trampling on anyone's scene."

"You do that. And make it quick." She clicked off.

"Well, that went well," I muttered as I typed out a text to Sierra, asking her to meet me at A Purrfect Pose. My phone pinged almost immediately with a thumbs-up emoji. With that done, I gave Luna a few parting pets, and then I was out the door.

The walk to my yoga studio was brisk and invigorating. Last night's rain gave the air a crispness that almost stung whenever I took a deep breath. I had to step around a few puddles here and there, but otherwise, most everything was dry by now, and that included the sky, which was bright blue and clear.

"What is this I hear about someone dying?" Sierra was waiting for me outside the studio, two to-go cups of coffee in her hand. They were from a local coffee shop named Shakes that we both loved. She handed one of the cups over.

I sipped from it gratefully. "I'm not sure what happened yet," I said. "But he didn't just die; he was killed and posed inside A Purrfect Pose."

"Posed? As in . . ." She stuck her tongue out of the corner of her mouth, contorted her body awkwardly, and nearly fell.

"The child's pose," I said. "Facedown, on his knees, hands extended before him."

Sierra shuddered. "They put him like that on purpose? Who'd you piss off?"

I stuck my tongue out at her, before motioning for her to follow. "We have to go in through the back."

Sierra followed me with a yawn. Next door, I noted Mr. Leslie watching, dog in hand, with a smile on his face. I was surprised he didn't come out and harass me, but I supposed he figured his job was now done and there was no need.

The alley was a whole lot less scary in the light of day than it had been last night. Sunlight lit across the small half-wall that separated the alley from a tree-lined green where pedestrians could be seen, walking dogs, or listening to music as they power-walked their way to better health. It was hard to imagine someone had been killed here the night before, or any night, for that matter.

We reached the back entrance to A Purrfect Pose. I tested the door and found it locked tight, as it should be. Using my key, I unlocked it and let Sierra in before me.

"We're supposed to stay in the back," I said. "I'm going to handwrite a sign to stick to the front door to let my students know I'll be closed for the foreseeable future, so I'll need to pop into the office for a minute or two. Could you feed the cats and make sure they have fresh water for me?"

"Sure thing." Sierra made for the front, peeked into the main room. "It looks . . . normal."

"There wasn't much blood." It was my turn to shudder. "He was stabbed, but it was pretty clean. I'm not sure any got onto the floor." Just the yoga mat.

"A clean stabbing?" She made a face. "The killer a neat freak or something?"

I spread my hands and shrugged before heading for the office. Clean freak or not, it was strange that they'd taken the time to lay out a mat. It made me wonder if it was one of mine, or if Jonas or the killer had brought their own.

If it was the killer's, it should make identifying them easy.

I entered the office and then stopped dead in my tracks.

Papers were scattered across the desk and floor. Drawers were hanging open, as was my filing cabinet. White powder was peppered all over my things. Even the small trash can by my desk had been emptied and left on its side on the floor.

Mouth hanging open, I did a quick check and found that everything important was still there, just not where it should be. Apparently, finding a killer included ransacking my office.

I had half a mind to call Chief Higgins and demand he come clean up after his officers, but decided against it. If he knew I was there, he'd be liable to arrest me for interfering with his crime scene, and then he would use me as bait for Hunter. And while I might be able to use Olivia to explain why I was there, it would in turn land her in hot water, something I didn't want to do to family.

"I'll deal with this later," I muttered, finding a marker and loose sheet of printer paper. I handwrote a brief note, found some tape, and then carried the page to the front door. I taped it on the inside, and then headed back to where Sierra was sitting on the floor with a bonded pair of young cats in her lap.

"Do you think Herman needs a friend or two?" she asked when I entered. "Like, do you think he's lonely by himself?" Seeing me, the cats left her lap to come wind their way around my ankles.

"I think Herman needs a diet."

I helped Sierra to her feet.

"That, he does." She scanned the room and nodded. "All fed and watered and safe. What's next?"

"Next, we head to the shelter so I can talk to Kiersten." A call would work, but I wanted to do this in person. It's harder to say no to someone when they can fall to their knees and beg in front of you. I knew the shelter was struggling for space, but I wasn't sure where else to go.

We headed out the back, and just as I was about to close the door, I remembered Lulu's adoption application. It was somewhere in my office, though with the mess, I wasn't sure where.

Still, since I was heading to see Kiersten, I figured I should look for it and take it with me.

"I need to grab something from inside real quick," I said. "Meet me at your car?"

"Okey dokey." Sierra saluted, and then walked away, humming under her breath.

Before heading back inside, I paused and looked around the alleyway, hoping to spot some sort of clue that would tell me that the murder had taken place out here, or who the killer might be. What was I looking for? I had no idea. Maybe a lost glove. Or perhaps droplets of blood. Anything would do.

The alley looked like, well, an alley. Debris was scattered across the pebbly surface. Sticks, discarded pop cans, and other trash lined the wall, though not as much as you'd expect.

A random white sock that was so old and filthy, it was stiff, lay near the alleyway door of Bark and Style.

If there had been any clues, they were long gone. The police would have searched the area, and if Jonas was killed out back and then dragged in through the alley door, any blood that might have spilled would have washed away in the rain.

Somewhat relieved—I didn't want to find any sort of bodily fluids, helpful or not—I headed inside and hurriedly searched through the office for Lulu's adoption application. I found it on the floor, under the desk with a handful of blank applications. I retrieved it, leaving the others lie, and then headed for the back again. I was about to open the door when I noticed one of the storage shelves—the same one Hunter had leaned against the previous week—had been moved.

I immediately imagined a black-clad figure dragging Jonas through the back door, bumping into the shelf, and knocking it askew as they passed. The image was so vivid, I actually stepped aside, as if to let them pass.

The thought that a killer might have been *right there* had invisible fingers running up and down my spine. I shoved the shelving unit back into place with a loud groan of metal feet scraping across the floor, not caring if the police wanted it left as it was. When I stepped back, I noticed the corner of a page sticking out from underneath the repositioned shelf.

Brow furrowed, and without thinking, I bent over and picked it up. The page was thick, glossy on one side, and I'd quickly deduced it was a printed photo, even before I'd turned it over to look at it.

And when I did . . .

My head spun so fast, I had to back up until I was leaning against the wall lest I fall. I stared at the photo, willed the image on it to change, but it remained stubbornly static and real.

The photo was in full color, taken during the evening, just

before the sun had gone down. Shadows stretched from the brick building which served as a backdrop to what was happening. Jonas Valentine had his arm extended, with something that might have been an envelope in his hand, but I couldn't be sure.

And standing with him, hand extended to receive the envelope—no, a small, wrapped package—was a hooded figure wearing a CLU hoodie that was becoming all too familiar. I couldn't see his face clearly, but I didn't need to.

Based on the clothing, the stance, and the build of the man, I was pretty sure I was looking at my brother.

"I was thinking that when we finish up here, we could meet up with Aaron and Henna. They're planning on . . ." Sierra trailed off, looked me up and down. "What did I miss?"

My heart was pounding in my ears, so I almost didn't hear her. Hunter and Jonas. Together. And someone had taken a photo of them. But why? And why was the photo left at A Purrfect Pose?

"Earth to Ash." Sierra waved a hand in front of my face. "You okay?"

"Yeah. Fine. I'm fine." I somehow managed to smile, despite how my anxiety was through the roof. "Aaron and Henna sounds great. Let's get to the shelter."

Sierra gave me a lingering look, but started her car without complaint.

I was torn on what to do with the photo. Take it to the police and Hunter might end up in jail. Do nothing and then I might be concealing evidence in Jonas's murder. I had no doubts that it *was* evidence, but of what? Maybe Hunter did nothing wrong and just happened to be in the wrong place at the wrong time.

My phone jangled, causing me to jump, which in turn startled Sierra, who swerved on the road before correcting herself.

"Sorry," I said, tugging my phone free and answering.

"Hi, Ash. It's Walker."

Oh boy. Was I ready for this? "I saw."

He laughed. "I guess you did. You sound busy, so I won't keep you. I just wanted to check in and make sure we're still on for tonight?"

"I, um . . ."

"If you don't want to, I understand." Hurt marred his words.

"It's not you." I took a deep breath, calmed my nerves. Walker had done nothing wrong, and the photo pretty much proved it. "And yes, we're still on. I've got a lot on my mind, so I'm a bit scatterbrained at the moment."

"We've all been there." He sounded relieved, which made a ball of warmth form in my chest. Maybe the day wouldn't turn out to be so bad after all. "Pick you up at seven?"

"Sure thing." I almost left it at that, but I *had* to know. "Hey, do you know a guy named Jonas Valentine? He was in my Friday morning yoga class. The one you attended."

There was a long pause before, "Can't say that I do. Why?"

"No reason. See you at seven." I clicked off before he could ask me anything more.

"That sounded awkward," Sierra said. "Hot date?"

"Remember that guy from Snoot's?"

She took her eyes off the road long enough to widen them at me. "You mean the hunk of meat with the smoldering good looks and stupid name?"

"His name's not stupid."

"Walker Hawk," she said, deepening her voice. "Buffalo wrangler by day, secret agent by night."

I laughed. "Stop it. But yes, it's him."

"Well, it's about time you got out of your apartment and lived a little. I was afraid you might shrivel up into an empty husk when you and Drew split."

"Hey! I still go out."

"Uh-huh. With us. And then you go home to be alone while the rest of us are still out having fun."

"I'm not alone. I have a cat now."

"That might actually make it worse." She paused, smiled. "Maybe Herman could come visit sometime so I can see how he'd handle another cat."

"We'll see. I need to get Luna settled in first before inflicting Herman on her."

"Hey! He's not that bad."

"He might squish her."

Sierra laughed. "That, he might."

We arrived at the animal shelter, which was directly across from Cardinal Lake University. The campus was buzzing with early-morning activity. Of course, campus might be too grand of a word for the trio of buildings that held classes and the two long, single-story dorms that housed the few students who couldn't commute and didn't want to rent one of the over-priced rentals around town. CLU was most definitely more of a local college than one that drew out-of-state students.

It struck me as strange that one of the professors there had been murdered, and yet classes went on like nothing had happened. I wondered if the school had called in a replacement, or if Jonas's classes had been cancelled. How did you adjust when someone was murdered like that and the kids had paid so much to attend his classes?

I shook off the thought as Sierra parked. Thankfully, that wasn't for me to decide. "I'll be just a minute if you want to wait here?"

"Sure." She sat back, phone already in hand. "I'll make sure Aaron and Henna are still good with meeting up. It's still pretty early for them, especially since they were together late last night, if you know what I mean?"

"They should get married and get it over with," I said, climbing out of the car.

Sierra snorted. "I'll tell them that."

"You'd better not." I closed the door and headed for the shelter.

The Cardinal Lake animal shelter wasn't exactly well funded, but they got by. As soon as you walked through the door, you were hit by the smell of wet dog and ammonia. The volunteers did what they could to mitigate the smell, but with so many animals, it was an impossible task.

"Hi, Ash." A teenaged Tyra Potts waved from her seat behind the counter as I entered. "You looking for Kiersten?"

"I am. How's school going?"

Tyra made a face that included crossed eyes and a tongue, which was pierced, sticking out of the corner of her mouth. I assumed that meant it was going okay.

Tyra had volunteered at the shelter from the moment she could walk. Her parents let her get away with pretty much anything, hence the tongue piercing, but that didn't mean she was trouble. In fact, she got good grades, was popular enough to not to get bullied, but not so much that she turned mean like so many others that age do. I liked her immensely, as anyone should.

"Kiersten's in the back with the cats. Got a new batch of kittens in today from the Holloway farm."

I suppressed a sigh. The Holloways had barn cats they refuse to neuter or spay, which in turn, made more cats than they needed. They figured it was good for the town because that meant there was a never-ending supply of kittens for people to adopt, not thinking that there were already too many homeless animals and they were just making things worse. No amount of explaining seemed to get it through their heads.

Needless to say, the Holloways weren't Kiersten's favorite people.

"I'll tread carefully," I said, heading for the door on the right, which led back toward the cat section.

Tyra's "It won't help," followed me through the door.

I found Kiersten in the far back of the shelter, mewling kittens milling around her feet. I was glad to note that they were weaned, and weren't so young that they would need to be bottle-fed.

"Looks like you've got your hands full," I said, which brought a half dozen tiny pairs of eyes swiveling my way. It was followed by the smallest—and cutest—stampede known to man as the kittens rushed over to investigate the newcomer.

Kiersten shot me a glare that evaporated as I scooped up a pair of the muted calicos. They immediately started playing with my hair.

"I'm about to go give Harlan a dressing down. Look at this, Ash! We don't have room for any more kittens, not after the ones that jerk left on the library doorstep last week."

"Well," I said, snapping my head sideways just in time to avoid a misaimed paw meant for my ear. I set the kittens down, and they immediately began to wrestle with one another. "At least they're cute."

"And small, I suppose," Kiersten said. "But if they're here for more than a month, I'm going to be overwhelmed."

"Maybe this will help." I stepped forward and handed her Lulu's application. "That's one less cat we need to find a home for."

Kiersten scanned the sheet and then set it aside. "One down, hundreds to go."

An exaggeration, but honestly, not by much.

I walked a circuit around the room, a trail of kittens tumbling in my wake. With every step, my heart sank a little more.

"What's going on, Ash? You've got that look on your face."

"What look?"

"The one that says you've got bad news that I'm not going to like."

I stopped my meandering and turned to face Kiersten. "Someone was killed at A Purrfect Pose last night."

Her mouth dropped open. "What? I didn't hear anything about it."

Kiersten wasn't one to follow the news or social media. She had her hands full here, and often sequestered herself to make sure the animals had her full attention. That often meant she was the last to hear of anything happening in town or otherwise.

"The police are working on the case, but in the meantime, they don't want me to open the studio."

Kiersten put it together quickly. "Which means you need someone to take the cats."

"I thought maybe you could bring them back here temporarily, but . . ." I motioned toward the kittens.

Kiersten leaned against the table and rubbed at her temples. I noted she had a dozen tiny superficial scratches on her hands, likely caused when she was giving the kittens a brief examination before calling in the local vet, Doctor Lewis, who often agreed to come to the shelter in situations like this.

"If there's nowhere else, I'm not going to say no," Kiersten said. "I mean, they are still technically shelter cats."

They were, yet I'd already taken to them as if they belonged to me and the studio.

I made a snap decision then. "Let me talk to the police," I said. "I can see if maybe we can leave the cats in place and go in to take care of them. It's not like there's any evidence left for them to find." I pointedly ignored the voice in the back of my head screaming about the photo I'd found.

Kiersten's shoulders sagged. "That would be great if they'll allow it. We're packed right now, and that could lead to a lot of sick animals." She hesitated a moment before asking, "Who died?"

"A man named Jonas Valentine." I waited to see if she'd react, but she didn't appear to know him. "He was a professor at CLU."

"And he was killed at the studio?"

"Or dragged there afterward. I'm not sure which."

"That's terrible." One of the kittens started meowing its tiny little head off, drawing Kiersten's attention. "Okay, okay. It's time for food," she said, scooping the furball up. "I should get back to it."

"Have fun," I told her. "I'll let you know what the police say."

"Do that. And if they say it's okay for us to go in, I'll help out as much as I can. I still have a key, so I can go in to feed them when you can't."

"Great." I left as the kittens swarmed Kiersten.

"See you, Ash," Tyra said as I made for the door. Her feet were propped up on the counter and she looked as if she might be preparing for a nap.

"Be good," I told her, and then I stepped outside.

As I walked back to the car, I found my gaze moving to the CLU campus across the street. I'd been to the shelter countless times, and yet I didn't recall ever paying the college much attention, let alone the people in it.

But now I couldn't help but look. Most seemed unaware or unfazed by what had happened. Some walked together and chatted. Others solo, often with earbuds in their ears, heads nodding along to music only they could hear. I couldn't make out faces from this distance, but I got the impression that life was moving on as usual.

I'd just reached Sierra's car when I caught sight of a familiar woman stepping out of a car and making for one of the campus buildings. No, I couldn't see her features, but I knew the stride and body shape.

Fay? What was Fay Valentine doing at school the day after her husband was murdered?

And then: *What if she doesn't know?*

It seemed unlikely, but it was always possible that the police had tried to reach her and she'd been out or her phone had been turned off and they'd given up.

With a "hold on" gesture to Sierra, who was watching me from behind the wheel of her car, I crossed the street, hoping I wasn't about to deliver the news to Fay Valentine that her husband was dead.

CHAPTER 7

The only time I'd ever been on the Cardinal Lake University campus was when I'd decided to walk the walking trail that weaved around the outskirts of the campus and all the way back into the small wooded area behind it. I'd parked in the main parking lot, hit the trail, and that was it. No exploring. No stopping in at one of the buildings. Just the trees and open air.

The campus green wasn't big. A handful of students lounged on the lawn, enjoying the weather. Another couple of people were walking the trail, arms and legs pumping. The parking lot, I noted, was only about halfway full, but it was still early. I'd often seen it packed, with cars lining the side of the road in front of the dorms because there were no more spaces left.

When I approached the brick building I saw Fay Valentine enter—Carter Hall, according to a plaque by the door—I didn't know what to expect. These days, with all of the security precautions schools take to keep the students safe, I half expected to find the doors locked to anyone who didn't have a school ID badge or to be frisked by an overzealous security guard the moment I was through the door.

But when I tugged on the door, it opened with no resistance.

A couple of students slid outside past me as I entered, none of them paying me much mind as they chatted with one another. An unmanned desk sat just inside to the right, and a campus security guard sat in a chair in the corner across from it. He didn't so much as glance up from his phone as I walked over to a large board behind the desk that listed department floors and teacher offices.

I perused the board, looking for Fay's name. There was no schedule of classes, so if she was teaching, I'd have no idea where to find her. I knew from her conversation with Topher on the first day of yoga class that she taught English Lit, but that didn't mean it was the only thing she taught. And the entire building seemed devoted to literature and language arts, so I couldn't even narrow my search down by floor or wing.

Students filtered by. No one seemed to notice me as they passed, nor did anyone come to the desk to see if I needed help. I considered the security guard, figuring if anyone would know where Fay Valentine might be, he would. Then again, he might ask me why I was looking for her, which could lead to an awkward exchange about Jonas I most definitely didn't want to get into with a stranger.

Her office it is, I decided. If nothing else, it was a place to start.

My footfalls echoed on the tiled floor as I crossed the room to the stairs. Fay's office was on the third floor. I climbed upward, mentally practicing what I was going to say once I saw her. How did you tell a woman her husband was dead? And if she already knew, then how did you ask her why she wasn't sitting at home, bawling her eyes out?

I paused at the second-floor landing and considered turning around. This wasn't my job. The police were the ones who should be here, talking to Fay. All I could do was make things worse.

But she was one of my students. Sure, we'd only met a couple of times, and we had never really talked beyond simple pleasantries, but that didn't mean I didn't care. If nothing else, I could give her my condolences because there was no telling if I'd ever get another chance.

With a nervous huff, I continued upward.

I reached the third floor. It looked like every other floor I'd passed, though there were far fewer students in the hallways here, and most of the doors were closed. I noted a small group of what I assumed were teachers standing in a doorway, sipping coffee, and staring down the hall toward an open door.

It didn't take a genius, let alone a college professor, to figure out they were staring at Fay Valentine's office.

Eyes swiveled my way briefly as I passed by. There were three of them, two women and a man. One of the women raised her mug fractionally toward me in salute, but otherwise, they remained grim-faced and silent in their vigil.

Fay might not know about Jonas, but these people sure did.

It wasn't until I was an office away from Fay's own that I heard voices. Voices I knew.

"You're making a mistake, Fay. Don't do this."

"I have to, Topher. I . . . I can't do this."

I came to a stop, uncertain whether to proceed or wait. I could make out Fay's tear-marred voice, along with Topher Newman's own stressed one, but I didn't know if they were with anyone else.

"We all care about you," Topher said. "We can be your support system. *I* can be if you need me to. You don't have to do this alone."

Fay sniffed and I imagined her dabbing at her nose and eyes with a tissue. "Thank you, Topher. It means a lot to me, it really does, but I can't. I just can't. Not with everything that's happened. Jonas and his—" She sucked in a breath as if she'd said more than she'd intended. "I can't."

"Please, at least think about it more before you make such a rash decision," Topher said, voice speeding up. "Forget everything else. Forget about me if you must. I know it's hard, but you're needed here."

"I've already decided." There was a rustle, and then Fay strode out of the office, carrying a cardboard box stuffed with what appeared to be the contents of her desk. The corner of a framed photograph stuck out the top, and I wondered if it was of Jonas or someone else important in her life. "Oh!" She jerked to a stop when she saw me. "Ash. What are you doing here?"

Topher stepped out into the hall behind Fay, wearing an Aerosmith T-shirt. He looked almost as frazzled as she did. Fay's face was red, her eyes puffy and swollen. One eye looked almost bruised, but it was hard to tell for sure through her tears.

"I'm so sorry, Fay," I said, mind blanking on everything I'd considered saying on my way up. "About Jonas. I was at the animal shelter when I saw you across the street coming in here and I . . ." I trailed off, not sure how to continue.

Fay closed her eyes, causing fat teardrops to squeeze out from their corners. She didn't bother wiping them away. They left a faint trail in her makeup as they slid down her cheeks and onto her blouse.

"I . . . Thank you, Ash," she said. "I apologize that it happened at your studio. The cats. And Jonas. I don't know why he was there, but . . ." She sucked in a trembling breath. "You shouldn't have been dragged into this."

The question *Dragged into what?* was on the tip of my tongue, but I bit it back. Now wasn't the time.

"Mrs. Valentine," Topher pleaded. "Fay. Please."

"No, I've made up my mind, Topher." Fay took a deep breath, steadied her gaze past me. "I appreciate your concern, and I do wish things could be different, but I can't stay here. Not after Jonas. What he's done." She took a deep, steadying breath. "Please, if you'll excuse me."

Before I could say or do anything, Fay strode past me, box clutched in her arms so tightly, she looked close to crushing it. Her colleagues muttered condolences to her as she passed. Fay didn't appear to have heard them as she made for the stairwell. She didn't look back before vanishing through the door.

"She doesn't deserve this," Topher said as the door closed behind her. "None of it."

"What did she mean?" I asked. "Is she quitting?"

Topher ran his fingers through his hair, fingers bunching briefly in his frustration. "She put in her resignation this morning. I was heading to class when I saw her and since I heard about Professor Valentine, I wanted to make sure she was okay. We all love her here. I think she's everyone's favorite teacher, whether you had her in class or not."

I could see that. Fay was somewhat reserved during the yoga sessions, but I thought that had more to do with Jonas's presence than anything. When she was playing with the cats, or talking to one of the other students, she let her guard down and would smile and laugh like anyone else. It made me wish I'd taken more time to get to know her. I had a feeling that I wouldn't be seeing her at A Purrfect Pose again, and honestly, I didn't blame her.

"She should have left him a long time ago."

"Pardon?" I asked, startled by the harshness in Topher's voice.

"Mrs. Valentine." He paused. "Fay. She should have divorced Professor Valentine months ago. She wasn't happy with him."

"Why do you say that?" I asked. I'd noticed tension between the couple, but nothing that hinted that their marriage was at risk.

Topher glanced up and down the hall, as if making sure no one was listening, before he spoke at a near whisper. "They fought," he said. "I don't know if you noticed her eye, but that bruise isn't because of her crying. I think she got into it with Jonas and he hit her."

"Did she tell you this?"

Topher chewed on his lower lip, stuffed his hands into his pockets, and shrugged. "Not directly. But you could tell." He took a step closer to me. "This happened a couple days ago, I think. I saw her in class yesterday and noticed she was wearing extra makeup. She was hiding the bruise, and had done a good enough job of concealing it, I'm pretty sure she's done it before."

I wanted to smack myself. If Fay had been wearing more makeup than usual, if she'd had a bruise under her eye on Friday, I should have noticed. Did it make me a bad person because I'd completely missed it? Or was I just unobservant?

Topher seemed to notice my frustration because his tone softened. "She did a really good job hiding it," he said. "I only noticed because the light hit her just right while you were out talking to the dog guy."

"Mr. Leslie?"

"Yeah. I wanted to ask her about it, but thought better of it since Professor Valentine was there and I didn't want him to overhear. I just know they'd been fighting recently; the Valentines, I mean. Like, a lot. It got so bad that she stayed with someone for a few days earlier this week." Another glance down the hall and another dip in volume. "I think she was seeing someone else."

"Fay?" I couldn't believe it. "She was cheating on Jonas?"

"I don't have proof, but I'm pretty sure she was."

"How do you know this?" I asked. I couldn't imagine that Fay would have confided in a student, even one she shared yoga class with.

"The rumor's been going around," he said with a dismissive shrug. "They had a big blowup here at the school earlier this week. I think it was Monday, maybe? Could have been Tuesday. That's when she moved out. Professor Valentine screamed something about her spending too much time with 'that guy.'" He made air quotes.

My mind was racing. Fay was cheating on Jonas, and he'd found out about it. They'd fought. He'd given her a black eye, or so it appeared. Not a bad one, but one that was noticeable by those who'd gotten close enough to her to see it. They hid their troubles well because I sure didn't notice them. And then . . . what?

I tried to imagine a scenario where Fay Valentine murdered her husband for striking her and I just couldn't make it work. Jonas killing Fay for cheating? Sure. You hear about that sort of thing all the time. But the other way around?

A new thought: if Jonas had hit Fay and her lover had found out about it, they'd be angry, maybe angry enough to kill.

"Do you know who she was cheating on him with?" I asked.

"I don't know for certain," Topher said. He was worrying at the hem of his well-worn shirt. It was clear that talking about this was making him nervous. Considering Jonas's murder, it was no wonder. "But after class Friday, Professor Valentine got into an argument with someone. I didn't hear what they said, but I'm pretty sure it had to have been about Fay because she looked upset by it."

"Who was he arguing with?" I asked. Could Fay have been seeing one of my other students? Someone like George?

"I don't know his name," Topher said. "But it was the new guy, the one who came to class without a mat."

By the time I made it back downstairs and was walking out of Carter Hall, I felt like a zombie. There was only one new guy who Topher could have been referring to: Walker Hawk.

I kept seeing him after class that day in my mind's eye. Red-faced, chest heaving, and looking like he was upset by something. I'd thought it was the yoga, maybe a little nervousness about talking to me, but no, he'd gotten into an argument with Jonas while I'd been in the office, helping Lulu with her cat adoption application.

He'd said he had something to do that night. Vague. Just "something." No clarification. And then, that very night, Jonas Valentine is murdered and left at A Purrfect Pose. Coincidence? I was beginning to think it wasn't.

A horn honked from the parking lot as I paused outside the Carter Hall doors. Sierra popped out of her car, which was now parked in the lot outside the building. She waved me over.

"I figured I'd save you the walk," she said as I mechanically opened the passenger side door and sat down. "So, you going to tell me what that was all about?" She gestured toward the English building I'd just come out of.

"Fay."

She blinked at me. "Like fairies and magical beings and stuff like that?"

"Valentine." I closed my eyes, forced my brain to break from the loop being played of Walker's red, sweaty face. "Jonas's wife."

"The widow?" Sierra looked at the doors to Carter Hall, but Fay Valentine was long gone. "She was here?"

I nodded and started picking at my thumbnail. "She resigned."

I knew I wasn't making much sense, and thankfully, Sierra didn't press too hard. I had no idea how I could explain it without freaking out. She *did* look worried, however.

"Are you going to be okay, Ash? You're pale and acting all fidgety and weird."

I jammed my hands under my thighs to keep from picking at

my nail. "I'm okay." I considered. "Well, not really *okay*, but I will be. I'm just a little shaken up right now is all."

Sierra turned in her seat. The car was running, but we had yet to move. "There's more to it than just you bumping into a woman whose husband was recently killed. Tell me."

"I could be wrong." I paused, considered. "Actually, I prob-ably *am* wrong."

"I don't care. Tell me."

I wasn't sure where to start, so I went with the most recent development first. "I think Fay was cheating on her husband with Walker."

"Walker? As in, *your* Walker?"

"He's not *my* Walker."

"You know what I mean, Ash."

I did, and so I let it go. "I guess Jonas got into an argument with Walker yesterday. It was likely about Fay, and then Jonas was killed later that night, and . . ."

"And you think Walker might have done it?"

I nodded as tears tried to force their way out. I blinked them away.

"Oh, Ash, come here." Sierra pulled me into an awkward hug, before pulling back, curious. "Wait. Didn't you ask him if he knew this Jonas guy on the phone earlier?"

"I did."

"And what did he say?"

"He said he didn't." Which, I was finding, had turned out to be a lie. And if he'd lied about that, what else had Walker Hawk lied about?

"That creep!" Sierra said. "You should call him up and give him a piece of your mind."

"Yeah, that sounds like a good idea. Let's call a guy who could bench-press me with one hand, and who might have killed a man in my studio, and yell at him. I don't see how that could possibly go badly for me."

Sierra made a face. "Yeah, I guess you're right." She shook her head. "Jeez. I can't believe it."

"You and me both." I almost left it at that, but it was nagging at me. "There's something else."

"There's more? Is the guy like some sort of mob boss or something? Should I be watching out for guys with no necks lurking around my house or something?"

"It's not about him." I turned in my seat so I could reach into the back where I'd left my purse. I took the photo I'd found at A Purrfect Pose from it and handed it to Sierra without explanation.

She looked at the photo for a solid two minutes, front and back, before handing it back. "I take it one of those guys is the dead one?"

"Jonas," I said with a nod, pointing him out.

"He knew Hunter?"

My heart sank. I'd hoped Sierra wouldn't have recognized him, because if she thought it might be someone other than my brother, then perhaps I'd been wrong and Hunter wasn't involved.

"I don't know," I said. "But this photo seems to indicate that he did."

She drummed her fingers on the wheel while she stared out the windshield, thinking. I let her do it because right then, I needed the time to organize my own scattered thoughts.

Jonas was dead. Hunter was in the photo found at the scene of the crime. Walker had argued with Jonas, might have been sleeping with Fay. How did it all connect?

Could Hunter have known about the affair somehow? Could he have gone to Jonas, convinced him to pay him so he could tell him who his wife was cheating on him with? It didn't sound like something Hunter would do, but then again, I didn't know everything about my brother.

But how did that lead to *Jonas* getting killed? Did Walker find out about the black eye and decide to punish Jonas for it? If that was the case, then how did the photo come into play? Had Walker stumbled upon the exchange between Jonas and Hunter and he decided to take a picture and then blackmail Jonas? But why do it at A Purrfect Pose of all places?

I replayed Walker's and my first encounter over in my head. I'd had coffees in hand and had bumped into him. I'd blamed myself. He'd said he wasn't watching where he was going, yet he *had* insinuated he'd seen me with my friends before our little accident. I'd thought that meant he'd noticed me because he was interested in me.

But what if it was because he'd been *following* me in the hopes of finding Hunter?

It seemed far-fetched, but I wasn't sure what else to think at that point.

"Let me see the photo again," Sierra said, holding out her hand. I handed it over automatically and watched as she looked from it, out the windshield, and then back to the photo again. "Interesting."

"What is?" I asked as she opened the car door and got out. I followed her. "Sierra?"

She was walking toward Carter Hall, but stopped before she reached it. She looked at the photo again, and then turned toward another building, one to the right of the first. After considering it a moment, she started walking.

"Sierra? What are you doing?" I hurried to catch up with her and fell in stride next to her.

"See that?" she asked, pointing at the photo.

"The blurry bit on the side?" There was a slight blur in the upper left corner of the photo.

"Yes. And that?" This time, she pointed toward the brick background.

"Yeah. Why?"

She kept walking, past the second building, onto the trail leading into the wooded area behind the college. Sierra glanced back toward the buildings, and then abruptly stepped off the trail in front of the trees. She would take three or four steps, pause, look at the photo, the building, and then do it again.

Finally, she stopped, and grinned. "There," she said, handing the photo back to me.

"There what?"

"Look." She pointed toward the back of the building we were facing. I could see movement through the windows as students and teachers milled around inside. It appeared as if they were between classes.

"Okay?" I asked. "What am I looking at?"

With a sigh, Sierra grabbed the photo and held it up. "See it?"

It hit me like a slap. "It was taken here." A window could be seen at the top of the photo. It was subtle, so much so I hadn't noticed, but standing here now, it was as obvious as day. "Hunter was here."

"Not only that," Sierra said, turning toward the trees. She pushed aside a bit of brush, and then pointed. "I think the person who took the photo was standing there."

I looked at where she was pointing, but saw nothing interesting. The brush looked a little smooshed, but that could have been caused by anything.

"I think someone took that photo without being seen," Sierra said. "They were here, saw what was going on, snuck into the trees, and took the picture. See that branch?" She pointed to a low-hanging branch that was about shoulder high. "That's what's in that corner." She pointed to the dark blur in the photo.

"They were being followed?" I asked, once more thinking of Walker.

"That, or someone was walking the trail, saw what was happening, and decided to take a picture of what was happening." "For what purpose?" I asked, more confused than ever. Sierra shrugged. "No clue." She started walking back to her car. "But if we find out who took the photo, then there's a good chance we'll uncover the identity of a killer."

CHAPTER 8

Henna Korhonen lived in a small house in a subdivision just off Cardinal Lake. It wasn't much bigger than my apartment, but thanks to the location, the price tag when she'd bought it two years ago—with help from her parents—had been eye-popping. I didn't even want to think what it would cost to buy it today.

Sierra and I were sitting on the back patio with Henna and Aaron, sipping espressos Henna had made with her latest splurge purchase. I couldn't see the lake from where we sat, but I could smell it on the breeze. Every so often, voices and boat engines could be heard as the sound echoed through the trees. Normally, it would be relaxing, but today, I doubted anything would calm my nerves.

"I can't imagine Hunter being involved in something this . . . this . . ." Henna looked to Aaron, who finished the thought for her.

"Murderous."

"Neither can I," I said with a sigh. The photo depicting Hunter with Jonas Valentine was sitting on the round patio table between us, being held down by a decorative nymph. Unlike much of the artwork around Henna's house, this nymph was clothed, albeit barely. "But he's in the photo."

"He *might* be in the photo," Aaron said, holding up a finger. "I'm not convinced it's him."

I desperately wanted to believe him, but I knew my brother. The more I looked at the image, the more I was positive it was Hunter. It was in the stance, the way he bunched his shoulders, as if he *knew* someone was taking his picture.

And what if he did? Could Hunter have been the one setting Jonas up? If so, for what?

A car drove by, drawing everyone's attention briefly. A Ferrari coasted to a stop outside the house next door, which was twice the size of Henna's own, and likely cost it. The car rumbled there for a good long couple of seconds before the driver used the driveway to turn around and speed off.

"Another lost soul," Henna said with a shake of her head. "I swear, they need to fix the signs around here. Do you know how many times I've had to call delivery services to complain about my packages never arriving?"

"You could always make signs of your own," Sierra said. "Hang them up on the trees."

Henna laughed. "I might do that."

"Any idea what's in the package-thing?" Aaron asked, nodding toward the photo.

"None," I said. "It could be money, I suppose."

"For?"

I shrugged, sipped my espresso. Knowing Hunter, it could be anything from a reward for some petty theft to payment for mowing the guy's grass. But if it was the latter, why make the handoff at the back of a building on the college campus where very few people could see them? And if it was an innocent exchange, why would someone take a picture of it and then bring the resulting photograph with them to murder Jonas Valentine?

"Hunter probably pointed him toward some new customers," Henna said.

"New customers?" I asked. "Jonas was a teacher."

"He was," Henna said. "And I guess he was pretty good at it when he wasn't dipping his toes into other professions."

"She doesn't mean he was looking to become a professional swimmer or anything like that," Aaron said with a smile that earned him a kick in the shin from Henna's bare foot.

"What are you talking about?" I asked.

The couple shared a look before Aaron answered. "It's just a silly rumor," he said. "At least it was back when we were younger and were students at CLU."

"Yeah," Sierra said with a laugh. "*Way* back, like all of two years ago."

"That's a lifetime with this dope," Henna said, bumping Aaron on the shoulder with her own.

"You know, that stings; it really does." He smiled as he said it.

"What rumor?" I asked. My heart was thumping in my chest so hard, I was sure they could all see it. Normally the banter between the lovebirds made me smile, but I wasn't feeling it today. "Do you know something that might tell me where Hunter is?"

Aaron frowned. "I don't know about that."

"And we don't even know if there's any weight to the rumors," Henna said. "You know how people talk. If there was any truth to it, I would imagine the school would have done something about it by now."

"What was the rumor?" I had to measure my words to keep from shouting them.

Another shared look between the couple. It was Aaron who finally spoke.

"Professor Valentine—Mister, not Missus—was rumored to have been selling stimulants to students."

"Homemade stims," Henna added. "Like, he made them in his classroom or office during off hours or some such. It had to be a difficult thing to pull off without anyone noticing."

"It's possible that he bought the pills at the store and sold them like he'd made them himself," Aaron said. "From what I heard, they were pretty potent. I have no idea how he managed it without getting caught, which is why I'm not so sure the rumors are true."

Henna swirled her espresso before speaking. "I knew a girl who might have bought some of his pills. She never admitted to it, so don't take this for gospel; I might be wrong. But this girl was definitely on something and she was taking chemistry with Professor Valentine at the time. She was fine at first, just your normal overachiever, but as the year went on, she started getting all twitchy and red-eyed. She hardly slept. The next thing I knew, she was gone. Whether she dropped out of college or transferred, I have no idea."

"That doesn't mean she was buying drugs from her teacher," I pointed out. The stress of college could have gotten to her. Or something in her personal life had put too much pressure on her. You know, like an overbearing mother who insisted she was doing the wrong thing with her life.

"No, it doesn't," Henna admitted. "But it does make you wonder."

That, it did. If Jonas was selling stimulants, homemade or otherwise, it could have gotten him into trouble with the school, the police, and students and their parents, if he were ever to be caught.

"Why would Hunter be involved in something like that?" Sierra asked, scrunching up her face. "It doesn't make any sense. He's never been into drug stuff before."

None of us had an answer to that.

"Even if Hunter was involved with Jonas and his pills," I said, "I don't think he would have killed him."

"No, of course not," Henna said as the others shook their heads.

"Who do you think did?" Aaron asked.

I considered it. I didn't like where my mind went, but it

made the most sense. "I'm starting to think it might have been Walker Hawk."

"That's the guy you were ogling at Snoot's, right?" Aaron asked.

"I wasn't ogling him."

Sierra snorted a laugh, while Aaron and Henna grinned at one another.

"I wasn't! I bumped into him and that's all that happened." I leaned forward. "But now that I've thought about it some, I don't think our meeting was an accident."

A bang caused a huge flock of birds to take flight from the surrounding trees. The sky briefly blackened before the birds resettled on their perches. Laughter followed the noise, and then died away.

"How so?" Henna shivered. By reflex, Aaron scooted his chair closer to put an arm around her.

"When we parted that night at Snoot's, he told me I should get back to my friends and he motioned toward our table," I said, suppressing a shiver myself. "That means he had already seen me. Seen *us*."

"You mean, like he was scoping you out?" Sierra asked.

"Or something like that," I said. "It feels like too much of a coincidence that I run into a guy who just so happens to have known the Valentines before he came to the yoga class, and when he does, it's the same class they are in. And then, that very night, Jonas dies."

"Wait, hold up," Aaron said. "He knew Professor Valentine?"

"That's what I heard." I explained what Topher had said about Jonas and Walker fighting while I'd been occupied with Lulu. "And when I talked to him on the phone this morning, Walker said he didn't know Jonas, which can't be true if he fought with him yesterday morning."

Sierra nodded, expression grave.

"So, one of them is lying," Aaron said.

"But which one?" I asked. I didn't want to believe either of them were. I supposed it was possible that Walker *didn't* know Jonas and the argument was about something that had happened while I was in the back with Lulu. Topher could have simply come to the wrong conclusion, especially since he already suspected Fay was cheating and Walker was a good-looking man.

"It should be pretty easy to figure that out," Henna said. "You say the argument happened after class?"

I nodded. "When I saw Walker afterward, he looked off. I thought it was because he was nervous or that we'd just spent the last thirty-odd minutes doing yoga."

"But he got into a fight with Jonas?" Aaron asked.

"An argument. I don't think it came to blows or anything." That, I would have heard about almost immediately.

"Well, it's likely others in the class saw what happened," Henna said. "If you ask around, maybe someone will have some more insights, like they overheard exactly what was said or something."

"I don't have that much time left," I muttered.

At Henna's and Aaron's questioning looks, Sierra said, "She's got a hot date with Walker tonight."

"You're going on a date with a guy who might have killed someone?" Henna asked, eyes wide.

"I didn't know that when I agreed to it!" I said. "In fact, the date was set up *before* Jonas was killed, so cut me some slack here."

"You should cancel," Henna said. "Call him up right now and tell him to shove it."

"Why?" Aaron asked. "Ash could interrogate him, ask him about the fight, how he knew Professor Valentine."

"Interrogate a killer?" Henna asked. "That sounds like a fantastic plan if you want to get killed yourself."

"That's what I said," I told Henna. "But Alexi said pretty much the same thing as Aaron. She thinks I should get Walker somewhere public, somewhere where he can't hurt me, and start asking him some questions."

"Sounds risky to me," Henna said.

"But what if we're all there?" Sierra asked. "You know, we serve as your backup? You go on your date and we, I don't know, stake out the place?"

"Or just so happen to be on dates of our own," Aaron said, taking Henna's hand and squeezing.

I didn't like any of this. Going on a date with a guy I'd only recently met was hard enough. But to do it with a guy I suspected might be a murderer? No way.

But looking around the table, I knew it was a losing battle. Even Henna seemed to be warming up to the idea as they talked about it. I had a feeling that if I were to put my foot down, I'd still find myself on the date, doing my best not to get murdered.

"Text me the details as soon as you have them," Sierra said. "I'll be sure to be there, no matter where you go, or how steamy it gets."

"And we'll be sitting a few tables away," Aaron said, while Henna nodded. "If this Walker guy tries anything, we can intercede."

The word "no" was on the tip of my tongue. All I had to do was open my mouth and say it.

"He's picking me up at seven" was what came out. "I'll text you the moment I know where we're going."

It looked like I was going to go on a date with a man who might be a killer, whether I wanted to or not.

Two hours later, I was standing in the middle of a pack of cats, contemplating doing something that would get me into a whole lot of trouble if anyone—namely, Chief Dan Higgins—were to find out about it.

After we finished our discussion on how to catch Walker Hawk in, well, *something*, my friends and I had hung out for a little while longer before I asked Sierra to drive me back into town and drop me off outside A Purrfect Pose. I then spent the next twenty minutes scouring the alley, looking for any sign at all that the murder had taken place out there—or that Walker had been there—but there was nothing.

So, I'd gone inside to take care of the cats, and do the one thing Chief Higgins had instructed me not to do.

I snooped.

It was my business, after all. I should know if someone was killed inside the building or if they'd been dragged in and posed after the fact. What difference it made? I wasn't sure. Jonas had ended up inside A Purrfect Pose, no matter where he was killed. That could mean someone was specifically trying to frame me, or it could mean that, like Alexi had said last night, they could have tried all the doors in the alley and mine was the only one that had opened.

But what about the security system? I'd been alerted to the door being ajar, but the cameras were unresponsive. That meant the killer knew about them, right? Or could the system have been down? A mere coincidence?

And what about the person I'd seen outside in the CLU hoodie when I'd come to check on the door? Could it have been the killer? A thief?

Hunter?

That was what I was there to find out.

I started in the cat room because, well, I was already there, and the door had been opened the night of the murder. I had no idea what a thief, Hunter or otherwise, would want out of the room. Even the killer would have no reason to open the door, not unless they thought the cats would somehow cover their tracks.

A quick look around told me that nothing was missing, and

that included the cats themselves. It was entirely possible the door had been opened by mistake, and I was wasting my time. But my office? *That* seemed like a better place to start.

I gave each of the cats one last pet before I closed them in, safe and snug. A few meows followed me across the hall, into the office, before they died away as the cats began playing with one another.

Thanks to Chief Higgins and the police, my office was a disaster, but at least my valuables were easy to find. The money was still secure in the small safe I kept in the corner. My desk had been ransacked, but that could have been from the police, not a thief. As far as I could tell, nothing was missing.

I stopped and surveyed the room, hands on my hips. If nothing was missing, what did that mean?

Honestly, I had no idea. I wasn't a police detective. I wasn't even an armchair sleuth who spent time watching murder mysteries or reading the books that would give me some insights into the mind of a killer, fictional or otherwise.

Anxiety churned at me as I left the office. The person in the CLU hoodie bothered me. They were too small to be Walker Hawk. But as noted before, Hunter was just the right size. But so were a lot of people.

If it was him, did that mean Hunter was the killer? Or had he come here, looking for me, and witnessed the murder? It might explain why he was missing now. If the killer had seen him, Hunter might be hiding, just so he wouldn't be next.

I entered the front room of A Purrfect Pose and then just stopped and stared at the empty space in the middle of the floor. The yoga mat Jonas had been posed upon was gone. The police had taken it, and I expected never to see it again. A quick count of the mats on display told me that none of them were missing. The same went for the ones on the storage shelf in the back; I'd counted them earlier.

So, that meant Jonas or the killer had brought their own mat. Who brought a yoga mat to a murder?

I walked a circuit around the room. Alone, the space felt too big, too quiet. My footfalls echoed, causing the hairs on the back of my neck to rise. I wondered if I'd ever feel comfortable inside here again, or if Mr. Leslie would get his wish and I'd be forced to move elsewhere, just to escape the ghosts of what had happened.

I paused by the big window and looked outside. Traffic was flowing around the square in fits and starts. A horn blared when a car shot through the square, not bothering to yield. They nearly hit a pedestrian crossing the street. It took me a moment to realize said pedestrian was Zaria Williams. She screamed at the car, fist raised in the air, before she continued on her way.

Anger sprang from anxiety and found a target in Zaria. Before I knew what I was doing, I was out the door and giving chase. I zipped past Bark and Style—which was where Zaria had come from—and crossed the street at a sprint, nearly getting hit by a car myself as I did.

I caught up to Zaria just as she was about to climb into a tiny electric vehicle parked at the side of the road.

"Zaria! Wait!"

She glanced up and scowled the moment she saw me. "What do *you* want?"

What *did* I want from her? The short chase had caused most of the anger to burn off, leaving me somewhat befuddled as to what to say next.

"You and Mr. Leslie want me gone," I said, not sure where I was going with it, but riding with it anyway.

Zaria's smile was of the mock sickly sweet kind. "What makes you think that? Oh, maybe it's because you imprison innocent animals."

Here we go. I forced myself to ignore the comment and pressed on. "Someone was killed at A Purrfect Pose. You wouldn't know anything about that, would you?"

"Why would I? Oh, wait, I know, you think *I* killed them

because I don't agree with you. Am I close?" Before I could respond, she laughed. "Of course you do. People like you never *think* before you jump to idiotic conclusions."

Welp, there it was again; the anger. "*I'm* the one jumping to conclusions? You're the one who acts like she knows what's going on inside my studio without actually ever stepping foot inside it!"

"I don't need to. I know what kind of person you are. My uncle told me all about you."

"Your uncle?" It dawned on me then. "Mr. Leslie is your *uncle?*"

Zaria rolled her eyes, shook her head, and then climbed into her car like I no longer mattered. She drove off without so much as another glance, leaving me standing alone on the sidewalk, feeling like an idiot.

I trudged back to A Purrfect Pose, silently fuming, and then locked up, making sure the back door was firmly closed. A part of me wanted to go over next door to yell at Mr. Leslie, but what good would that do? He, like Zaria, would just tell me how bad of a person I was being and then promptly ignore me.

I can't keep doing this. I felt bad for the cats, for leaving them alone at A Purrfect Pose, despite someone coming in to check on them regularly. If I thought I could manage it, I'd take them all home with me, but I was worried that it wouldn't work out, that I'd lose one of them or they would cause my landlord, Ian, to toss me out.

No, my apartment wasn't an option. Not yet anyway.

What I needed to do was open the studio again, and there was only one way I was going to be able to do that: talk to the man who was preventing me from doing it.

The walk to the Cardinal Lake police station wasn't a long one, which was a shame because by the time I was stepping through the front doors, I still hadn't figured out what I was going to say that would make Chief Higgins change his mind about letting me open. I guess that meant I was just going to have to wing it.

"Ash? What are you doing here?" Olivia was leaning on a desk, talking to another officer, when I entered. She straightened and joined me at the door. "We don't have anything new for you."

Oh, but I do. My purse suddenly felt like it weighed a hundred pounds. The photo of Jonas and Hunter together was tucked away inside. "I need to talk to Chief Higgins," I said. "About the cats."

Olivia's expression hardened. "You aren't going to tell him—"

"No, I'm not going to bring you into it," I assured her. "But the cats do need to be taken care of and the shelter is overwhelmed, so they can't go back there."

"I see," she said, before sighing. "Let me see if he'll talk to you."

I waited out front while Olivia went looking for Chief Higgins. It gave me more time to think about the photo, about how I *should* give it to the police, but in doing so, I'd be sentencing Hunter to . . . I wasn't sure what, but I knew with Higgins involved, it wouldn't be good for him.

If I don't hand it over, am I any better than the killer? Withholding evidence was a crime. I could be hurting the investigation by not turning it over. The killer might walk free because of it.

But . . . Hunter. I just needed to talk to Hunter first.

"Ms. Branson?" Chief Dan Higgins approached without Olivia. He'd likely told her to remain behind because of her connection to my family. "You want to talk?"

I crossed my arms to keep my hands from my purse. "I do."

Higgins rubbed at his chin, considered me, and then mirrored my stance. "Okay. Talk."

"It's about the cats." I explained about the shelter, the need to care for the animals, and the lack of anywhere else to take them. "And I see no reason as to why I can't hold classes. You've already collected all the evidence." My ears burned as I said it.

Higgins appeared unmoved, so I was surprised when he answered with, "You can go in and take care of the cats as often as you like."

I blinked at him. "Really?"

He nodded, relaxed. "We might not see eye to eye, but that shouldn't mean animals should suffer for it. I have a cat. I couldn't imagine leaving her on her own with no one to take care of her."

I couldn't help it; my mouth fell open and I asked, "*You* have a cat?"

He laughed. "What? You think just because I'm a big guy, I don't have a soft spot?"

"No, of course not," I said. "I, uh, thank you." I dropped my arms. "Would it be okay if I started holding classes at A Purrfect Pose again?"

"No."

"Come on! It's not going to hurt anything."

"You don't know that," he said. "At this point, we don't know if the killer was targeting you and your place, or if they were after Mr. Valentine. Until we know for sure, I don't want you putting yourself at risk."

"I won't be at risk. There's always ten or more people with me during class. I could cancel the night classes, only hold morning and afternoon sessions. I won't be alone."

"And after class?" he asked. "Are you telling me you leave when everyone else does, that you are never there alone?"

I clamped my mouth shut. I could have said something about how letting me in to feed the cats meant that I'd only ever be inside the studio by myself, but I didn't want to lose that privilege. Besides, unlike classes, the times when I'd show for the cats would be random and hard to predict for someone intent on doing me harm.

"I'm looking out for you here, Ash, whether you want to believe me or not," Higgins said.

"Mr. Leslie is Zaria Williams's uncle." I hadn't meant to say anything, but it just popped out in my frustration.

Higgins stared at me. "And?"

"And?" Then I got it. "You already knew! Why didn't you say something before?"

"Why would I?" he asked. "As far as I can tell, neither Ms. Williams or Mr. Leslie had anything to do with the murder."

"But they—"

Higgins raised a hand and cut me off. "Take the win, Ash. Feed your cats. Let me do the police work, all right? I'll find the killer and then you can go back to doing your yoga."

A "but" was on my lips, but I choked it back with a nod. I knew from experience that Chief Higgins wouldn't relent, and pressing him would only make him reconsider what concessions he had already made.

Grudgingly, I thanked him and then left the police station. The sun was shining, but in a few hours, it wouldn't be. Dinner was fast approaching, and I wasn't going to be doing it alone.

Maybe going on a date with Walker Hawk wasn't such a bad idea. If it helped me get to the bottom of the murder and let me open my studio again, then the risk, I thought, would be worth it.

CHAPTER 9

A series of tiny meows urged me to move faster as I filled the cat dish with food. Luna was pacing back and forth at my feet, rubbing my calves with every pass.

"Okay, okay, it's coming," I said.

She meowed once more and then threw herself bodily onto her side, paws reaching toward me, as if she'd collapsed from hunger and was trying to let me know that she was on her last breath.

Talk about a drama queen.

As the food dish hit the floor, she popped up and ran over, suddenly full of life again. She attacked the food with the relish of one who expects to never see it again.

I was watching her eat with a combination of amusement and love when my phone rang. One look at the screen and my already stressful day took a turn for the worse.

Bringing the phone to my ear, I tried not to sigh when I said, "Hi, Mom."

"Ashley Cordelia."

I closed my eyes. I could hear the satisfaction in her voice, the sheer glee at being right, and all she'd done was say my name.

"I don't have long," I told her, glancing at the clock. I had twenty minutes to get ready for my date, less if I wanted to be waiting for him outside. "If we can talk about this tomorrow, I can call you first thing in the morning."

"No, no, this won't take long," Mom said. "I just figured I'd reach out and let you know you are still welcome at Branson Designs. I've heard that you have some dissatisfied customers as of late and that could cause a ripple effect." She paused. "You call them customers, right? I don't know how to describe any of what you do."

"They're my students. How did you—Never mind." Of course she knew all about the murder and subsequent backlash I'd received from, as she put it, dissatisfied customers. My inbox had been blowing up all day with emails from yoga students wondering about the studio. Two asked for their money back, saying they could never return, even if things got worked out with the police. Another pair had decided to cancel the monthly sub and would reconsider *if*—and they stressed the if part—I opened again.

I had a feeling it was only going to get worse the longer the investigation drew out.

"It's a shame what happened, of course," Mom was saying. "Don't get me wrong. But it's not entirely unsurprising, either."

"You expected someone to get murdered?" I asked, mind flashing on a rather unkind thought. *Did she set it up just to ruin me?* Mom could be cutthroat when it came to getting what she wanted, but to murder someone? That seemed a bit much, even for her.

"No, I don't mean I thought someone would die at your little place, but I was positive *something* would happen. When you make decisions without thinking through the consequences, it's inevitable that something will go wrong. It's simply the way the world works. I tried to teach you kids that, but it appears as if it has fallen on deaf ears."

Don't argue, Ash. Don't argue. "I should go," I said, voice tight. This was exactly the sort of conversation I didn't want to have. Ever.

"Ashley, please," Mom said. "I'm not trying to upset you. I hope you understand that I'm simply looking out for your best interests. I always have."

"I know." And, deep down, I did. She just had a crappy way of showing it.

Mom sighed dramatically into the phone, making sure I understood her displeasure with me. She'd probably expected me to grovel and tell her how right she was. "Well, I suppose I should let you go do whatever it is you think is more important than talking to your mother. It was nice talking to you."

It was my turn to sigh, though mine wasn't nearly as dramatic. "It's not that, Mom. I really do have somewhere to be. I've got . . ." I checked my Fitbit. "Fifteen minutes to get ready or else I'm going to be late."

"Oh?" Curiosity was slathered all over the word.

Instead of answering—and enduring the barrage of questions that would follow—I asked, "Have you seen Hunter lately? I've been trying to reach him."

A pause. "No, I haven't heard from *Reginald*. Why?"

That was another rabbit hole I wanted no part of. "No reason. He wanted to talk last week and we haven't had the chance to get together since then."

"I see. Well, if I talk to him, I'll be sure to mention you. Not that I expect to see him, that is. You know how he can be. He acts like I've done him some great disservice, all because I want to help him climb out of the hole he's dug for himself. And when I *do* offer my services, what does he do? He takes what he needs and then is gone again, without so much as a thank-you. It makes me feel unappreciated."

Somehow I felt the last was aimed at me, more than at Hunter. "Thanks. I'll call you soon."

"And let me know about your decision. I really do think you should come back to Branson Designs, where family can keep you safe."

I rolled my eyes, said a silent prayer for strength. "I will. Goodbye, Mom."

"Ashley Cordelia."

I clicked off and then, with one last frantic look at my Fitbit, I hurried into my bedroom to get changed.

I didn't overthink my outfit, but made sure I was comfortable and mobile. No heels. No tight skirts or flowing dresses. If Walker Hawk turned out to be a killer, I needed to be able to run away without tripping over a too-long dress or staggering around in heels, though I supposed I could use the latter as a weapon if it came down it.

Besides, this was just dinner in Cardinal Lake. Even the fanciest restaurant by the lake was more of a jeans and nice shirt kind of place. There was no reason to go overboard.

It took less than ten minutes to find something I liked and to touch up my makeup. By then, Luna was in a food coma on her cat perch by the window. She looked so content and relaxed, it eased my mind. I mean, how could the rest of my day go badly when she looked that cute?

Voices outside my door had me tensing. I eased closer until I could make out Pavan's voice. It was followed by Edna's raspy laugh, and then Walker Hawk's chuckle.

I froze, suddenly panicked. Was I really going to do this? I had my phone, and would have it with me throughout the night. A group chat with Alexi, Sierra, Aaron, and Henna was a finger press away. As soon as I knew where I was going, I'd fill them in and they'd do whatever it was they planned on doing to make sure I stayed safe.

But it wasn't just the thought that Walker might be a murderer that had my skin crawling and my anxiety spiking through the roof. I was bombarded with memories of Drew, of how he was the only guy I'd ever dated. Quiet moments. Big fancy dinners. Lunches on the beach.

It was supposed to last forever, and then I had to go and realize that I liked him better as a friend. Did I make a mistake? Was I making a mistake now?

A knock at the door had me debating the merits of leaping out the window and running away before sense returned. I could do this. Just because dating was new territory for me didn't mean it had to be scary. People did it all the time. Only a small percentage of them ended up murdered.

I took a calming breath, brushed imaginary lint from my shirt, and then I answered the door.

Walker Hawk stood in the hall, a bouquet of flowers in hand and an aw-shucks grin on his face. He was dressed, thankfully, in jeans and a nice shirt that showed off his physique. Behind him, Edna and Pavan were smiling like fools as they watched from Edna's doorway.

"Hi," I said, trying my damnedest not to look at my neighbors.

"Hi." Walker presented the flowers. "I know it's cliché, but it felt weird coming here empty-handed."

"Thank you." And then, against my better judgment, the words "Do you want to come inside a moment?" popped out.

"Sure. Thank you."

I stepped aside, allowing Walker in. As I closed the door, Pavan shot me a thumbs-up, while Edna winked before tittering something to Pavan that caused him to laugh.

Those two were going to be unbearable tomorrow, I just knew it.

Luna's head rose as Walker entered my apartment. She took one look at him, and then decided he must be safe enough, because she went right back to sleep. Good omen? I sure hoped so.

"Let me put these in water and then we can go."

Walker nodded and proceeded to glance around my apartment from the doorway. "Nice place," he said, with no hint of ridicule in his voice.

"I haven't unpacked," I said, finding a tall glass. I filled it with water and then added the flowers. I had a vase somewhere, but it, like almost everything else I owned, was still boxed up.

"I see that."

I carried the flowers to the table and set them down. I noted the flowers were all cat-safe and wondered if he'd taken that into consideration when he'd bought them or if it had happened by chance. Either way, I couldn't help but give him a few brownie points for it, murderer or not.

"I'm ready if you are," I said, grabbing my purse and slipping my phone inside.

Walker bowed his head and opened the door for me. "After you."

Mentally steeling myself, I stepped out into the hall.

"I'm impressed," I said, lifting my beer. I almost had to shout above the noise, it was so loud. "I thought you might go for something fancy."

Walker laughed. "I thought about it. But then I realized I don't know enough about you to know whether or not you'd like something like that. We met at Snoot's on the Lake, so I figured, why not bring you back here?"

Snoot's was rocking since it was a Saturday night. The music was turned up and the place was packed wall to wall. I'd hoped to get a seat on the deck outside, but that too was a mass of people, many of whom were so young, they made *me* feel old.

Instead, we'd found a corner table that still had crumbs scattered across it and claimed it before anyone else could. A quick brush-off, and it was as clean as it was going to get.

When Walker had left to get our beer and put in a food order, I sent a quick group text to my friends before stuffing my phone back into my pocket. It buzzed three times in rapid succession in what was likely a series of emojis wishing me luck. I didn't get a chance to check before he was back.

"This is definitely within my comfort zone," I said.

"That's good to hear."

Of course, being within my comfort zone was dangerous. I was already finding myself relaxing and wanting to enjoy the evening, despite my trepidation about Walker. I loved Snoot's, and Walker bringing me here had earned him even more brownie points, so many in fact, I was starting to believe there was no way he could be a killer and be this charming.

Yet for as much as I wanted to sit back and enjoy the date without thoughts of murder, I had burning questions that needed to be asked. But how to do it without raising Walker's suspicions?

"I'm sorry to hear about what happened at your studio," he said, giving me the opening I needed without me having to force it. "It has to be tough."

"It is," I said. "Especially since I just opened a week ago and the police are forcing me to close until they solve the case."

"They say all press is good press," Walker said, making a face that said he didn't quite believe it. "Maybe it will somehow work out in the end."

"But a murder?" I said. "I doubt someone dying inside A Purrfect Pose will make people want to roll around on the floor." I paused long enough to take a drink before saying, as casual as I could manage, "You didn't know the victim, Jonas Valentine, did you?"

Walker, like me, used his beer to give himself a moment to gather his thoughts. "No." The briefest pause. "Not well, anyway."

I raised my eyebrows at him over my glass.

"When I told you before I didn't know him, I might have stretched the truth a bit."

My heart thudded hard enough I feared Walker could hear it. I swallowed a large gulp of beer that had my head spinning ever so slightly before I asked, "Oh?" You know, hard-hitting questions.

"I went to CLU," he explained. "It was about four years ago. I transferred to Michigan after a two-year stint." He smirked. "I know, I know, an Ohio guy should go to Ohio State."

"I was thinking Ohio University."

"That *would* be better, but Michigan had what I wanted."

I considered that, and then asked, "Why did you transfer?"

Walker rubbed the back of his neck, eyes on his sandwich, which he'd barely touched. Granted, my food was also sitting untouched on my plate, growing colder by the moment.

"I'd like to say it was because I was looking for a better education than what CLU would get me, but that's not entirely true. I could have stayed at CLU and still have done what I'm doing now."

I almost asked him what it was he did for work, but caught myself. If I derailed the conversation now, we might not ever get back on topic. I did file the question away for later, just in case.

"What was it then?" I asked. "Jonas?"

Walker frowned, and then nodded, before spreading his hands. "Sort of. Professor Valentine . . . Well, Fay."

I got the distinct impression that bringing up Fay wasn't what he was originally going to say, but her name caught me off guard so much, I asked, "What about her?"

"You know her. She's younger than Jonas, right?"

I nodded, though I had no idea. She *looked* younger than her late husband, but I'd never asked her if she was or not. People aged differently, so it was entirely possible they were the same age and she'd just done it more gracefully than he had.

"Everyone at the college noticed, let me tell you. And seeing her at your studio, I can say that she still looks much the same now as she did four years ago, maybe even better in some ways."

"What does this have to do with you leaving CLU?" I asked.

Behind Walker, I noted Henna and Aaron pushing through the door and the mass of people clustered around it. They were scanning the crowd, likely looking for me, but they didn't appear to see me, even when their eyes passed right over our table.

"This was four years ago," he reminded me, almost defensively. "She's what? In her forties now? I think she was in her late thirties then. She used to look to be in her twenties, and I guess she still does to my eyes today."

Aaron and Henna vanished in the direction of the bar. I eyed the doorway, but neither Sierra or Alexi appeared. I assumed that meant they were waiting outside.

"She's an attractive woman."

My attention snapped back to Walker. "You have a crush on her?"

"*Had.*" He toyed with his beer. His ears and neck were turning a deep crimson and he refused to meet my eye. "It's embarrassing. All the guys thought she was pretty. And, I don't know, Jonas wasn't a nice person then, and he didn't seem to be all that friendly when I saw him at your studio. It made many of us feel like we could save her or something. You know, stupid college-kid stuff. Save the world, or in this case, the damsel in distress."

"Is that why you argued with Jonas that day?"

Walker's head snapped up, eyes going wide. "You know about that?"

I could have kicked myself, but it was too late to backtrack now. "I was told about it, yes. Was it about Fay?"

Walker didn't answer. He dropped his head and instead focused on his sandwich.

My ears were ringing and I wasn't so sure it was from the noise of Snoot's. Walker had a crush on Fay Valentine and then later transferred from CLU to Michigan for what? To get away from Jonas? Why would he feel the need do that?

Because he made a move on Fay and Jonas found out.

Could it be that simple? Walker flees to Michigan to get away from an angry husband. He returns to Cardinal Lake, Ohio, years later, thinking it all behind him, and joins the yoga class that the Valentines are attending. Coincidence? Maybe. He then argues with Jonas, possibly about Fay, and then later that night Jonas ends up dead.

I'm no detective, but it sounded like motive to me.

Of course, how did Hunter play into any of this? That photo didn't appear at A Purrfect Pose all by itself, meaning I was missing something.

"Back when you went to CLU, did you hear anything about Jonas selling stimulants to students?" I asked.

The red was fading from Walker's face, but he still looked uncomfortable. He was picking at the crust of his sandwich, seemingly lost in his own thoughts.

"Walker?" I asked, raising my voice.

"Sorry," he said, finally meeting my eye. "I hate talking about it. I was just a kid back then with a stupid crush on a woman I had no business thinking of that way. I'm over it now, and I explained that to Jonas when I saw him." He spread his hands, smiled. "That's all there is to it."

Sure, other than how Jonas had ended up dead later that night; a night when Walker had said he had "something to do."

The song changed, and with it, a cheer erupted. I didn't know the tune, but it was upbeat and had most of Snoot's jumping up and down and dancing. There might not be a DJ, but the pub definitely had the feel of a party zone, one I wasn't feeling.

"Do you want to get out of here?" Walker asked, noting my discomfort. "We could take a walk on the beach and get some fresh air. Once again, cliché, I know, but I could use the break from the noise." He paused, gave me a sheepish look. "That is, unless I've upset you?"

Had he? I had to admit, when he'd mentioned having a crush on Fay Valentine, I'd felt a pang of jealousy, despite my concerns about him possibly being a killer. Would it really be so bad to get to know the guy, just in case he turned out to be innocent?

"Sure," I said, rising. I even managed to smile. "A walk sounds great."

Walker took me gently by the hand and, like a gentleman, he led the way to the door.

My lips tingled as I approached the door to my apartment complex after having left Walker in his car. The walk on the beach had been calming to the point where I almost forgot about his admission to once having a crush on Fay Valentine and the possibility that he might have killed her husband because of it.

Unfortunately, it was the almost part that ruined things.

Every time I started to relax, I'd think of some small thing he'd said and I would tense up or pull slightly away from him. He noticed, and by the time we were in his car, headed back to my apartment, I could tell it was bothering him. Even the kiss good night was quick and close to mechanical.

But it *was* a kiss and I found myself wanting to try again, perhaps with a bit more gusto on my part.

I crossed the central courtyard, lost in my thoughts. The four buildings that made up the apartment complex surrounded me, and I'm pretty sure eyes were following me from a few of the windows. I shot the group a text, telling everyone I was safely back home as I entered my building through the front door and climbed the stairs to the second floor. I hadn't seen Alexi or Sierra at the beach, but something told me they'd been there, watching.

It was a little past ten when I reached my apartment door. Edna and Pavan were both gone, and likely asleep, which saved me from having to talk about Walker and my conflicted feelings about him before I'd figured it out myself. I doubted I'd be so lucky in the morning, where they'll likely be waiting for me outside my door like a couple of good-natured vultures.

I removed my keys, inserted the apartment key into the lock, and turned it, only to find the door was already unlocked.

My entire body went numb as fear zinged through me. Had Walker beat me to my own door somehow and was waiting for me inside? My brain alternated between imagining him standing naked in the middle of the room amid a scattering of rose petals to him holding a knife while being covered in blood.

Slowly, common sense took over. No, Walker couldn't be inside my apartment. I'd watched him drive off, so there was no way he could have beat me to the door, even if he'd sprinted. I'd been distracted when we'd left for our date and I hadn't double-checked the door to make sure it had closed properly; that's all it was.

But I *had* locked it. If it had stuck like it was wont to do, that was one thing. This was different.

When I pushed open the door, I did so slowly, my free hand bunched into a fist I wasn't afraid to use. No one leapt out at me. A light was on in the living room, but I'd left it on when I'd left with Walker so I wouldn't be coming back to a dark apartment. Luna wasn't on her perch, but it was late. She was likely waiting for me in bed.

I entered my apartment and closed the door behind me. As soon as I did, the toilet down the hall flushed.

Someone was here!

This time, I lost all control of rational thought. I snatched up an umbrella I kept propped in the corner by the door and held it by the closed canopy, leaving the wooden shaft exposed to be used as a weapon. As the sink in the bathroom turned on, I hurried across the living room, to the hall, and positioned myself outside the bathroom door.

A brief *Why would a thief or killer use my bathroom?* flashed through my mind, but I didn't have time to consider it. The water shut off and the intruder stepped toward the door, grasped the handle, and pulled.

And with a scream that had to have been heard throughout the entire complex, I brought the umbrella down hard upon the intruder's head, just as he stepped out of the bathroom, a purring Luna trailing in his wake.

CHAPTER 10

"I'm sorry!" I said for what had to be the tenth time in as many minutes. "I didn't know it was you."

"You could have asked." Hunter adjusted the bag of lima beans I'd given him, pressing it to the side of his head a bit higher than he had been. "If you were any stronger, you would have given me a concussion."

If I'd been any stronger, I might have done more than that. The umbrella was now lying in the hallway in two pieces. If it hadn't broken, I'm pretty sure Hunter's skull would have.

"Why were you in my apartment, anyway?" I asked.

Hunter scowled, wouldn't meet my eye. "What? I can't pay my sister a visit every now and again?"

"Not when you haven't answered said sister's calls for two days. Not when no one could find you. Not at"—I glanced at the clock—"a quarter past ten at night." I paused to calm myself. I was starting to yell and didn't need to wake the entire complex. "Where have you been, Hunter? We've been worried."

He licked his lips, and then winced. "I bit my tongue."

"Do you want an ice pack for that, too?" It came out harsher than I'd intended, but I was waffling between relief and anger. I was glad Hunter was okay and felt comfortable enough to break into my apartment. But he'd *broken into my apartment!*

"No." Hunter held out a hand for Luna, who'd only recently come sneaking back out from my bedroom after I'd conked my brother on the head, scaring her half to death. She eased closer to him, sniffed, and then let herself be pet. "But thanks."

I paced the living room before finally sitting on the couch next to Hunter. "What's going on, Hunter? A man was murdered and left in A Purrfect Pose, and then you up and vanish."

He dropped the hand holding the limas into his lap. He studied the bag, as if searching for answers in it.

"Hunter!" I demanded. "Do I need to call Mom?"

"No." Sullen. "I didn't kill no one."

Grammar aside, that was good to hear. "But you knew him?"

He didn't respond. He just stared at the beans.

"Please, Hunter," I said, scooting closer. "Tell me what's going on. I can't help you if I don't know what's happening."

He sighed, set the lima beans aside, and then stood to take my place pacing. "It's not my fault."

"Okay. Great. Whose fault is it then?"

"I don't know."

"Hunter—"

"Seriously! I never got a name."

Uh-oh. I didn't like the sound of that. "You'd better start from the beginning."

It took him some time to get around to explaining himself. He crouched to pet Luna, carried the frozen lima beans back to the freezer, and then resumed his pacing before he finally spoke.

"About two weeks ago, I got a message from someone who went by VH."

"VH?" I asked.

"Yeah. That's how they signed off. Didn't get a name or anything like that."

My chest tightened. VH wasn't that far off from WH, aka Walker Hawk. Could it have been a typo? An intentional shortening of the first initial?

"What did the message say?" I asked, pushing those thoughts out of my head. I'd deal with them later.

"That I was to go to CLU in a CLU hoodie so I'll fit in with the other students, and pick up a package from someone."

I already knew, but I asked, "From whom?"

Hunter rubbed his nose, wouldn't meet my eye. "I didn't know who it was at the time. I was just told where to be and when to be there. I showed, got my package, and then I left."

"His name was Jonas Valentine," I said. "*Professor* Jonas Valentine."

"I know that now," Hunter said. "When I saw him at your studio last week, I kind of freaked out. And then when Olivia showed up, I knew I was in trouble, so I beat it."

"Why would you be in trouble, Hunter? What was in the package?"

He moved to the window, parted the curtain to peer outside. He was acting like a guy afraid that the police would bust in at any moment, which made me even more worried. His explanation wasn't helping.

"Pills."

"Pills?" Heart sinking further, I moved to the edge of the couch. "Like, stimulants?"

Hunter glanced at me. "How'd you know?"

"Rumor had it that Jonas was selling stimulants to CLU students."

"Well, I don't know nothing about that, but I do know that's what he gave me. A big old bag of 'em. I didn't realize it until I was out of there and I took a peek inside out of curiosity. Then . . . Oh, man." He ran his fingers through his hair, grabbing on and tugging as he did. "I'm so screwed."

"Did you take them to the police?" Dumb question, but I felt it needed to be asked.

"Are you nuts?" Hunter said. "I take something like that to the police, good intentions or not, and Chief Higgins would have me sitting behind bars for the rest of my life. You know that."

Unfortunately, while I doubted Hunter would end up in prison, I could see Higgins pushing for some serious jail time for accepting the handoff.

"Okay, if you didn't take them to the police, then what did you do with them?"

"So, I was supposed to get the package and take it to a drop-off spot at the lake. Once that was done, I was to leave, then come back an hour later and I'd find my money in the same spot."

"You did it for money?" I asked, disappointment warring with the *Well, duh, why else would he have done it?* thought that went through my head.

Hunter shrugged, as if it was a no-brainer. "It was good money. I should have known it wasn't on the up-and-up as soon as I saw the figure, but man, I could have used the cash."

I noted the phrasing. "You didn't follow through?"

"No, of course not." Hunter paused in his pacing long enough to scoop Luna up and pet her as he began again. "You know I'm not into drugs or anything like that. I'm a screwup, I admit, but not in that way."

I could have pointed out that they were just stimulants, not hard drugs, but did it really matter? The point was that they were being sold, likely illegally, and Hunter had gotten himself mixed up in it.

"Where are the pills?" I asked.

"Not here, so don't worry."

"I'm not worried about that." Though I was glad he hadn't hidden them in the back of my toilet or in a light fixture somewhere. "I'm worried about you."

"Don't be. I'll be fine." Luna started squirming, so he deposited her on her perch. "I realized something was off and hid the package where no one will find it, then once I saw Olivia at your studio, I decided to lay low for a bit."

"And hide from your family?"

"I wasn't hiding." The chagrin in his tone said otherwise. "But I thought that the police were onto the whole deal and might be there to pick up that guy—"

"Jonas."

Hunter nodded. "And that I'd be pulled into it through no fault of my own."

Once again, I had to refrain from pointing out the flaw in Hunter's logic. I mean, he didn't have to take the job. Who in their right mind accepted something like that over the phone? In a mostly anonymous message, no less.

"You never talked to this VH?" I asked. "Never saw them in person?"

"Nah. Just the texts."

"Can I see them?"

Hunter hesitated before tugging his phone out of his pocket. He fiddled with it longer than it would have taken to find the texts, telling me he'd likely deleted something else before he handed it over.

The message was simple, stating exactly what Hunter said it did. The ten-thousand-dollar payment for the job was bigger than I'd expected, but it *was* eye-catching, especially for someone like Hunter. If it had been me, I would have been skeptical from the start.

Then again, if it had been me, I wouldn't have considered doing it, no matter the price tag.

The message was signed, as Hunter had said, with a simple *VH*. I handed the phone back.

"Were there more messages?"

Hunter shook his head as he slipped his phone back into his pocket. "Just the one."

Strange. I'd have figured his contact would have followed up with him, especially after the pills didn't find their way to the drop spot at the lake.

The word *SETUP!* screamed through my head, blinking on and off in all caps.

I rose from the couch and went to the table where I'd left my purse. I removed the photo I'd found at A Purrfect Pose, studied it briefly, and then carried it back to Hunter. He took it and paled.

"Where did you get this?"

"I found it," I said. "Near where I'd found Jonas's body."

Hunter's hands started shaking. "Someone was watching me?"

"I'm guessing it was this VH who contacted you. Do you have any idea, any at all, of who might have asked you to do this?"

"No! Oh man." He started moving erratically, and I got the impression that he was about to bolt. I moved so that if he tried, I could step in his way.

What I'd do afterward, I had no idea. I couldn't tackle him and hold him there forever.

"Listen, Hunter," I said, keeping my voice calm. "You need to talk to the police. To Olivia."

"I can't."

"You can. It's obvious this was a trick designed to catch someone doing something illegal."

"Yeah, me."

"Maybe. But I don't think so."

He gave me back the photo and then rubbed his hands on his jeans, as if touching it had made him feel dirty. "I'm the one they contacted. I'm the one right there in that picture. Of course they're after me."

"Jonas is also in the photo," I said. "It was taken at the college where he works. And," I added, "he's the one who ended up dead."

That gave him pause. Hunter dropped down onto the couch, head in his hands. My heart broke for him. His life hadn't been easy, but he *did* have a support system in place, namely me and Alexi. I just wished he would use us a little more often.

"What am I going to do?"

Pushing him to talk to Olivia wasn't going to work, at least not tonight. "Stay here," I said. "Get some rest. I don't have a spare bed, but the couch is comfortable enough. I'll get you some blankets, a pillow, and you can stay the night."

"I don't want to get in your way."

"Hunter, you won't. I want to help."

He glanced up at me, and I noted the moisture in his eyes. "Thanks, Sis."

"We can talk about what to do next in the morning," I said, fighting back tears of my own. "You're not going to get into trouble for this."

As promised, I unpacked a blanket and pillow for Hunter, and set him up in the living room. Then we talked about just about everything *but* the murder and possible setup. By the time we were done, it was near midnight and I was dead on my feet. Hunter looked no better and as I'd snapped off the light and headed for my bedroom, his eyes were closed and he was snoring softly on the couch.

I left my bedroom door open a crack so Luna could get in and out, and then I settled into bed, tired and worried. Hunter had gotten himself into a jam and, thanks to his history, I knew it wasn't going to be as easy as him explaining himself to the police to get him out of it.

But we'd figure it out. All we needed to do was talk about it in the morning.

"You have got to be kidding me!"

Sunlight filtered in through the parted curtains, illuminating the couch.

The *empty* couch.

I'd slept through the night, which had been a mistake. I should have checked on Hunter every hour. I should have . . . what? Tied him down?

My eyes moved toward where I'd left the photo last night.

It was no longer there.

"Hunter, you didn't."

Oh, but he did. I scoured the entire living room and couldn't find the photo. I checked the trash cans, the bathroom and toilet, everywhere. It appeared he'd taken it with him.

On the table sat a single piece of paper torn from a notepad I kept on the kitchen counter to jot down my grocery lists. Hunter's near-indecipherable scrawl was on the page. I snatched it up and read, anger growing with every word.

> *Ash,*
> *I did nothing wrong, but Higgins won't see it that way, even with Olivia speaking up for me. I can take care of this on my own. Don't know how, but I'll figure it out.*
> *Don't worry about me. I've got this.*
> *Thanks for everything, though.*
> *Hunter*

I read and reread it, fighting the urge to ball up the page and throw it across the room.

Instead, I set it back down, picked up my cell, and dialed.

"Hunter is an idiot," I said as soon as Alexi's tired voice answered.

"That, we knew," she said through a yawn. "What time is it?"

With creeping dread, I glanced at the clock. "Just after six," I said with a wince. "Sorry."

"No, no, I needed to get up anyway." There was a rustle, which I assumed was Alexi sliding from bed. "Evan's already up with the kids. You'd think they'd want to sleep in on the weekends, but nope."

"He was here."

"Who? Evan?"

"No, Hunter. He broke into my apartment last night and told me about some pills and some anonymous text asking him to pick them up. Then he took the picture of him with Jonas when he snuck out while I was asleep."

"Wait. Hold up and back up. What's going on, now?"

I did a mental reset and then went through the night, just after my date had ended. Alexi knew all about that, so there was no need to rehash how my evening with Walker had gone.

"And he was gone this morning?" she asked when I was done.

"Yep. Left me a nice note, though."

She laughed. "I bet." Water ran in the background. Alexi's next words were spoken through toothpaste. "Any idea where he went?"

"None. I *can* tell you where he didn't go." The police. Mom's. You know, anywhere near anyone who could actually help him.

Alexi spat, rinsed out her mouth. "Gah. I couldn't take it. Morning mouth sucks."

I ran my tongue around my own mouth. Having not brushed my teeth yet, I tended to agree.

"We should go to Mom," Alexi said. "Tell her what's going on."

"That sounds like a pleasant conversation. 'Hey, Mom, just wanted to let you know that your son, *Reginald,* got himself involved with a guy pushing pills on his students. Oh, and this guy just so happened to get himself murdered the other day.'"

Alexi laughed. "Well, it's a place to start."

"I suppose." I sighed. As much as I hated to admit it, she was right. Mom would know what to do. Or, at least, she'd have the resources and determination to find Hunter before he got himself into deeper trouble.

We just had to convince her it was worth her time.

"Meet me at Mom's?" I asked.

"Give me an hour." A pause. "Make that two. Evan's cooking breakfast and I should probably spend some time with the family before I go. I doubt Hunter will do anything too dramatic this early."

"I hope not." But I agreed, two hours sounded good. It would give me time to come up with a plan. "I'll see you there."

"This is going to be fun!"

I groaned as I clicked off just as there was a knock at my door. Thinking it might be Hunter, I stomped over to it and jerked the door open, harsh words on the tip of my tongue. I swallowed them when I saw who was waiting on me.

Edna's sweet smile and twinkling eyes took me in. Behind her, Pavan was grinning ear to ear.

"I'm sorry to knock so early, Ash," Edna said. "But I heard you talking, and figured you wouldn't mind."

"Hi, Ash," Pavan said from behind her. "Did you have a good evening?"

"Yes. How was your evening?" Edna asked before I could speak. "That nice young man who was here to take you out seemed enthusiastic." She leaned forward. "These walls aren't as thick as they should be."

"Wait. You think . . ." I suppressed a smile. "Walker didn't come home with me last night."

"Oh?" Both Pavan's and Edna's smiles faltered. She was the one who spoke. "But I heard sounds last night."

"Loud sounds," Pavan said.

Mental note: don't bring dates home with me unless I want the entire complex to listen to whatever we're up to.

"And someone snuck out early this morning," Edna went on. "I just figured it was your date leaving after . . . well, now, I shouldn't say."

"No, it wasn't him. It was my brother, Hunter."

Pavan's eyes widened, causing me to roll my own.

"I didn't know he was here, so I kind of broke an umbrella over his head. He startled me."

Pavan and Edna shared a look. It was Pavan who spoke next. "So, your date didn't end well?"

I thought about it and decided on a diplomatic answer. "It was fine. We've only known each other a week, so we're taking it slow."

Edna's lips pressed together, as if she disapproved. "Well, don't take too long. A man like that won't last on the market."

"I won't," I said, glancing at my Fitbit. "I'm sorry to cut this short, but I need to get ready. I'm meeting someone in a little bit."

"Oh no, we don't want to keep you." Edna stepped back. Pavan rested a hand on her shoulder, which she patted with her own. "You do what you have to do."

"Thanks." I started to close the door, but paused halfway there. "What time did Hunter leave this morning?"

Edna glanced at Pavan, who shook his head. "I suppose it was a little over an hour ago," she said. "I'm an early riser, but I wasn't paying much attention to the time."

That meant Hunter had, at best, five hours of sleep. Probably less. Important? Probably not, but it told me how long of a head start he had.

"Thank you," I said. "I'll talk to you both later."

"Have a good day, Ash," Pavan said as I closed the door.

I immediately went into the bathroom and brushed my teeth and showered, making sure to hurry, just in case Hunter caught a case of common sense and came back. When I was done, a message was waiting for me on my phone.

Still blindly hoping that every contact might turn out to be Hunter, I hurriedly checked it. I should have known better since it wasn't a text, but rather, an email sent to my business address.

Hi, Ash, it's Lulu O'Brien. I'm having everyone over for yoga at my place this morning at seven. I know you don't normally have classes on Sundays, but I thought it might be fun since we can't have them at the studio. No cats, which is a shame, but I hope to remedy that soon! Hope to see you, but don't fret if you can't make it. It's short notice, I know. Here's my address.

I checked the clock with a frown. It was almost six thirty, meaning I had just enough time to get dressed and drive over to Lulu's if I wanted to make it for yoga.

But Hunter . . .

I could stay for forty-five minutes and still meet Alexi at Mom's. It might make me a minute or two late, but it wasn't like Mom was expecting us. A few minutes late wouldn't hurt anything.

Besides, I could use the stress relief. Seeing Lulu, George, and the others would be good for my mental state. And it might help keep them engaged long enough that they'd come back to A Purrfect Pose once Chief Higgins let me open again.

And hey, maybe I'd learn something about Jonas's last day,

something I'd missed that would help me prove my brother's innocence.

"What do you think, Luna?" I asked the kitten, who was watching me with wide, interested eyes. "Should I go?"

She popped up and went to her empty food bowl. There, she meowed, and then flopped over onto her side, suddenly too weak to stand.

"Okay," I said with a laugh. "I won't leave until after breakfast."

Once she was fed, I took a few moments to watch her eat, and then I was out the door.

CHAPTER 11

Lulu lived in a gigantic house about as far away from the lake as you can get without leaving the town of Cardinal Lake itself. The driveway rose on a gentle slope and meandered through an open gate, up to the front of the house, which had a four-car garage and its own personal cul-de-sac. It wasn't as opulent as some of the other houses in town, but it was damn close.

I parked beside a trio of cars already sitting in front of the house. I never imagined Lulu in a place like this, but then again, I didn't know much about her outside of yoga. As I got out of the car, I wondered what Cal and Lulu O'Brien did to earn their money. In the short time I'd known her, Lulu had never said.

The front door was dominated by one of those decorative oval windows that had to cost a fortune. It was frosted just enough that I couldn't see much more than vague shapes inside. A video doorbell lit up at my approach. Before I could press it, the door opened, and there stood Lulu, dressed in her favorite yoga outfit, grinning like a fool.

"Ash! I'm so glad you came." She wrapped me in a warm hug before pulling me inside. "George arrived first and he was running the show in your absence, but now that you're here, you'll take over. Two of the younger kids are here too. Kelly and . . ." She frowned before it came to her. "And Chad. I don't know their last names yet. I should remedy that."

"I can't stay long," I said, head on a swivel as we moved deeper into the house. It was decorated less like someone with money lived here, and more like two people with two very distinct personalities were at war with one another.

Half the decorations were bright and colorful. Paintings of fields filled with blooming flowers of all types and shades. Bright, inviting rugs and tapestries hung from the walls and covered the hardwood floor. A table was filled with various rainbow-colored figurines that looked breakable enough that I made sure to give it a wide berth.

And then there were the antiques. Guns, tables, tattered flags and memorabilia that had to have come from a war, though I couldn't tell you which one. One wall was full of books that were of the informative type, not something you'd read for fun. There was an entire room glimpsed through a cracked doorway that looked like a Civil War museum with busts and uniforms surrounding a hardwood desk.

"Is Cal here?" I asked, figuring the latter stuff to be his. I was curious to meet him and see how he and Lulu coexisted with such wildly different tastes.

"No. As soon as he heard I was having friends over for yoga, he sprinted right out the door like his butt was on fire. He's not into this sort of thing, and I'm okay with that. We've always had our own interests, as you can see." She motioned toward one of Cal's ancient rifles hanging above a doorway.

We entered the living room, which was large and inviting. The couch and chairs had been pushed to the side, leaving a big open space for everyone to spread out. George was at the front of the room, hands on his hips, a stern expression on his face.

"Kelly, that's not how you do the *add ho muck a savanna!*"

Kelly, who was indeed doing downward dog incorrectly—she had her feet spread so far apart, she was practically doing splits—groaned and shifted positions. She was doing her poses on the hardwood floor, without a mat, and while wearing socks, which was likely what caused her feet to slide apart. I'm pretty sure I heard her mutter, "That's not how you say it."

"Everyone, everyone!" Lulu clapped her hands, drawing the group's collective eye. "Look who's here!"

Heads turned. Both Kelly and Chad looked relieved when they saw me, while George merely sighed.

"I can't stay long," I said. "But maybe I can run us through a few poses before I have to go."

George relinquished the front of the room to me and before I knew it, we were going through an abbreviated version of the Friday morning routine. I wasn't entirely on my game and slipped up a few times, which George promptly pointed out. Every time I glanced up, my mind went to Jonas and whether anyone in the room knew anything.

"And breathe," I said, finishing up the last pose. I'd cut it rather short, which caused George to frown, but I wanted time to talk with everyone before I needed to head to Mom's. "So—"

A tone sounded, causing Lulu, whose face was awash in sweat, to start. "Oh! Someone else is here." She hustled out of the room.

That left me with the three others. Kelly and Chad were talking to one another in the corner. Kelly was smiling, while Chad was alternating between staring at his feet and looking her in the eye. I could feel the tension between them clear across the room.

I decided to leave them to it and start with George, who was rolling up his mat.

"You were doing a good job when I got here," I told him. "I hope it's okay that I took over. Lulu thought—"

"It's fine," he said, cutting me off. "I wasn't trying to step on your toes or take your job or anything like that. I figured that since you weren't here, I could try my hand at running a class. You know, see how I'd do? It's harder than I anticipated."

"From what I saw, you were doing fine."

He shrugged, didn't appear to believe me. He might like to correct others—often incorrectly—but George wasn't a confident man. He wanted to be, don't get me wrong, but there was a reservedness to him that came out whenever you got him one-on-one. Like now.

"It's a shame what happened to Jonas," I said. "Did you know him well?"

George finished rolling up his mat before answering. "Not really. Only thing I know about him is that he didn't much enjoy your classes."

"Did he tell you that?"

"No, but I could see it in his posture. He wasn't a happy man. Don't understand why not. His wife seemed nice enough."

"Did you talk to her much?" *You know, about Jonas and maybe how she wanted to kill him?* I didn't say the last out loud, for obvious reasons.

"Maybe a word or two." George wiped an arm across his forehead and then smoothed back his thinning hair. "I wish I would have taken the time to talk to them more. Now it's too late." He sighed. "I do hope they allow you to open the studio again. It's a terrible thing that happened there, but it shouldn't force you out of business."

"I hope so too."

"I'm not sure if you've noticed, but I don't make friends easily. Your classes . . ." He looked away.

"I understand," I said, resting a hand on his shoulder. He tensed briefly before he relaxed into it.

"I should finish getting cleaned up," he said. "I'll, uh, I'll talk to you later."

George hurried over to the corner where he'd left his bag.

He didn't look back, but I could tell he was painfully aware of me watching him by the hunch of his shoulders.

I turned to Kelly and Chad, who were still chatting with one another. At my approach, they both abruptly stopped talking and looked away, as if embarrassed to have been caught together.

"Hi, Chad. Kelly. I'm happy to see you here."

Chad cleared his throat, nodded. Kelly fidgeted a moment before she broke out into her typical Kelly-sized grin.

"I'm glad you came, Ms. Branson." She paused. "Ash. I feel weird calling you that."

"Don't. I much prefer you to use my given name."

"It's just . . ." She shrugged. "You're like a teacher, and I always called all my teachers Mister or Miss. Never their real names."

"Well, at my studio, we're all equal as far as I'm concerned. No need for any of that formal stuff."

Kelly tugged on her slip-on shoes. "I hope we can go back to A Purrfect Pose. This was nice and all, but I miss the cats. It's just not the same without them."

"Will they let us?" Chad asked. "Go back to the studio, I mean. After . . . well, you know?"

Oh, did I ever. "I think so. The police are being overly cautious at the moment, but I'm pretty sure they'll let us go back soon." Or so I hoped.

"What if they don't find the killer?" Chad asked. "Do you think they'll, I don't know, condemn the place? I'm not sure what they do in situations like this."

Before I could answer, Kelly paled. "Are we safe? Is there a yoga-killer out there somewhere, hunting us down one by one like in one of those movies on Shudder?" She hugged herself.

"We're safe," I said. "I don't think Jonas's death had to do with yoga or the studio."

Chad started rolling up his yoga mat, taking far less care

than George had with it. "I hope so. I didn't think I'd like it there, but I've actually had a pretty good time." He shot Kelly a quick glance, which said more than words what he found most appealing about the class.

Kelly bit her lip. Her eyes were on me, so she missed Chad's glance. "It's all just so weird," she said. "First, there's a thief, and then Mr. Valentine is killed. It's like someone is targeting the studio and those who go to it."

"Wait. There's a thief?" I asked. "Something was stolen?"

"My mat." Kelly frowned as Chad tucked his own mat under his arm. "After class on Friday, Chad, Topher, and I decided to hang out together. It wasn't until I got home later that day that I realized my mat was gone."

"You probably left it at the beach." At my questioning look, he explained. "We did a little post-lunch yoga at the lake." He smiled. "We got a lot of odd looks."

"I swear I put it back in the car when we were done," Kelly said. "In fact, I remember doing it because I accidentally knocked a bunch of textbooks out of the car."

"It wouldn't shock me if Topher took the mat as a joke," Chad said. "He does that sort of thing every now and again. We should ask him when we see him next."

"Where is Topher today?" I asked. "I'm surprised he's not here with you."

Chad shrugged. "He's been pretty upset lately. Professor Valentine's death hit him hard. He always liked him, talked about him quite a bit, though I don't know why. I always found Mr. Valentine to be something of a jerk."

"Chad!" Kelly's hand flew to her mouth. "That's not nice."

"I'm sorry, but he was. I guess Topher's more understanding than I am. I don't like it when people talk down to me, and that's the one thing Mr. Valentine was good at."

"He talked down to you?" I asked. "At A Purrfect Pose?"

"Nah, at CLU," Chad said. "He barely spoke to me at the

studio. In college, he was one of those professors that insisted you come to class every day or else he'd mark you down a letter grade, no matter what reason you gave for not being there. You could be dying and he'd dock you points for missing his class."

"That sounds horrible," Kelly said, before turning to me. "I didn't go to CLU, so I didn't meet either of the Valentines until A Purrfect Pose."

"Did you ever hear anything about Jonas selling stimulants to students?" I asked Chad.

"Did he?" Chad asked, seemingly surprised by the question. "If he did, I never heard anything about it. I wouldn't be surprised if he did, though. He seemed the type."

"Do you think Topher bought anything from him?" I asked, hating it as I did.

"No chance," Chad said as Kelly shook her head. "He liked the guy, but he wouldn't do anything like that. He's too . . ." He looked to Kelly, who answered for him.

"Straitlaced, I guess you'd call it. Topher wouldn't do anything that would make him look bad in front of others."

With nothing else to ask, and with my time quickly running out, I thanked the two of them and then went looking for Lulu so I could tell her goodbye.

She wasn't hard to find, thanks to the cursing coming from a room down the hall. I followed the sound into the dining room, where Lulu was kneeling in front of a man with red hair and a beard that was so long and bushy, it could double as a blanket in a pinch.

"I'm fine!" the man said, though his pained expression told me otherwise. "It's just sore."

"It's swollen, Cal," Lulu said, touching her husband's knee, which was indeed red and swollen. "It might be sprained."

"If it is, I'll take care of it." He looked past her, to me. "You've got company. You don't need to fuss over me."

"I didn't mean to intrude," I said. "I wanted to say goodbye to Lulu. I've got to go."

Lulu worked her way to her feet, using Cal's good knee for support. "I hope you're not leaving because I abandoned you. Cal twisted his knee on his walk and I wanted to make sure he's okay."

"I'm fine!" he said with a scowl.

"No, I really do need to go," I said. "Thank you for inviting me over. Your house is beautiful."

Lulu beamed, and I'm pretty sure Cal blushed, though it was hard to tell through all the hair. "I'm so glad you came, Ash," she said. "I hope we can do this again, though I do pray your studio opens soon."

"Thank you. I agree." I considered asking her questions about Jonas, but with Cal there, it didn't feel like the right time. "I'll let you know as soon as the police get back to me about opening. It shouldn't be much longer."

"You do that. I suppose I should check on the others since *someone* is too stubborn to see the doctor." She glanced over her shoulder at Cal, who snorted.

"The doctor will tell me to stay off my leg for a few days and to take something for the pain. I can do that without wasting his time and mine."

Lulu rolled her eyes and then followed me to the door. "Really, Ash, I do appreciate you coming. You don't know how much your class means to me."

"I'm glad you like it," I said. "I hope Cal will be okay."

"He'll be fine." She waved off my concern. "I like fussing over him. He acts all rough and tough, but he enjoys the attention. And the back-and-forth between us adds a little, I don't know, spice, if you know what I mean?"

I didn't see how, but hey, I wasn't one to judge.

"I'll see you soon, Lulu."

"Have a good day, Ash. Don't let what's happened get you down. Everything will work out, just you wait and see!"

* * *

Alexi's car was already sitting in the driveway when I arrived at Mom's a short time later. The house was surprisingly normal, especially if you knew anything about Cecilia Branson. It fit the family comfortably back when we'd all lived together in what felt like a lifetime ago, without too much wasted space. One more kid and it might have been too small to contain us.

Mom had kept the house when she and Dad had split. With her here alone, she had more than enough space for her and her larger-than-life ego.

Alexi was waiting for me in her car. When I parked beside her, she climbed out and nodded to a motorcycle resting near the closed garage door. I'd missed it when I'd pulled in, but I wasn't surprised to see it.

"Are you ready for this?" I asked her.

"Hey, I'm just here for moral support."

"Gee, thanks." I stuck my tongue out at her, just as the front door opened and a man in a leather jacket, jeans, and with hair down to his shoulders came out. He hesitated when he saw us, before he hurried over to his motorcycle.

"Ashley," Mom said from the doorway as the guy walked the motorcycle around our cars and then hopped on. He gunned the engine and tore out of there like we might chase after him. "Alexandra. What are you two doing here so early in the morning?"

"Who was that?" I asked as the sound of the motorcycle faded.

Mom shrugged and folded her robe across her chest. She was wearing a thin slip underneath. "I didn't get his name. Barry-something, I think?"

I opened my mouth to respond, but closed it again. What *could* I say? I wanted to know nothing about Mom's sex life. This little tidbit was more than enough for one lifetime.

"May we come in?" Alexi asked.

Mom looked like she might say no before she heaved a

patented Cecilia Branson sigh. "I suppose I can give you a few minutes of my time. I am quite busy today."

"Busy with some random guy named Barry, apparently," I muttered under my breath.

Alexi snickered as we followed Mom into the house.

"Coffee is an hour old, but should still be hot," Mom said, taking a seat at the dining room table. "Why are you here?"

Alexi moved to stand beside the coffeepot in the kitchen, though she didn't pour herself a cup. I stood across the table from Mom, too nervous to sit.

"Have you talked to Hunter recently?" I asked.

"Haven't we been over this?" Mom sounded bored. "I haven't seen or heard from him in a while. I don't expect to anytime soon. Why?"

I looked to Alexi, who gave me a reassuring nod. There was nothing I could do but dive in headfirst.

It took the better part of twenty minutes to go through it all, thanks to Mom's constant flippant comments. By the time I was done, she was frowning so hard, I took a step back to keep from getting scorched by the heat of it.

"What do you think?" I asked her, not quite sure I wanted to know.

Mom drummed perfectly manicured nails on the table a moment before answering. "I think you should come back and work for me."

"What?" It came out as a shout. "Are you serious? After all that, *this* is what you say?"

"What else do you expect me to say, Ashley? Reginald makes his own choices. We've gone over this time and time again. I've tried to help him, and recently at that, but it has apparently fallen on deaf ears."

"Wait," I said, as Alexi perked up. "You've tried to help Hun—" I caught myself, even as Mom's eyes narrowed. "Reginald? *Recently?*"

"Of course I have. He's made mistakes, but he's still my son."

Alexi walked over to stand beside me. "How did you help him?"

"*Tried*," Mom corrected. "He came to me a little while back, asking for money."

"I thought you said you haven't talked to him recently," I said, trying to keep the anger out of my voice.

"I haven't. This was about two months ago. He'd gotten himself into some scrape or another and needed a couple of thousand dollars to get out of it."

"A couple of *thousand?*" I asked, incredulous. Hunter often made mistakes, but nothing of that magnitude.

Mom shrugged it off like it was nothing. "He didn't say what it was for exactly. I assume it was to pay off some sort of debt. When I didn't hear from him afterward, I figured he'd taken care of it."

"So, you gave him the money?" Alexi asked.

"I did." Mom sagged, some of the sternness fading from her as she did. "I understand I'm not easy, but that doesn't make me callous. Reginald needed help, and I did what I could. His father couldn't help him, which is understandable, considering the circumstances."

I ignored the bit about Dad, other than taking note that it sounded like Hunter might have gone to him for help first. If I got nothing out of Mom, perhaps Dad would know something.

"Why didn't you tell me this before?" I asked.

"Why would I?" Mom countered. "It had nothing to do with you. Reginald made a mistake, he was looking to settle up for it and atone. And since he asked me to keep it to myself, I decided to honor his wishes. But hearing all of this about him accepting money to what? Pick up drugs?"

"Stimulants," I said.

She scoffed. "It's thrown me for a loop, to be frank. I honestly thought he'd taken care of his money problems. Apparently, I was wrong."

"Do you think he accepted the job so he could pay off this debt of his?" Alexi asked. "That your money wasn't enough?"

"I suppose I do," Mom said. "I gave him everything he asked for. If he'd asked for more, I'd have given it to him. Perhaps something came up and he owed more than he expected."

Yeah, but what?

I couldn't imagine Hunter getting himself involved in any situation in which he'd owe someone thousands of dollars. It *would* explain why he'd jump at an opportunity to make ten thousand, no questions asked, especially when it had to have been obvious the exchange wasn't on the up-and-up.

"That's all I know," Mom said. "Whatever Hunter has gotten himself into, it's his mess. I don't think either of you should get involved. He'll have to find his own way out of it."

Alexi and I left a short time later. Mom insisted she knew nothing else, and no amount of asking would get her to change her tune.

"We need to find out who Hunter owed money to," Alexi said as soon as we were back outside. Mom hadn't even walked us to the door.

"Do you have any idea who that might be?" I asked. "Or why he would owe anyone anything? I didn't think Hunter gambled."

"Neither did I," Alexi said. "But maybe he just started. Or what if he . . . ?" She shook her head. "Honestly, I have no idea what he could have done that would cause him to fall so far behind that he'd be willing to come to Mom for help."

"What if it's all connected?" I asked, dread making me shiver, despite the warmth of the day.

"What do you mean?"

"Hunter needed money, so he goes to Mom and asks for a loan."

"Okay?"

"He gets the money and then pays off his debt, whatever that debt might be. This is a month or so ago, right?"

"Right."

"Well, what if the guy he paid off decides he wants more? He might think Hunter is an easy mark and can't do anything to stop him, so he sets Hunter up by having him collect the pills from Jonas, takes the photo of the two of them together and . . ." I trailed off, seeing where this was going and not liking it one bit.

"I don't like that look, Ash," Alexi said.

"I don't like what I'm thinking." I paced the driveway, trying to come up with some alternate explanation, but it made too much horrible sense.

"And that is?" Alexi asked.

"I originally thought the photo I'd found was taken to blackmail Jonas Valentine," I said. "He was killed and left at A Purrfect Pose, and that's where I found the photo, so it made sense that Jonas was the target."

"The killer lured him there and used the photo as proof that he was doing something illegal."

"Right. But what if the target wasn't Jonas, but Hunter? He was the one that was contacted to meet with Jonas by this VH guy. If he was the one Hunter owed money to . . ."

Alexi frowned. "But if Hunter was the target, why would Jonas Valentine be the one who ended up dead?"

For a moment, I thought Alexi had given me an out. Why kill Jonas if Hunter was the real target?

Because Jonas Valentine was the one doing the blackmailing.

I hated it, but it made sense. Jonas is selling stimulants. Hunter gets involved with him somehow. He asks Mom for money, gives it to Jonas, but Jonas isn't satisfied. He sets up the meet, has someone take the photo, and then goes on to blackmail Hunter, who what? Kills him? That's where the theory runs off the rails for me. Hunter was a lot of things, but he wasn't a killer.

"We're missing something," I said. "Hunter says he didn't

know Jonas until after they'd met outside the college. He also says that he never delivered the pills or collected his pay. I can't see him agreeing to meet Jonas or anyone else when he is already afraid of getting caught. He was scared *before* Jonas was killed."

"Okay. So, where do we go from here?" Alexi asked.

Hunter was missing again, so asking him about it was out. Jonas was dead. Who else knew about Jonas's side hustle? The students who bought the pills? Fay Valentine? The college?

The person who took the photo.

VH. Whoever VH was.

"I need to check on the cats at the studio," I said. "Maybe while I'm doing that, I'll come up with a plan." Because right then I had no idea what to do, or where to go.

Alexi nodded. "I'll talk to Evan. If nothing else, he can call Olivia and see what she can tell him about what the police are thinking. It's possible they have a lead we're unaware of that would fill in some of the blanks."

And exonerate Hunter.

But I had a sinking feeling that both Alexi and I were hoping for a miracle that was never going to happen.

CHAPTER 12

It had only been a few days, yet A Purrfect Pose felt like it had been abandoned for months when I slipped in through the back door. It was something in the air, a staleness that shouldn't have been there since someone was constantly stopping in to check on the cats.

Speaking of which, I was met by a chorus of meows and tiny paws as every last one of the kitties tried to climb me as soon as I opened the door to the room. One black cat purred so loudly, he sounded like a miniature lawnmower as he rubbed up against my shins. I made sure to take a few moments to show each and every cat the attention they craved before I checked on their supplies.

"It looks like Kiersten was already here," I said, noting the full water, clean litter boxes, and semi-full food dishes. "That means I have more time for cuddles."

And boy, did I ever need those.

I sat down on the floor and spent the next hour playing with the cats and doing my best to forget my troubles. Sure, I could have scoured Cardinal Lake for Hunter or made more in-quiries into Jonas Valentine, but where could I possibly start? I'd already talked to everyone I could think of, checked all of

Hunter's favorite places. The stress was getting to me, and taking the time to focus on something soft and loveable that needed me was the best way to lower it.

Once I was all cuddled out, I made a quick pass through the office, but decided to leave the mess where it was. I could worry about cleaning later. My time with the cats had me feeling better, and worrying about tidying up would only make me angry at Higgins again for leaving the mess in the first place.

I left through the back door, humming to myself. I started to walk toward my car, but veered off to the front of A Purrfect Pose instead, thinking I'd check to make sure my handwritten note could be seen clearly through the door.

Instead, I found myself looking at another type of note entirely.

AVOID! ANIMAL EXPLOITER!

It was written in all capital block letters by an angry hand using a thick, black marker. Anyone so much as glancing at the door would have been able to see it and read it, even from the street.

There was a moment where my brain didn't quite comprehend what I was seeing. Who would do such a thing? Why?

And then it hit me. Who else?

Fuming, I snatched the page from the window. I turned to my left, eyes zeroing in on the door next door. I noted the OPEN sign on the window of Bark and Style, gritted my teeth, and then I marched right in, ready to throw down with the first person who got in my way.

Mr. Leslie was sitting in a chair at the back of the room, fiddling with his phone when I stormed in. Even though Ginger was the only dog in attendance, the place smelled of wet dog and too much shampoo. The empty grooming stations were clean, with no sign of dog hair, despite the smell.

"What is this?" I demanded, waving the page in front of Mr. Leslie's face. You know what? Screw it. *Jordan's* face.

He glanced up from his phone long enough to shrug. "A piece of paper?"

My fist tightened on the page, crumpling it. "I know you put her up to this."

"I haven't the slightest clue as to whom you are referring." He cocked his head to the side. "Shouldn't you be cleaning out your studio by now?"

"I'm not giving up!" I shouted, which caused Ginger to hop to her feet and start barking. "I get that you don't like cats, don't like my studio, but that's no reason to treat me like this."

Jordan sighed, tapped his phone screen, and then set it face-down on the counter behind him. "I don't dislike cats, per se," he said. "But your presence next door has hurt my business, whether you want to believe it or not. Just look at this place! Empty."

Maybe you should check your attitude if you want to know why no one is here. Diplomacy won out and I didn't say it out loud.

"Call Zaria off," I said instead. "Tell her to stop doing this." I shook the page at him for emphasis. "If she continues to harass me, I'll have no choice but to call the police."

Jordan narrowed his eyes at me. "You wouldn't dare."

"Wouldn't I? You did it to me."

A staredown ensued. At our feet, Ginger's head bounced back and forth, like she was watching an especially exciting tennis match.

Finally, Jordan heaved a sigh and stood. "Fine, I'll talk to her if it'll make you happy."

I was so geared up for a fight, his concession caught me by surprise. "Really?"

"Really. Here." He held out a hand. "Give me that and I'll destroy it."

I knew that the real reason he wanted the page was so I couldn't give it to the police, but right then I only wanted the harassment to stop. I handed it over and Jordan balled it up and tossed it into the trash can behind the counter. He made a show of wiping his hands.

"There. All done and gone." He sat back down and crossed his legs as he leaned back in his chair. "Is that all?"

Was it? No, I didn't think it was.

"You knew about the cameras," I said. "Did you tell Zaria about my security system?"

Jordan's face crinkled. "Why on earth would I do that?" And then it dawned on him. "You think one of us *killed* that man?"

I crossed my arms, suddenly defensive. Hearing it out loud, I found it to be unlikely. Jordan Allen Leslie might be annoying, but he didn't look like he could hurt anyone. "I don't know," I said. "Did you?"

"Of course not!" He blinked rapidly, almost as if he were fighting back tears. "I can't believe you could think such a thing of me."

"I . . ." I felt like a jerk. "I don't. But someone broke in and killed one of my students. The cameras were down when it happened."

"And that makes you think I did it?"

"No. But if you told someone . . ."

"I didn't." Jordan appeared genuinely hurt. "To think I'd murder someone over some petty spat."

And just like that, I felt like the world's meanest, most insensitive person.

"Can we call a truce?" I asked. "There's no reason why we can't coexist."

Jordan's foot started wagging at high speed. He was as highstrung as a Pomeranian. "I suppose that would be for the best," he said. "For now."

It would have to do.

I left Jordan sitting at the counter, still not convinced he was going to leave me or A Purrfect Pose alone long term. If he held off until after the police caught Jonas Valentine's killer and I was back on my feet, then perhaps I would enjoy a little rivalry between us. Just as long as it didn't turn hurtful, it might be good for me.

Once I was back in my car, I just sat there, staring ahead, with no idea what to do next. I'd put everything into the studio, my entire world, and it was on hold until Jonas's killer could be found. Did that mean my life was on pause too? It sure felt like it.

I didn't know what to do, where to go. Hunter was out there somewhere, doing who knows what. A killer was stalking Cardinal Lake and I had no idea if they'd kill again, or if it was a onetime deal. The police were doing what they could. And me? I just wanted someone to tell me everything would be okay and somehow make me believe it.

And I knew just who to call.

I picked up my phone, found the correct contact, and then let my finger hover over it for a long couple of seconds. Did I really want to do this?

Yes, I realized. Yes, I did.

I pressed the button and brought my phone to my ear.

"Ash?" Drew's voice was a comfort that struck me so hard, I found an actual tear forming in the corner of my eye.

"Drew." Voice choked, I cleared my throat. "Sorry. I probably shouldn't have called."

"No, it's okay. I'm glad to hear from you. It's been too long since we had a chance to catch up. How have you been since we talked last?" A pause. "Dumb question. I heard about what happened."

"It's been tough," I admitted. I considered leaving it at that and then hanging up. We were still friends, sure, but Drew and I hadn't had a real sit-down conversation since I'd broken up with him.

But right then I needed a friendly face and a return to something familiar. "Can we meet?" I said, biting my lower lip as I did. "To talk." I glanced at the dash clock. "Lunch, maybe?"

Drew sounded surprised when he answered. "Yeah, sure. That'd be great, actually."

"How about The Hop? I'm close by." And it was a nice and public place that wouldn't cause our lunch to appear romantic in any way, shape, or form. At least, I hoped it wouldn't.

Ginny is going to kill me.

"Sounds good. Give me . . ." I imagined him checking his watch, calculating. "Fifteen minutes?"

"Perfect. I'll grab a table."

"See you then." A short, almost uncomfortable pause. "I'm glad you called, Ash. We really should talk."

I hung up wondering if I was making a mistake. I had no intention of ever getting back with Drew Hinton romantically, but as a regular friend I saw on a weekly, maybe even daily basis? I think that was something I needed, just to bring some semblance of normal back to a life quickly spiraling out of my control.

When Drew crossed the patio and sat down across from me, memories of our time together flooded back. I don't know how many times we'd met at The Hop back when we were dating, but it was a lot. The familiarity of it hurt just enough to make me turn away before our eyes met.

And still, despite those old feelings and memories resurfacing, I didn't want to go back to him. Even here, sitting across from him, I realized I'd done the right thing in breaking up. I cared for him deeply, but as a friend. It had taken me years to realize it, and, apparently, I was still learning.

"This place never changes," he said, not bothering with the menu when the waiter came over to take our orders. Soft drinks and sandwiches, just like always. "It's good to see you, Ash."

"Yeah, you too." I took a breath. "I wasn't sure I should call. Ginny—"

"Knows we are just friends. She might get jealous every now and again, but so do we all." He smiled, causing his eyes to sparkle in the sunlight. "I've missed this. Just . . . talking."

Yeah, well, I was pretty sure he wasn't going to like the topic of conversation once I got around to bringing it up. "It's been tough the last couple of days," I said. "After the . . . you know?"

"The murder." His expression darkened briefly before his smile returned. "I'm sure you'll get through it just fine. You always do."

"I wish I could be so confident."

"Why wouldn't you be?" Drew asked. "You've accomplished a lot, Ash. You've endured even more." He didn't need to say it, but I was pretty sure he was talking about my family. "This is a bump in the road. A big, ugly bump, but a bump nonetheless."

"You really should stop saying 'bump.'"

Drew laughed. I missed that sound. "You're probably right." He reached across the table and patted my hand. "If you ever need to talk, please call me. Even if you just need to scream at someone, I'll be there. I can take it."

I sagged back in my chair. "Thanks, Drew. It's just . . ." The waiter returned, deposited our drinks and sandwiches without much more than a mutter. I waited until he was gone before I said, "Hunter is involved."

"In the murder?"

"With the murdered man, at least," I said. "It's complicated."

He took a bite of his sandwich. "Hit me with it."

So, I did just that. I told him about everything from Hunter showing up at A Purrfect Pose and acting strange the day I opened for the first time, to me finding the photo after the murder, all the way to Hunter absconding with said photo after breaking into my apartment. I hated that almost everything appeared to revolve around my brother. It made me feel like I was accusing him of the murder when all I was doing was listing the facts as I knew them.

Drew listened with typical Drew attentiveness. He didn't ask questions, didn't try to correct me when I stumbled over words or contradicted myself whenever I got the details confused. He let me tell it like I needed to tell it before he set the remains of his sandwich aside, a grim expression on his face.

"That doesn't sound good for Hunter," he said.

"No, it doesn't." I sighed. "I don't know what to do. Hunter wouldn't kill anyone, but what if someone is after him? And what if Chief Higgins finds out about his involvement? You know he'll try to pin everything on Hunter if given the chance."

"He wouldn't do that." At my incredulous look, Drew doubled down. "He *wouldn't*, Ash. Chief Higgins might have a beef with your brother, but he's a good cop. I can see him giving Hunter a good hard look, probably harder than he deserves, but if the evidence doesn't point to him being the killer, then Higgins won't arrest him out of some personal vendetta."

"I know." And, deep down, I supposed I did. Chief Higgins had never manufactured evidence as far as I was aware. He'd never gone after Hunter for something he didn't do. Question him? Sure. But he'd always followed the evidence to a logical conclusion.

But this was different. This wasn't a missing watch or a case of petty vandalism. Someone was dead. That changed things.

Didn't it?

"Have you talked to the police about any of this? Olivia?"

I fiddled with my drink. "Not all of it."

"You should. Just hand over what you know and see what happens."

"And if they go after Hunter? Drew, I couldn't live with my-self if I'm the one who gets him arrested."

"You're not getting him into anything, Ash." Drew started to reach across the table for my hand, but caught himself. He grabbed his drink instead.

"I know. It just feels that way sometimes." And I hated it. "It's not like I can give them the photo now that Hunter has taken it. I have no physical evidence of anything. Just hearsay."

We both fell silent. My stomach was in knots, as were my thoughts. I knew what the right thing to do was, yet I couldn't bring myself to do it. If it was anyone but Hunter . . .

"Look, Ash," Drew said after a few quiet moments. "I know it's hard to believe, but things will work out. The police will do their jobs and the killer will be caught and you'll be back to teaching yoga classes with your cats in no time. Hunter will be Hunter and he'll get a slap on the wrist for being a bonehead, but he's not going to go to jail for something he didn't do."

"But what if the killer wasn't after Jonas Valentine? Or Hunter? What if he's after me and all of this is some round-about way to ruin my life?"

Drew's eyebrows rose. "Who would want to do that?"

"I don't know," I said. "Ginny."

"Ginny?"

When I'd originally said it, I'd been joking, but now, having said it out loud, I found myself wanting to believe it. "You re-member when we ran into one another at Snoot's last week?" I asked.

Drew nodded, amusement dancing in his eyes.

"She had a few words for me while you were gone. Nothing too terrible," I added, not wanting to cause friction between them. "But she thinks I'm trying to win you back. Who knows? Maybe she's the one who set all of this up, just to get rid of me."

"I know all about Ginny's concerns, trust me," Drew said. "But she wouldn't kill a man over them."

I sagged in my seat. "I know. I just can't think of anyone else. I mean, who do I know that would *kill* someone? Why would they do it at my studio if I wasn't somehow a target? Why pose him like that? Why leave the photo with Hunter? Why—"

Drew abruptly stood and rounded the table. "Come here."

I rose on shaky legs and allowed him to wrap me in a hug. The panic that had been bubbling up dissipated like smoke and I leaned into him, wishing that a simple hug could make all of my troubles disappear.

Instead, they seemed to make them manifest.

I'd closed my eyes when I leaned into the hug. I'd wrapped my arms around Drew by reflex, as one often does when receiving a hug from a close friend. There was no romantic intent behind it.

Yet when I opened my eyes, head pressed against Drew's chest and shoulder, I found someone watching us as if they thought we were about to climb into bed together.

"Walker!" I jerked out of Drew's grasp so quickly, I just about pulled him off-balance. "What are you doing here?" Dumb question, but I couldn't help myself. He'd caught me by surprise.

Walker cleared his throat, hooked his thumbs through his belt loop, and adopted a casual stance, though I could see tension in his shoulders. "Stopped in for some lunch," he said, before his gaze flickered past me, to the table and the remains of Drew's and my meal. "Guess you did as well."

Seconds passed where I didn't know what to do. I hadn't done anything wrong, yet I felt like I'd just been caught with someone else's husband.

"I'm Drew Hinton," Drew said when it was clear I was at a loss. "Ash's friend."

"Walker Hawk."

The two men shook. I was glad to note Walker didn't try to break Drew's hand in some manly display of strength.

"Walker, this is Drew." I could have smacked myself, considering they'd just introduced themselves, but I plowed on nonetheless. "He's an old friend. We met for lunch."

"I see that." Walker smiled and seemed to relax ever so slightly.

"Drew, Walker and I . . ." We were what? Dating? I didn't think our one night out constituted dating. And considering the first date had happened only last night, it wasn't like Walker had time to ask me out again.

"We've known each other about a week now," Walker said, saving me. "So, I guess that makes me a new friend."

"Ash needs as many of those as she can get," Drew said, nudging me with his shoulder.

"Hey! I do not!" I thought about it, reddened. "I don't mean that I don't want you as a friend, Walker."

Both men laughed. Great, now my ex and, I suppose I'd call him my crush, were bonding.

And what if Walker Hawk just so happens to be the mysterious VH who'd contacted Hunter?

The thought lingered long enough to stomp all over any welling good mood I might have had. I had no proof Walker was VH, but I didn't have proof he wasn't, either.

Walker must have caught some of my discomfort because he stepped back and put a hand on the back of his chair. "I should probably eat. I've got some things to do today, so I don't have long."

"Yeah, no, you do that," I said. "Drew and I were just leaving anyway." My half-eaten sandwich said otherwise, but at that point, I wasn't hungry anymore.

"It was nice to meet you, Walker," Drew said.

"You too." Walker sat and picked up the menu.

As Drew and I paid and left, I noted Walker was watching us over the menu. He was frowning ever so slightly, and when I looked directly at him, his eyes dropped back to the menu and didn't rise again until after we'd left.

Drew and I stopped on the sidewalk once we were outside.

"Don't say it," I said when I saw Drew's grin.

"Say what?"

I narrowed my eyes at him.

He laughed. "Come on, Ash. It's good that you're moving on. I'm not hurt by it. You deserve to be happy."

I could have said all sorts of things then. About my worries that Walker might have had something to do with Jonas Valentine's death. About how he could be tied to whatever was going on with Hunter. That we'd just recently met and that while, yeah, I liked him, he might no longer feel the same way about me after our date. And after what had just happened.

But all I managed was "If you say so."

Drew put an arm around my shoulders, squeezed. "Oh, I do, Ash. I do. Maybe I'll head back and put in a good word for you. Lord knows you could use the help." He laughed.

Great. Just what I needed: my ex trying to hook me up with a new boyfriend. There was no way *that* could ever go wrong.

And yet, when Drew and I parted, I found myself smiling. It was good to have Drew back in my life, even if his presence did cause a few extra complications in the relationship department.

Sometimes those complications make life worth living.

CHAPTER 13

I wish I could say I spent the rest of my Sunday scouring the streets for Hunter and discovering who killed Jonas Valentine. I wanted to be proactive, I really did, but my morning had been draining, and I couldn't bring myself to do much more than check on the cats at A Purrfect Pose before I decided to go home.

I spent most of the afternoon playing with Luna, and at one point, napping on the couch with her curled up on my stomach. Every sound caused me to startle, and before long, I was pacing my apartment, glancing toward the door every few seconds, expecting it to burst open and a killer to come waltzing through.

Unfortunately, Hunter was often the killer my mind's eye materialized.

By the time I was ready for bed, I was so paranoid, I dragged a pair of heavy boxes of kitchen supplies in front of the door. That was after I tugged on the door a couple dozen times to make sure it hadn't stuck when I'd tried to close it and that the lock was indeed engaged. Luna eyed the boxes, measured them, and then hopped up on them. She immediately settled in for the long haul.

Sleep didn't come easily that night, but I did sleep. When I woke, I was groggy, but determined. To do what? No clue. I only knew that I had to do *something* lest I drive myself insane with worry. I couldn't keep living like this.

Monday arrived warm and sunny, so I decided to walk to A Purrfect Pose for my morning cat check-in. On the way, I made a mental list of everything I wanted to do that day. Finding Hunter was on top of that list, of course. The only problem? Where did I start?

I turned down the alley, went in through A Purrfect Pose's back door, and spent a good hour with the cats, before I paused to look out at the empty studio floor.

I need to talk to Chief Higgins. The cats. My students. They deserved to have their studio back. *I* deserved it. He might tell me no, might be annoyed I even asked again, but darn it, I needed to get back to some semblance of normal here.

When I left, I had it in my mind to walk all the way to the police station and demand Chief Higgins allow me to reopen. By the time I'd walked the alley and had made my way around to the front of A Purrfect Pose, I wasn't so sure that was a good idea. I wanted to open, yes, but what made me think I'd get my way by hounding Higgins about it in the middle of a murder investigation?

I found my gaze drifting to the building across the square: Branson Designs. After a moment's thought, I decided, *what the hell?* and I started that way.

A car shot around the square, not bothering to yield to other cars, *or* me in the crosswalk. I just managed to sprint the last few feet to the opposite side of the road as horns blared and the driver shouted something especially unflattering at me as she zoomed past.

"Learn to drive," I muttered, resisting the urge to flip her off. The fountain in the middle of the square was nice and all, but the square was a deathtrap. It was a wonder more accidents didn't happen than they already did.

I reached the door to Branson Designs without getting run over, and then just stood there, hand on the handle. I'd spent the better part of my youth here. First, as a kid, thinking it was exciting to go with Mom into work, and then later, bored out of my mind while I waited for her to let me go play with my friends instead of listening to her prattle on about the best T-shirt designs. And then, for a few miserable years, I worked at the front desk, taking orders. Mom didn't think I had enough of a creative mind to design anything.

Honestly, she was probably right.

I *so* didn't want to go in there.

But I felt I had to.

I opened the door and stepped inside.

Branson Designs didn't look like much. The showroom, as Mom liked to call it, displayed the flashiest of her designs hanging on the wall, or on strategically placed mannequins. Shirts, purses, masks. Anything that could catch someone's eye and draw them in. A book on the counter had pages upon pages of other designs for customers to choose from, including popular custom requests.

Leaning against the counter, my cousin Juniper Branson was staring at her phone, looking as bored as I'd always felt when I'd been in the same position. A year my junior, Juniper was doing the Branson thing by working at Branson Designs, but she'd told me once that she planned on finding her own path somewhere down the line.

What that path might be, she had no idea. Just that she'd like to do something for herself, and not have to think about how it might affect the family. She had the good looks and smarts to do just about anything.

When Juniper saw me enter, she set her phone aside, facedown, and plopped her chin into her upturned palms.

"Well, well, well," she said. "Who do we have here?"

"Hi, Juniper," I said. "How's things going?"

"Ash." She glanced behind her out of reflex, likely to make sure Mom hadn't heard her use the shortened version of my name. "I heard about what happened."

By now everyone in Cardinal Lake knew. "It's been tough, but I'm working it out."

"The police aren't letting you open?" she asked, glancing toward the window, though she couldn't see A Purrfect Pose past the fountain.

"Not yet."

"Sucks." She picked up her phone. "Aunt Cecilia's in her office. Everyone else is having meetings or something."

"Thanks." Meetings meant most everyone would be there. Hopefully one of them knew where Hunter might be. "I'm going to pop in the back and say hi to a few people."

"Knock yourself out." The store phone rang and Juniper snatched it up. "Branson Designs. What can we make for you?" She rolled her eyes at me as I passed by chuckling.

Nope, I didn't miss this one bit.

The door to the back was closed with a large EMPLOYEES ONLY sign hanging on it. I ignored it as I opened the door and stepped into the hall beyond.

And directly into someone coming from the other side.

"Oh, Ashley! What are you doing here?" Uncle Cliffton—never Cliff—said. Behind him were the handful of offices where all the, quote, unquote "important work" took place.

"Hi, Cliffton," I said. "I thought I'd stop in and see how everyone was doing."

Uncle Cliffton placed his bulk squarely in front of me so that I couldn't see—or walk—past him.

"It's a very busy time for us, Ashley," he said. "Cecilia is looking to expand and we're brainstorming new ideas." Meaning, he didn't have time for me.

"I won't stay long," I said. "I wouldn't want to interrupt."

Cliffton's lips thinned as he pressed them together. "Well, that's the thing, Ashley. You *are* interrupting. You know what they say? Time stops for no one and all that. I'm sure you understand."

"Really," I said. "This will just take a minute." And then, before he could protest, I asked, "You haven't seen Hunter lately, have you?"

Uncle Cliffton made a face like I'd just dropped a sack of manure in front of him. "Why would I have seen your brother around here?"

"Not just here. Anywhere. I've been looking for him and haven't been able to track him down."

Cliffton shook his head, that same disgusted look on his face. "No, I can't say that I have. If you do find him, tell him to clean up his act. Cecilia is apoplectic because of him."

Considering I'd just talked to Mom yesterday, I knew that was an exaggeration, but I let it slide.

"Well, if you do see him, could you have him call me?" I asked. "It's important."

"Sure, but I don't expect to hear from him any time soon. We don't typically run in the same circles."

Despite being family. I wanted to say something snarky to him about it, but Uncle Cliffton was much like his sister, my mom, when it came to caring about something other than himself.

Okay, maybe that was going a bit too far, but still . . .

"I should probably ask around the office," I said. "Maybe someone else has talked to him."

Uncle Cliffton didn't budge. In fact, he seemed to swell to fill the entire hallway. "Sorry, Ashley. You know it's employees only back here."

I stared at him, shocked. "What?"

"Employees only. I'm sure you saw the sign on the door."

"Yeah, but . . ." That couldn't possibly apply to me. I mean, I'd been allowed back here all my life. I was family, and this was a family-run business.

Uncle Cliffton crossed his arms and spread his feet, effectively blocking my path. He wasn't obese or anything, but he *was* a large man. There was no way I was going to move him or slip past him.

My phone pinged before I could come up with something to say that would convince him to let me pass. I glared at him a moment longer before pulling my phone from my pocket and checking it. One look at the text and my heart dropped.

We need to talk. Face-to-face. Now.

Olivia.

With a groan, I turned and walked out without so much as a goodbye to Uncle Cliffton. I felt bad, but right then I thought he deserved it.

"Bye, Ash," Juniper said, not looking up from her phone as I stepped outside, onto the sidewalk.

There, I dialed, heart thudding in my throat.

"Hi, Olivia," I said when she answered. "Where do you want to meet?"

A Frisbee whizzed past my head, missing me by inches. It bounced off a three-foot-high supporting brick wall that was currently the perch of a half dozen college students, before it fell to the sand. A belated "Look out!" was followed by a "Sorry!" as a blond-haired kid chased after the wayward Frisbee.

When I'd asked Olivia where she wanted to meet, I expected her to ask me to come down to the police station to chat about Hunter. Her tone in both text and call were not what I'd call cordial.

So imagine my surprise when she told me that she'd be waiting for me lakeside.

The manmade beach wasn't terribly big, so it didn't take long to spot her amongst the morning revelers. She was standing near the water with her shoes, laces tied together, dangling from her shoulder while she stared out into the lake, where boats and swimmers alike floated lazily in the sun.

I left my shoes on as I crossed the sand—imported from a real, natural beach somewhere, I imagined—to where she stood. It wasn't cold out, but here by the lake, there was a chill to the air that made me wish for a jacket.

Olivia glanced over at me when I joined her. She was in full uniform—sans her socks and shoes, of course. She looked tired. No, more than that. She was exhausted.

"It's strange how a place where everyone is yelling and screaming can feel so peaceful and quiet," she said.

On cue, a kid stated screaming her head off behind us, while a burst of laughter came from a boat on the lake. And yet, despite the noise, calm washed over me in time with the gentle sluicing of water against the shore.

"It's the open air," I said, shielding my eyes so I could see Snoot's across the lake. I wondered if I should drop in on Sierra after I was done with Olivia. Breakfast would be wrapping up and they'd be closing soon afterward, meaning she'd have some free time before her evening shift. She often pulled doubles on Mondays.

"I imagine so," Olivia said before she sighed and turned to face me fully. "Where's Hunter?"

I couldn't look at her when I answered. "I haven't seen him."

"At all?"

I hesitated, which was a mistake.

"Look, Ash, Chief Higgins is on the warpath. He thinks Hunter is avoiding him, which makes him suspicious. It's gotten to the point where he's snapping at me, like he thinks I've tucked your brother away somewhere. I need to know what's going on or else I can't do anything to help. So, where is he?"

"Honestly," I said. "I don't know. He showed up at my place Saturday night and he crashed on my couch. When I woke up, he was already gone."

"And you haven't seen him since?"

"No. Both Alexi and I have looked all over for him. We even talked to Mom, hoping she'd know something."

Olivia scowled. She knew as well as anyone that if we went to Cecilia Branson, we were desperate.

"This isn't good, Ash. Not for any of us. Evan called me early this morning, asking me questions he knew I couldn't answer. Something's up, and I want to know what that something is."

I kept my eyes on Snoot's, on the lake. Anywhere but on Olivia.

"Ash. Look at me."

Grudgingly, I did.

"I can't help him if you don't tell me the whole story here. Chief Higgins is convinced Hunter is into something, and it's distracting him. If Hunter were to come to him, talk to him, then he could get the whole mess sorted out. Then we could turn our focus onto who really killed that man at your studio."

"Hunter knew the victim," I said, blurting it out before it could get stuck in my throat. "Not personally, but he'd had contact with him."

Olivia scowled. "So, he *is* involved."

"Not on purpose." I took a deep breath and explained everything I knew about Hunter and his involvement with Jonas Valentine, including my theories that it was a setup of some kind.

"And where is this picture you found?" Olivia asked when I ran out of steam.

I looked down at my sand-covered shoes. "Hunter took it."

"He what?" She threw her hands up into the air, paced away, and then stormed back over, clearly PO'd. "You found evidence at a crime scene and didn't immediately contact us? And now that evidence is gone, taken by someone who might have some insights as to what is going on in Cardinal Lake?"

I felt tiny, and my voice matched the feeling when I said, "Yes."

"I . . . You . . . Ugh!" Olivia scrubbed at her face. "How am I supposed to explain this to Dan without him tearing me a new one?"

"You don't?" Sheepish.

Olivia just glared.

"I mean, you tell him what you have to, but think about it, Olivia. Someone is trying to set Hunter up." I hoped. "He was tricked into thinking he was picking up a simple package, that he'd get paid, and that he could take care of his other problems." Whatever they were.

"A package," she said, flat. "Even Hunter's not dumb enough to think that someone was paying him to pick up something legal."

"I know." And that was something I'd have to talk to him about when this was over. "But still, someone was there, watching. They took the photo, and then had it with them when Jonas was killed."

Olivia considered that. "That makes the photographer a rather intriguing suspect."

"It does," I said, confidence growing.

"Do you know who said photographer might be?"

"No. But I do know Hunter wouldn't kill anyone. You know him. He might do a lot of stupid things, but not murder."

Olivia nodded, though she wasn't happy about it. "I do. And, while I personally don't think he's a killer, that doesn't mean Chief Higgins is so inclined."

"Mom said Hunter asked her for a few thousand dollars a few months ago. She gave it to him, but if it wasn't enough, it would explain why he agreed to pick up the package." I paused, hopeful. "You don't know what he needed the money for, do you?"

"I wish I did." Olivia turned back to the water and stared out over it. "I'll have to do some digging and see if I can find anything out." She glanced at me out of the corner of her eye. "I'll try to do it without Chief Higgins finding out, but you and I both know that if he comes asking me about it, I'm going to tell him."

"I know." And I didn't blame her for it. It was her job to follow and uphold the law. Keeping secrets for me, even for a little while and with good intentions, could cost her dearly. "Thank you."

She grunted.

"You don't think Chief Higgins would allow me to open tomorrow, do you?" I asked.

"Not a chance," Olivia said, before adding, "But I'll ask him again, just in case."

"Thanks."

We both fell silent as we stared out over the lake. The water was so clear, I could see the reflection of the clouds in it, almost as if I was looking into a mirror. Not even the ripples could dispel the image.

"I come here for peace sometimes," Olivia said after a while. "Even in the winter, when no one is here, I find it calming."

I could see that. In the winter, the closest I came to Cardinal Lake's beach was Snoot's. Every now and again, I'd see someone walking the shore, despite the cold. And maybe a daredevil or two risking their lives by sliding across the ice. It always struck me as odd, but standing here now, I could imagine looking out over the frozen water, coat pulled tightly around me as snow drifted lazily from the sky, and just letting all my troubles fly away.

"Today, it hasn't helped," Olivia said. "I'm unsettled. I don't know what your brother is into, but it worries me like nothing else. He's family. He might not be my blood, might only be tied to me through my brother's marriage to your sister, but that doesn't make the bond any less powerful."

"He doesn't want to hurt anyone," I said. "Hunter is . . ."

"He's his father's son," she said, with some amount of fondness. "They aren't much alike on the face of it, but look deep enough and you can see the similarities."

Which made me wonder if Dad might have some insight into where Hunter has gone. Maybe not specifically, but an idea. And maybe what he planned on doing next. Hunter couldn't hide forever. If they thought the same way, then perhaps they'd come to the same conclusions.

It looked like dinner with Dad was most definitely happening.

"Do you know anything about a man named Walker Hawk?" The question popped out of my mouth, seemingly from nowhere. I hadn't even been thinking of him.

"Walker Hawk?" Olivia made a face. "That his real name?"

"As far as I know, it is."

"Can't say that I know him. Why?"

I chose my words carefully. "He came into my life recently. We went out once."

"And you want to make sure he's not some sort of predator you should be careful of?"

I shrugged. "Something like that. He . . ." I frowned. "He knew Jonas Valentine. And Hunter said the person who'd contacted him about meeting Jonas signed the message with the initials VH. I know it's not the same, but Walker Hawk. VH. They're close."

"Close, sure, but you're right, it's not the same, not unless this Walker guy talks like those old movie vampires. 'Hello, I'm Valker Hawk.'"

Her impression was so spot-on, I laughed. "No, he sounds nothing like that."

"Then I doubt he's this VH character. I'm not sure I know anyone with those initials."

"Neither do I."

Olivia considered it a moment longer before pulling her shoes from her shoulder. "Welp, I guess I'd best get back to work." She started toward the parking lot, working at the knot she'd made in her laces. "These moments of peace are few and far between these days."

A new question hit me, so I kept pace with her, though I did lower my voice so no one else would hear. "Did you ever determine where the knife came from?" I asked. "The one that was used on Jonas."

Olivia nodded, but otherwise, didn't answer.

"Can you tell me?" I pressed. "Maybe if I knew where it came from, I'll be able to connect it to something else." What? I had no idea, but it sounded like as a good of an excuse as any to pry.

Olivia worked the laces free, paused at the wall to brush her feet off before tugging her balled-up socks out from inside her shoes and pulling them on. The shoes followed.

"Is there something you haven't told me that would allow you to make a connection I couldn't?" she asked when she was done.

"No," I said. "It's just . . ." I had no idea how to put it. I supposed I'd feel better if I knew. Like, if they had a lead that pointed to someone other than Hunter as the killer, then I could sleep peacefully at night.

I followed Olivia all the way to her cruiser, silently willing her to answer. She rested her arm against the car, just above the door, and turned to stare at me. Something must have convinced her I needed to know, because when she answered, she did so with a kindness normally reserved for giving someone bad news.

"You didn't hear this from me," she said. "Don't breathe a word of this to Higgins or I'll string you up myself."

I mimed locking my lips and throwing away the key.

"The knife that killed Jonas Valentine . . ." She glanced around, made sure no one was listening. "It came from the Valentines' very own kitchen."

CHAPTER 14

All my knives were present and accounted for.

I sat drumming my fingers on the table in my apartment, staring across the room to the knife block on the counter. I'd dug it out of a box, along with the last couple of knives I'd yet to unpack, and then set them on the counter so I could stare at them.

Why? Inspiration, I supposed.

I tried to imagine Fay Valentine pulling a knife from a block much like mine and taking it with her to kill her husband outside of A Purrfect Pose. Why not do it at home? Or lure him into the woods somewhere where no one might happen by and witness her killing him?

Answer?

The killing was impromptu.

But if that was the case, why did she have the knife on her in the first place?

Because she was afraid of Jonas and what he might do to her.

It made sense. Fay was rumored to have cheated on her husband. She had the eye of a lot of her students and likely quite a few of the faculty as well. Jonas finds out about the possible affair, gets angry, and they fight. He hits her, does so more than once. She becomes frightened of him, afraid that he might take it a step too far, so she decides to start carrying a knife in her purse, just in case.

That's where things start to get fuzzy for me. Were they out on an evening walk when Jonas grew angry with her again? Maybe she'd denied cheating and he refused to believe her. Maybe while they were walking on the green behind A Purrfect Pose, he confronted her again, got aggressive. It was evening. Perhaps they were alone. She panics, stabs him, and then drags him into A Purrfect Pose to hide the body until she could come up with a plan.

But how did the photograph play into it? Hunter and the stimulants? Why pose him in my studio at all? I hadn't done anything to Fay Valentine to warrant being framed or implicated in the crime. And how did she just so happen to do it while the cameras were down?

There was only one way I was going to find out.

I picked up my cell, but didn't dial right away.

If Fay was involved in her husband's death, then the police should already be nipping at her heels, thanks to the knife having come from her kitchen. Did I really need to be poking my nose into it when they could handle it themselves?

For Hunter's sake, I thought I did.

When students signed up for classes at A Purrfect Pose beyond the daily rate, they were required to leave an email address and phone number in case I needed to reach them. I eventually wanted to have a newsletter, or in cases such as this, the ability to send out email blasts to let students know when classes were postponed or cancelled.

I hadn't gotten around to putting all of that together yet, but I had taken the time to put the students' numbers into my phone.

I pressed on the Valentine name, which was tagged as for both Fay and Jonas. I assumed it was their home number.

It rang twice before Fay answered with a tentative "Hello?"

"Hi, Fay, it's Ash Branson from A Purrfect Pose." I winced, hating how robotic I sounded.

"Ah, yes, Ash. What can I do for you?"

Something in her voice gave me pause. There was a slight quaver to it, a hesitation that made me feel as if she was on the verge of having a massive breakdown. A result of her husband's death? Something else?

"Is everything okay, Fay?" I asked.

She laughed. There was no humor in the sound. "I don't know. Is it? Can it be?"

"I'm sorry, I—"

"No, don't be." She sighed. "I just got a call from CLU. They want me to empty Jonas's office, but I don't know if I can do that. To be alone in there with all his things . . ." I could hear her swallow through the phone. "It's going to be hard. I'm not sure I'm strong enough."

A big flashing OPPORTUNITY! sign flashed on and off in my head. It was quickly followed by a question: If Fay was this upset over cleaning out Jonas's office, could she really be his killer?

Guilt tended to do strange things to people, made them act in unpredictable ways. Yet, I didn't think it was guilt in her voice, but genuine pain. I wasn't an expert on voice analysis, of course, so I could be wrong and she was faking the whole devastated widow thing.

"When do they want you to go in?" I asked.

"As soon as possible. Today. Now." Another sigh. "I've been working up the nerve to do this even before the call. There's just so much to do, so much to worry about, that I feel like I'm being pulled from every which direction with no idea where to go to keep from being torn in two." A pause. "I'm sorry, Ash. I don't mean to dump on you like this. You called me for a reason."

"No, it can wait. You've been through a lot."

"I have." Her sigh seemed to drain her. "Still, it's no reason to put my life on hold. I should go in and get this over with so I can move on. If that's even possible."

"I can come," I said. "I can help pack boxes or can simply be there for emotional support. I don't want to get in the way, but in something like this, it's probably best if you had someone there."

"I wouldn't want to impose upon you."

"You wouldn't be. A Purrfect Pose is closed, so I'm free and willing to help." Did I sound too eager? I thought I did.

Fay was silent long enough I was pretty sure she was going to turn me down. I was debating the merits of showing up anyway when she finally answered.

"Thank you. I'd appreciate the company. I'll be there in twenty minutes if you want to meet me at Lester Hall. It's the science building. Do you need directions?"

"No, I know where it is. I'll see you there. Hold strong, Fay. You'll get through this."

"Thank you, Ash."

I clicked off, eyes drifting back to the knife block one more time, and wondered . . .

The CLU campus was buzzing with activity when I arrived. The parking lot was near full, forcing me to park about as far from Lester Hall as you could get and still be on the campus. Since it was a nice day, I didn't mind the walk. It gave me time to think.

I'd left my knives at home, figuring if I couldn't be safe on a college campus, then I wasn't safe anywhere. Even if I pressured Fay into confessing, I doubted she'd pull a weapon on me. If she'd killed Jonas, she'd done so in self-defense. It wasn't premeditated.

Or, at least, I didn't think it was.

As I walked, I kept an eye out for people I knew. Topher. Chad. Anyone who might be tempted to join in and help clean the office if they were to see me with Fay. It was kind of hard to ask someone about crimes they might have committed with an audience.

Thankfully, I didn't see anyone I knew as I made the long walk across the lot to the front door of Lester Hall. I debated waiting outside for Fay, but if she'd already gone in, I could be waiting awhile, so I went ahead and headed inside. A girl with round glasses and a short, stylish haircut sat at the desk. She looked up from a tablet when I entered.

"Ms. Branson?" she asked, catching me by surprise.

"Yes?"

The girl grinned. "Mrs. Valentine told me to keep an eye out for you and pass word that she's already upstairs."

"Oh. Thank you."

"No prob. Have a good day." She went back to her tablet.

I checked the board behind her, spotted Professor Jonas Valentine's name, took note of the floor and room number, and then headed for the stairs.

I spotted Fay standing outside Jonas's office door the moment I exited the stairwell, two floors later. The door was still firmly closed, and Fay wasn't making a move to open it. She was just standing there, staring blankly ahead.

She must have heard me coming because when I drew close, Fay, without glancing over, said, "I thought I could do it, but now that I'm here, I'm not sure I can." She was holding a keycard loosely in one hand.

"Do you want me to do it?" I asked.

Fay nodded and handed over the card. There were tears on her cheeks, and she kept chewing on her lower lip, which was already red and somewhat swollen from previous gnawing.

I rested a hand briefly on her back, and then I pressed the back of the keycard against the electronic lock. There was a clunk as the door unlocked. I opened it, revealing the dark office in which Jonas Valentine had spent much of his time.

Fay took the lead then. She reached past me and flipped on a buzzing overhead light before she entered the office. Her step was hesitant, but she was moving forward. Progress.

"I rarely came in here when Jonas was alive," she said. "I never had a reason to. It was his space, like my office is my own. It's like they were the part of our lives that we kept separate from one another. Secrets, almost." She sniffed. "It sounds silly, but I feel like I'm invading his privacy coming here now."

The office was tidier than I expected. Science books lined a small shelf behind a desk clear of debris. There were no calendars, no stack of ungraded papers. A small coffee maker sat on a table near the door. The pot was lined with a smudge of black where the remains of a pot of coffee had evaporated.

"Where do I begin?" Fay asked. "This was his life. I didn't belong before. I don't belong now."

She moved as if she might turn and flee the room, but at the sight of me behind her, she calmed.

"I'm being stupid, aren't I?" she asked.

"No, you're not. You sound like someone who's suffered a loss." And not like a woman who'd recently committed murder. I was really starting to doubt my theory that she'd killed her own husband.

Fay made a slow circuit around the room, which didn't take long considering the office's small size. "I didn't bring a box. Why didn't I bring the box I'd brought up from the car?" She raised a hand to her forehead and closed her eyes. "I'm so scatterbrained these days, it's a wonder I can function at all."

"We can always sort through his things and take a few of the bigger pieces down to your car," I said. "Like the coffeepot. We can grab a box then."

She nodded, almost too vigorously. "You're right. Let's see what we have." And then, under her breath, "I'm sorry, Jonas."

We spent the next thirty minutes sifting through Jonas Valentine's office, both of us with different agendas. There wasn't much to see, unfortunately. He was an orderly man who didn't bring outside materials into the office. I'd hoped to find something that might point to his killer, or at least give credence to the rumors about him selling stimulants to students.

But if he kept pills at the school, he didn't leave them here.

By the time we'd gotten through the desk and Fay had moved on to crouch in front of a small cabinet in the back of the room, she had calmed down enough that I thought I could ask her some questions without causing her to have a breakdown.

I started somewhere a little personal.

"I talked to a former student of yours," I said. "Walker Hawk? He went to school here a few years ago."

Fay paused, a stack of folders that had students' names on them in hand. "Walker Hawk? I remember the name, but not the face." She laughed. "The name is impossible to forget, isn't it?"

"It is," I admitted. "Walker said he transferred to Michigan after a few years here and only recently has come back. He was in yoga class on Friday."

Her eyes widened. "*That's* where I know him from. When I saw him, I recognized him, but couldn't place him. He and Jonas . . ." She frowned.

"They argued."

Fay's nod was slow, thoughtful. "It was brief, and I didn't hear what it was about. Honestly, Jonas rarely got along with anyone, so I didn't think much about it. You don't think this Walker Hawk guy killed him, do you?"

Did I? "I don't know," I said. "I don't think so, but it's possible." Now for the tougher questions. "I heard the knife found at the scene came from your kitchen." I watched her carefully as I said it.

Fay's entire face turned white and she braced a hand against the corner of Jonas's desk to keep from falling over. "It did. I could hardly believe it when the police told me, but I checked, and sure enough, one was missing."

"Any idea how it got there?" There being Jonas's back, but I didn't think that would be wise to point out.

Fay swallowed, sifted through the folders before dropping them back into the cabinet. "I assume Jonas took it with him. Or . . ."

When she didn't say anything more, I prompted her with a follow-up "Or?"

Fay closed the cabinet and rose from her crouch. I expected her to ask me why I was asking such personal questions or demand to know who I thought I was pressing her on such a sensitive topic, but all she did was sag against the wall and peer out the window before speaking.

"I wasn't home that night."

Bingo! my brain supplied. Now we were getting somewhere. "Were you with someone?"

Fay chuckled. "It's not what you think." She glanced at me out of the corner of her eye. "I know the rumors that have gone around about me and Jonas. Teachers talk. Students too. And it doesn't take long for the tales to get back to those being gossiped about."

"I don't mean to pry," I said, meaning to do just that.

"I know," Fay said, gaze returning to the window. "I was with family. My mom, in fact. She always told me that Jonas would be the death of me, and I suppose she was right. Or would have been if . . . Well, you know."

I nodded. *If Jonas hadn't died first.*

"We had a fight—Jonas and I—and I went to stay with Mom for a few nights to let things cool down. I was there the night Jonas was killed."

I thought back, frowned. "You were together at class Friday morning."

"We were." Fay rubbed her temples, closed her eyes. "It was for appearances, I suppose. And, despite our troubles, I still cared for him. I wanted to work it out, but didn't know how. I do have fun at your classes, and thought that perhaps if he saw me enjoying myself, he'd realize . . . Honestly, I don't know what I was hoping for. Maybe I was being delusional. I probably was."

"So, you weren't home with him the night he died?" I asked, just to make sure I was following her right.

Fay shook her head. "I wasn't. The knife . . . I don't know if he'd invited someone over and they took it, or if he'd taken it with him when he'd left. I wish I did. It would explain so much."

"Such as?"

"Who killed him, for one." She swallowed, took a trembling breath. "Whether he was cheating on me or if his late-night adventures were for something else."

"You think Jonas was cheating on you?"

Fay considered the question and then shrugged. "I don't know. Maybe? He was a hard man, but he once showed me a kindness that made me feel safe. He stopped treating me that way, and I suppose I began to wonder if he was doing it for someone else now. He'd vanish at times. Abruptly. He would be sitting in his home office and then would get a call and the next thing I knew, he'd be out the door without so much as a 'see you later.'"

For a date, I wondered. Or because someone needed pills?

"Have you gone through his things at home?" I asked. "Like a home office? Maybe there's a clue as to what he was up to there."

"I have a little. Not all of it. I . . . It's hard." Fay sucked in a breath and pushed away from the wall. "I'm going to take a few things down to the car now," she said. "I'm sorry I dragged you all the way out here, but now that I've started, I think I'd like to do this on my own. It's too . . . personal."

"I understand." And I was sure my questions didn't help matters any. I felt like a bully for bringing up her dead husband, but I didn't know how else to get to the bottom of what had happened to him. "I really am sorry about all of this."

Fay gave me a wan smile, and then we each loaded our arms full of his things to carry down the stairs and out of the building. I, of course, ended up with the coffeepot.

Once the pot was in the trunk of the car, Fay went back inside, a box in hand, leaving me to stand alone in the parking lot. I stared at Lester Hall, hoping that it would somehow reveal a secret, something that would allow me to put all of these horrible things behind me. The murder. Hunter's troubles. My trepidation about Walker Hawk.

The building itself didn't have an answer for me, I realized, but perhaps a place nearby would.

I left the lot feeling strangely like an intruder, despite the fact there were others who were clearly not of college age walking the nearby trail. No one paid me any mind as I crossed the lawn, toward where Sierra and I had determined the photograph depicting Jonas and Hunter making the handoff had been taken.

It looked much the same as it had when I'd been there the last time. There were no discarded cups or bubblegum wrappers. Just the slightly disturbed brush, which by now looked more like it should, telling me that the photographer—or anyone else—hadn't been back.

"Come on. Show me something," I muttered, looking for *anything* that might tell me who had hidden here.

The space wasn't large. I tried to imagine Walker crouching there to snap the photo, but it didn't work in my head. I didn't think the space was big enough for him to squeeze inside without sticking out like a sore thumb. Even someone as oblivious as Hunter could be would have noticed him there.

On a whim, I decided to climb into the small space myself. Perhaps, if nothing else, standing in the exact spot as a possible killer would put me in his or her shoes, as it were, and I'd have an epiphany.

The brush tugged at my clothes as I slipped in behind the tree with the low-hanging branch that had appeared in the corner of the photo. A stick poked out from the underbrush and scored across my shin as I settled in. Cursing, I tried to move, but there were briars behind me and they had latched onto my shirt the moment I'd gotten into place.

Another curse escaped me when I heard a tear as I scooted forward. I grabbed at my shirt, which now had a small hole in it about hip high.

"Great," I muttered, more annoyed with myself than anything.

No, there was no way Walker Hawk could fit back here and take a photo. Whoever it was, wasn't a large person. Even I was having a hard time fitting comfortably.

Dejected, but feeling as if I'd accomplished something, I climbed out of the brush, yelping as a branch caught my hair. I just about fell over as I stumbled out, rubbing at my scalp where the hair had been pulled. A kid in a bright orange tank top paused on the trail, grinned, and shot me a thumbs-up and a wink, before he jogged away.

Perfect. Now rumors would start going around about a disheveled woman getting her kicks in the trees at CLU. I figured it was time I got out of there before someone took a picture of me and posted it to social media, because the last thing I needed was Mom calling to lecture me about decorum and preserving the family name.

CHAPTER 15

"I think I've messed up," I said, tucking my feet under my rump. I was sitting on Brianna Green's overstuffed couch. "Walker couldn't have taken the photo. I've been treating him like a suspect ever since Jonas was killed."

"Just because he didn't take the picture, doesn't mean he's innocent," Bri said from her favorite glider rocker in the corner. A faint squeak accompanied every rock.

"I know." I heaved a sigh and let my head fall back against the couch cushion. "Why can't my life ever be easy?"

"You're a Branson."

Had truer words ever been spoken?

As soon as I'd left the CLU campus, I'd driven straight to Bri's. Out of all my friends, she was the most likely to be home, and sure enough, she'd just settled in to watch one of her favorite Norwegian crime shows on Netflix when I'd banged on the door to her apartment.

"Who do you think did it?" I asked, hoping her binge-watching had somehow turned her into a criminal mind savant.

"Taken the photograph? Or killed the professor?"

"Either. Both." I sat up straighter. "Who should I be watching out for?"

Bri considered it a long couple of seconds before answering. "Keep in mind, I don't have all the details."

I nodded. I'd told her what I knew, but there were a lot of holes that I couldn't fill. "Anything you have to say can only help."

"All right. So, the knife is from the murdered man's kitchen."

"Jonas Valentine."

"Right. He'd fought with his wife and she was staying with her mom on the night of the murder. That very likely gives her an alibi, but a weak one since her mom might be willing to cover for her."

"Let's assume Fay is innocent," I said. "Assume she was with her mom all night and couldn't have killed Jonas. Who does that leave then?"

"Okay. Let me think." Bri considered it with a frown. "If the wife didn't do it, then perhaps another woman did. You said Jonas was cheating on her, right?"

"He *might* have been," I said. "Fay isn't sure he was seeing anyone. His absences might have been for another reason."

Bri nodded, recalculated. "Then the murder probably ties back to the stimulants Jonas was purported to be selling. It makes the most sense."

"The stimulants Hunter picked up from him." My stomach churned at the thought.

"Someone took the photo and then brought it with them to the studio where Jonas was killed," Bri said. "Why do that? Blackmail?"

"That's what I've assumed."

"But for what purpose?" Bri asked. "And who? Was there a rival dealer out there who wanted him to stop infringing upon their territory? Another teacher who wanted in on the action? Or wanted Jonas to pay them so they wouldn't turn him in to the administration?"

"I haven't heard anything about a rival dealer or anything like that," I said.

"I hate to say it, but there's a lot of unknowns here, Ash," Bri said. "Who took the photo? Who contacted Hunter? Why Hunter at all? Why do it at A Purrfect Pose? Why kill Jonas? Why use his own knife? That makes me feel like it wasn't premeditated. The murder, anyway."

My head was spinning, so I buried it in my hands. "This is a disaster."

"There's a connection in there somewhere," Bri said. "You just have to find it."

But how? I'd tried talking to people, but nothing anyone said ever led to a breakthrough. Someone wanted Jonas Valentine dead. Either that, or they wanted to frame Hunter for the crime. Or frame me. Or maybe it was all one big coincidence and Jonas just happened to be in the wrong place at the wrong time.

With a knife from his own kitchen.

Outside my yoga studio where Jonas was a student.

Yeah, I didn't believe it either.

"What about my security cameras?" I asked, looking up. "They weren't working the night of the murder."

"That *is* interesting," Bri said, rocking back. "It points to someone who knew they were there and knew how to shut them off."

Which meant the person who'd broken in, who'd killed Jonas Valentine and posed him in my studio, wasn't a stranger to me.

It was someone I knew.

A friend. A relative. The killer might be someone I was close to.

The thought stuck with me as I left Bri's a few hours later. Someone I knew was a murderer. Premeditated or not, they killed him and posed him in A Purrfect Pose, leaving behind a photo that would incriminate Hunter. Who did I know that would do such a thing?

The only people who knew the password for the security system were me and Kiersten. The only other people who'd known the system even existed were Jordan Leslie, Alexi, Sierra, Kiersten, and me. Maybe Hunter. And I might have mentioned it to Mom or Dad, but I didn't think I had.

No one on that list seemed likely. None of them but Hunter were involved with Jonas Valentine as far as I knew.

Could Mom have been protecting Hunter and killed Jonas to keep her son out of trouble?

It was a wild thought. Hunter goes to her for money, but it isn't enough. He decides to take on the job provided by the mysterious VH. In doing so, he what? Tells Mom? And she decides to get her clothing torn and dirty so she can take a photograph and frame Jonas?

No, Mom wouldn't do that. But she *might* get someone else in the family to do it for her.

What are you doing, Ash? Mom? A relative? If I kept at it, I was going to start suspecting myself.

I pulled up in front of A Purrfect Pose a few minutes later, determined to put all thoughts of murder out of my mind. A group of three people were standing outside the doors. One was peering in through the large plate glass window, hands cupped beside their face to shut out the light.

I parked and climbed out of my car, drawing the trio's attention.

"Oh! Hi, Ash." Sissy Tom stepped away from the window, face reddening as if I'd caught her doing something far worse. She'd attended a handful of yoga classes, and, like the other two, were of college age. "We were just looking for you."

The others, Dylan Cole and Brittany Hamp, nodded.

"I'm sorry," I said. "The studio is closed for the time being."

"We know," Dylan said. "We got to talking about you and I guess we thought we'd come check the place out." The chagrined smile told me he was hoping to see more than me at the studio; likely a bloodstain or two.

"We miss the classes," Brittany said. "And the cats."

"Me too," I said. "After what happened, the police thought it best if I closed for a few days. I'm sure I'll be allowed to open soon."

"Oh." Sissy frowned. "I really hoped we'd be able to start back up today. When I saw movement inside, I figured it was you getting the place ready to open again."

An icy chill worked up my spine, causing my next words to come out haltingly. "Movement? Inside? A Purrfect Pose?"

Sissy looked suddenly uncertain. "Yeah. Someone is moving around in the back. Like I said, I thought it was you, but I never got a good look at them."

Someone I knew. Someone who knew the password. Someone who, like now, could get into the studio without tripping the alarm.

They're looking for the photo!

"Stay here," I said before turning and speed-walking toward the alley access. Someone was in A Purrfect Pose. A photo was left there, likely by accident. What if the killer had come back for it?

Now, if I'd been thinking straight, a few thoughts would have crossed my mind then. Why would a killer break in and snoop around A Purrfect Pose in broad daylight? Why would it have taken so long for them to realize the photo was missing and to come back to look for it? Why not call the police instead of investigating myself?

But thanks to my recent conversation with Bri, I was convinced I'd find Uncle Cliffton or Hunter ransacking my office.

As frustrating as they both could be, I didn't want to get either of them into trouble. Now, if one of them turned out to be a killer . . .

I hit the alley at a near run. My heart was pounding, sending blood racing through my veins. It was probably why I wasn't thinking clearly. At least, that's what I told myself later.

When I reached the alley door, I found it to be closed, but unlocked. I jerked it open, eyes immediately finding the cracked cat room door. A light was on inside and a chorus of meows sifted out. I stepped inside A Purrfect Pose, closed the alley door softly behind me, and then scoured the immediate area for a weapon. All I found was a broom propped in the corner. I grabbed it and tested my grip on the wooden handle. It would have to do.

I crept slowly forward, not quite sure what I would do when I opened the door. Bludgeon the intruder? Hold them hostage while I contacted the police? Some combination of both?

More than likely, I'd end up panicking, missing my swing, and getting knocked over as the intruder escaped scot-free.

As I neared the cat room door, footsteps rapidly approached from the other side. I clutched the broom handle with both hands, reared back, and was ready to strike when the door sprung open and someone walked out.

"Ash!" Tyra Potts yelped my name as she hopped back into the cat room, startling the cats who'd been following her. There was a scrabbling of claws on the floor and one surprised hiss. "It's me!"

I gasped and fell back a step of my own. "Tyra?" I had to speak around my heart, which was currently residing halfway up my throat. "What are you doing here?"

Tyra's eyes were wide, hands raised to ward off a blow. She eyed the broom, which I was still holding up like a weapon. I lowered it and leaned it against the wall before showing her my empty hands.

"Kiersten sent me," Tyra said, slowly relaxing. "You know? For the cats." She gestured toward the felines who were bravely peeking out at me.

"I . . ." I took a breath, let it out through my nose. "I'm sorry. You startled me. I'd come to do the same thing and didn't think anyone would be here."

Tyra's shoulders eased as she laughed. "Startled *you*? I think you just about gave me a heart attack."

"I almost clubbed you over the head." A half-mad laugh escaped me then. I was starting to think it best if I kept bludgeoning objects out of my hands before someone else I cared about got seriously hurt.

"I'm glad you didn't." Tyra let her breath out in a huff. "I could get to liking it here. The cats are amazing. I'm not so sure about the yoga."

"I think you'd enjoy it. Though you'd have to put down your phone for a few minutes in order to do it."

"Hey! I'm not a phone addict like the rest of my brain-dead classmates." She patted her back pocket where her phone was currently stuffed. "In fact, I've barely looked at it all day."

"A teen who isn't enraptured by her phone? Will wonders never cease?"

Tyra rolled her eyes at me, but smiled as she did it. "I've been too busy to scroll. Cats are fed and watered. The litter boxes are clean. And I took care of dangly toy time." She mimed playing with the cats, which caused a few of them to grow excited. "I was just about to run to the bathroom when you came charging in like a bull."

"I did no such thing." I tried not to blush when I said it.

"Well, it sure felt like you did. I really do think I saw my life flash before my eyes. I'm just glad I didn't pee my pants."

I laughed. "Me too." I stepped aside. "Go ahead. I wouldn't want you to make a mess all over my freshly cleaned floor."

"You're a funny one, Ash." Tyra slipped past me, and into the bathroom.

As soon as she closed the door, I sagged against the wall. The police needed find Jonas's killer and clear Hunter's name soon or else I was going to give myself a stroke. I longed to get back to worrying solely about cats and yoga.

And maybe, just maybe, about Walker Hawk, if I hadn't chased him away already.

While Tyra took care of her business, I went ahead and double-checked the cats, but Tyra had done a good job and everything was in order, leaving me nothing to do. I spent a few minutes petting the cats, which helped calm me down, and then I joined Tyra as she stepped out of the bathroom, wiping her hands on her shorts.

"You're out of paper towels," she said. "I should probably get back to the shelter and man the front desk. You know, where nothing fun ever happens."

"I take it you want to work with the animals at the shelter more?"

"I guess. Kiersten lets me do whatever I want, really, but I don't know." Her eyes went distant. "I suppose I expected more . . . *something*."

I considered asking her to come work for me, but stopped myself short. Now wasn't the time, not when I wasn't even sure there'd be a job for her here much longer. If and when Chief Higgins let me open again, I could consider offering it to her. And maybe after talking to Kiersten about it. I'd hate to poach an employee from her without her consent.

"Tyra, Kiersten gave you the password to the security system, right?" I asked, a new thought forming.

"Yeah." She grew nervous. "Wasn't she supposed to?"

"No, she was. I was just curious. You haven't given it to anyone else, have you? Or had someone ask about it? A friend?

Someone who claimed they knew me and needed to get inside for some reason?"

Tyra looked insulted. "Of course not."

"Okay, thanks." I smiled to tell her everything was okay. "I'll see you soon. Tell Kiersten 'Hi' for me."

She hesitated, looked as if she might ask me something, before she said, "Will do. See ya, Ash." And then she left through the alley door.

I followed after her a few minutes later, making sure the door was locked tight. By the time I'd worked my way back out front, Dylan, Brittany, and Sissy were gone. I guess they saw no reason to stick around to make sure I hadn't been mauled by a maniac.

My phone rang, causing me to jump. I snatched it out of my pocket, checked the number, which was unknown, and then answered with a tentative "Hello?"

"Ash. It's Chief Dan Higgins." Even though he was the one to call, he didn't sound happy about talking to me.

"Chief." I didn't know what else to say, so I left it at that.

"I need you to come down here to the station. We need to talk."

"Okay. When?"

"Now." He clicked off.

I groaned as I stuffed my phone back into my pocket. This day just kept getting better and better.

Chief Dan Higgins was waiting for me outside his office when I arrived at the Cardinal Lake police station. As soon as he saw me, he jerked a thumb over his shoulder and marched inside, leaving the door open for me.

It didn't look inviting at all.

"Let me explain," I said the moment I was through the door.

"Close it," he demanded as he dropped into the chair behind his desk. "Then sit."

I did as requested and then opened my mouth to speak, but Higgins cut me off before I could utter the first syllable.

"What are you thinking, Ash?"

"I, uh . . ."

"You're not a detective. You're not even a police officer. Or a private investigator. Or any role or title that would give you leave to question suspects in a murder investigation. You're not even a gosh-darn soul-sucking reporter!" He smacked an open hand against the top of his desk.

The sound was like a gunshot and caused me to jump. "Sorry?" I winced as I said it.

Higgins took a calming breath. It didn't appear to help. "This is a serious matter, Ash. You shouldn't be interfering."

"I'm not interfering!"

"You didn't talk to Fay Valentine? You didn't show up at the college where Jonas Valentine worked? You haven't been in and out of the crime scene like I specifically told you not to do?" He leaned forward, eyes narrowing, nostrils flaring. "You didn't withhold evidence?"

Uh-oh. Apparently, my conversation with Olivia had gotten out. "Look, I can explain."

"Please, do."

"I was going to give you the photo, I swear! But I wanted to talk to Hunter first. He's my brother. He might have been able to explain it and—"

"Did he?"

"Kind of." I flinched when Higgins scowled. "He didn't know anything. He said it felt like a setup, and I'm pretty sure it was. Hunter didn't mean to do anything wrong."

Even coming out of my mouth, it sounded lame. Of course Hunter knew what he was doing was probably a crime. Why else would someone need to hire him for the pickup if it wasn't illegal?

Chief Higgins heaved a sigh as he clenched and unclenched his big fists. "You've put me and Officer Chase in a tough spot here, Ash," he said. "I get that you're trying to protect your family, but a man is dead. His killer is out there somewhere. If bringing your brother in and locking him up for a few days would somehow help catch him, then I think it would be worth it, don't you?"

Put like that, I supposed I agreed, but didn't think Hunter would. "I know. I'm sorry."

"Sorry doesn't cut it. I could charge you, you know? I won't, but I could."

I wasn't sure if it was a bluff or not, and thought better of asking. "Thank you."

"I won't *yet.*" He leveled a finger at me. "But I want you to tell me everything you know. All of it. I don't want you to leave anything out. I don't care how insignificant you think it might be. Do I make myself clear?"

I bristled at his tone. I wasn't a child, though he was talking to me like one.

But, at the same time, I understood why he was angry. I'd screwed up. I'd cost him evidence, which in turn could have cost him time in the investigation. No one else had ended up dead, but what if that changed? Could I live with myself if someone else died because I hadn't come to Higgins with the photo right away? What if it was someone close to me, someone like Hunter?

So what if Chief Higgins made me feel small? Telling him was the right thing to do.

It took longer than it should have because I kept catching myself hedging around anything that touched on Hunter's involvement. I figured that Higgins already knew much of what I had to say, but that was okay. Maybe hearing it all laid out in front of him, he'd put it together with some piece of evidence I didn't have and it would lead him straight to Jonas's killer.

I had to hand it to him, Chief Higgins listened without interruption. He made faces, of course. Especially when I mentioned times in which I'd done something he didn't think I should have done, which was often. I should have turned Hunter in right away. I should have given him the photo as soon as I'd found it. I should have told him about Walker Hawk. About the connections between victim and suspects I'd learned over the course of my poking around.

By the time I was done, I was exhausted. I felt like I'd betrayed my family and friends, and most especially Hunter. It wasn't a good feeling.

"Is there anything else?" Higgins asked once I fell silent. "There's no other small detail you've left out, in order to protect someone, is there?"

I shook my head. "That's everything." I'd even included my theories as to who could have done it and why, which he'd hardly acknowledged, and probably for good reason. As he'd pointed out, I wasn't a detective. I had no business involving myself in any of this.

"All right," Higgins said, pushing his way to his feet with a thunderous cracking of knees that caused him to wince. "Here's the deal. You will tell me immediately if more evidence falls into your lap. You will contact me the *second* you hear from your brother. Understood?"

I nodded.

"I'm keeping you closed until Friday."

It took me a moment to grasp what he was saying. "You're letting me open A Purrfect Pose again?"

"I am, but on the condition that you stop holding back on me. I get why you did it, Ash, I really do. But I want it to stop."

"I will." And I meant it.

"I hope that keeping you busy with your studio will keep

you out of my business," he said. "You've got too much time on your hands right now. Go home. Get some rest. And then get back to work and let me do my job. Sound good?"

"Sounds great."

He grunted and stepped past me to push open his office door. He didn't say anything more as I left. He merely closed the door behind me. Good sign or bad? I had no idea.

And right then I didn't care.

Despite my meddling, Higgins was going to allow me to open again.

If that wasn't a cause for celebration, I didn't know what was.

CHAPTER 16

"Wait! Ash, come over here."

The urgency in Pavan's voice had me scrambling over to where he and Edna stood outside Edna's apartment door. They were staring down the hall, past my door, to the empty apartment beyond.

"What's happening?" I asked, shifting my bags from one hand to the other. I'd stopped at the pet store on the way home and bought new treats and toys for Luna. Yes, it was overkill considering she already had more than enough, but I couldn't help myself. I was so excited about being able to open again, I wanted to celebrate with her.

"Ian's here," Edna said. "He brought a prospective renter." She nodded toward the closed apartment door—apartment 203.

I cocked an eyebrow at them. "And you're standing guard, because . . . ?"

"Oh, you'll see," Pavan said with a grin.

Seconds ticked by where we just stood there, staring at the door. I was curious. Since the apartment was next to mine, it meant I'd be sharing a wall with whoever moved in.

"How long have they been in there?" I asked when the door remained closed a few minutes later.

"Ten minutes, maybe?" Pavan glanced at Edna, who nodded. "You just missed bumping into them."

"Should I be worried?" I asked.

"It depends," Edna said, fighting back a smile. "Do you have a peephole?"

Pavan laughed, which caused Edna to snicker.

Oh boy. I wasn't sure I wanted to know.

"I'm sorry about the other day," I told Pavan while we waited. "I wish I could have stayed for dinner with your family."

"It's all right. It just meant I got to focus more of my attention on Jae."

"I bet she was thrilled about that."

He chuckled. "She was something all right. Seo-Jun had to remind me she wasn't ten anymore at least a dozen times." He leaned closer. "It didn't help."

Edna rested a hand on his arm. "They're always your little babies, no matter how old they get."

I glanced at her out of the corner of my eye. Edna never had visitors, and that included children or grandchildren. It made me wonder if she had any or if they were estranged, but I couldn't think of a way to ask that wouldn't seem impolite.

The doorknob to apartment 203 rattled, drawing all our eyes. Pavan reached out and rested an anticipatory hand on Edna's wrist. Their excitement had me anxiously joining them in staring in rapt fascination, not quite sure what to expect when the door finally did open.

"You're going to love this, Ash," Pavan said, just as the door opened a crack.

Ian Banks's voice drifted out. "I handle everything you'll ever need. Just call and I'll be right over. The residents here call me the everyman handyman." He laughed.

Ian led the way out of the apartment. He was wearing his best suit, telling me he wanted to impress the prospective renter. His dark hair was combed back, just barely hiding the bald spot at the back of his head. He'd even shaved, which looked odd on him since I was used to a scruffier look.

The man who followed him was . . . wow.

"Mm-hmm," Edna said under her breath, just as Pavan whispered, "I knew you'd approve."

I didn't recall doing it, but I'd sucked in a breath and held it as the man stepped out of the apartment. He had the face and build of a model, and had shoulder-length brown hair, styled to perfection. He was smiling, and I swear angels were singing because of it.

"It's nice," the man said. His voice had a faint rasp that only added to his attractiveness. He looked past Ian and locked eyes with me, causing my knees to wobble.

"It's my very best, Mr. Fitzgerald, I promise you." Ian jerked to a stop when he saw the three of us standing outside Edna's apartment. He cleared his throat as his smile became strained. "And you won't find a better group of neighbors either."

"Please, call me Leon. It's a pleasure to meet all of you." He bowed his head ever so slightly, eyes never leaving mine.

While Edna and Pavan each managed pleasantries, I think the only thing that came out of my mouth was an elongated "Uh."

"If you'd like, I could show you another apartment." Ian was practically stumbling over his words, making me wonder who this Leon Fitzgerald really was. A movie star? A demigod? With his looks and charisma, he could be either.

"No, I think this one should suffice," Leon said. "I do enjoy the view."

"Great!" Ian was beaming. "We could head over to my office and can get the paperwork signed right now, if you'd like? I will have the apartment professionally cleaned, top to bottom, before you move in, of course."

The two men started for the stairs. Edna cleared her throat, then nodded toward my apartment door. "Now's your chance," she said.

It took me a moment to realize what she was talking about. "Oh!" I caught the men before they took the first stair. "Ian. Can I have a moment?"

"Ash," he said, shooting nervous side-eye at Leon. "I really should—"

"No, go right ahead," Leon said, cutting him off. "I'm in no hurry."

Ian winced, though he was still holding on to his smile. Barely. "What do you need, Ash?"

"My door. I called you about it sticking. Remember?"

Red rushed up Ian's neck, colored his face. "Yes, yes. I plan on taking care of that soon."

"Do you think it could be today?" I asked. "After you're done with Mr. Fitzgerald, of course."

The smile cracked. "Well, I . . ." Another side-eyed glance at Leon, before Ian sagged. "Of course. I should be back in an hour, two tops, to take a look at it."

"That'd be great!" I said, grinning. "I should be home all day." I turned to Leon. "Ian really is a great landlord. He sometimes gets so busy helping, it takes a few days for him to get to you, but it gets done."

Leon fought a smile of his own. It caused his eyes to sparkle like stars. Or maybe it was just the overhead lights that did it. "That's good to hear. I think I might like it here." He checked his watch. "I need to step outside to make a call. You two can work out the details of the repairs."

Ian held his composure until Leon was out of sight before he swung around to face me. "I know what you did there, Ash, and I don't appreciate it."

"It made you look good." Kind of. "And the door really does need to be looked at. What if someone were to break in? I'd have to call the police and with a new resident who has yet to settle in, that might look bad."

It felt petty laying it out like that, but Ian had tried to make *me* deal with it myself, when it was his job to fix it. It was in the contract.

"Fine," he said. "I'll look at it today, but I can't promise it'll be fixed right away. I might have to buy supplies."

"That's okay. Thank you." Ian started to walk away when a new thought struck me. "Hey, Ian?"

He heaved a sigh, turned.

"Do you know anything about security systems?"

"A little. Do you need one for your apartment?"

Probably, but that wasn't why I was asking. "I have one set up at my studio downtown. Someone broke in through the back door, but the cameras weren't working. I use an app that sends me alerts when it detects movement. Do you know of any way in which someone could have shut them down without alerting me?"

He considered it a moment. "Well, if they have the passcode, they could have done it."

"What if they didn't?"

He shrugged. "I'm sure it's possible. If they cut the power, and if your cameras don't run on batteries, that might have done it. And considering most of those types of systems need Wi-Fi to work, no power equals no signal, so that could have been it."

"I got an alert for the door," I said. "So, the power was working."

"Then someone got the code," Ian said. "That'd be my guess. You didn't write it down and leave it somewhere where it could be found, did you?"

Had I? I thanked Ian and considered it on the way back to my apartment door.

"Were we right, or were we right?" Pavan asked.

"You were right," I said, only half paying attention.

I can be scatterbrained at times. Forgetful at others. I vaguely remembered writing down the password to the security system, but where did I leave it?

I unlocked my apartment door and stepped inside with a distracted goodbye to Pavan and Edna, who were busy gossiping about our newest neighbor. Luna came over to greet me as I closed the door and leaned against it, thinking.

I hung the cameras at A Purrfect Pose myself. Then I'd downloaded the app while I'd still been there. I went into the office and then worked through the setup procedure while sitting at my desk.

And then what?

My eyes widened as it hit me.

I wrote the password down so I wouldn't forget it. Then I folded the piece of paper I'd written it on, and then went about setting up for the first day at the studio.

"My desk," I said, paling.

After setup, I'd stuck the password in my office desk drawer where anyone could have walked in and grabbed it without me noticing. I didn't leave the office locked. In fact, the door was normally hanging wide open while I had classes. The cat room was across the hall. The restroom was past it. Dozens of people had walked by, unsupervised. Anyone could have gone in and taken it.

But who would have done such a thing?

A meow caught my attention. Luna was staring at the bag in my hand like she knew what was in it.

"All right, all right," I said, turning my attention toward her. There was nothing I could do about the password now, not if the killer already had it, other than change it. I made a mental note to do that as soon as I'd played with Luna.

I carried the bag over to the table and pulled the tag off the cat toy, which was one of those sticks with a string with a bunch of feathers attached to the end. Luna's eyes went black as I flipped it into the air for the first time. The hunt was on.

The feathers never stood a chance.

* * *

After a thoroughly exhausting romp around the apartment with Luna, I spent the next few hours on the phone. First, I changed the password to the security system, as well as the one to the door, just in case. Then I contacted anyone and everyone I knew about Hunter. He had to be *somewhere*. And someone out there must know where he was.

But if they did, no one I talked to admitted to it. Alexi was likewise flummoxed, and by the time I'd settled in for the night, I was frustrated. Ian had come and gone, promising that he could fix the door without much trouble, though it might take a few days before he got around to do it. I had a feeling that if I didn't press him, those days would turn into weeks, and then to months.

Luna was snoozing soundly on her perch after a second vigorous play session and a hearty dinner that was followed up with a couple of catnip-laced treats. I was considering the merits of calling it an early night myself when my phone rang with an unfamiliar number.

Worried it might be Chief Higgins again, I answered with a tentative "Hello?"

"Ash! Get down here this instant."

"J. Allen?"

"Who else would it be?" Jordan said in a harsh whisper. "You need to get down here right away."

I stood and went to the window and looked outside. Nope, he wasn't standing in the courtyard. "Where are you?"

"At Bark and Style." He sounded frantic. "I was at home when I realized I'd forgotten Ginger's favorite furry friend at the shop and I just had to get it for her before she realized it. When I got here, I saw someone snooping around outside, acting all sneaky. I think they're scoping out your place."

"Did you call the police?" I asked, already on my way to the door.

"No, of course not. What if it's just someone who's lost? Or a kid looking to pull a silly prank? Besides, it's not *my* business they're poking around. You should get down here and check it out."

"I'm already on the way."

I clicked off as I left my apartment and all but ran down the stairs. This time, I played it smart and jumped into my car, rather than hoofing it. If it was the killer come back to commit some other heinous crime at A Purrfect Pose, I was going to stop them.

On the way, I put in a call to Olivia, but I got her voicemail. I wasn't sure how to feel about that. On one hand, Jordan might be right and it was just someone walking around, a drunk perhaps, and calling the police on them would be a waste of time. On the other, police backup would be nice.

I decided to wait and see. The police station was a button press away, so if I didn't recognize the culprit, I could call before getting out of my car.

I parked in front of Bark and Style a minute later, immediately noting that no one was standing in front of A Purrfect Pose. Was I too late and the prowler was already gone? I hadn't gotten an alert on my phone, so they weren't inside, not unless whoever it was shut everything down, including the door alert this time.

There's one way to find out.

I brought up the camera app. It was working, so no outage this time. A quick scan showed me nothing was out of place and no one was moving around inside.

Okay, that was good. No one had broken in to leave yet another body for me to find. But the culprit still might be lurking around outside somewhere.

I climbed out of my car, and as soon as I did, Jordan appeared in his window as if he'd been waiting for me. He mouthed, "In the alley!" before he vanished back into the depths of the doggie salon.

I could have gone all the way around to the alley entrance so I could sneak up on the prowler, but that would put me in a dark alley with someone who might turn out to be a killer.

I didn't think so.

I went into A Purrfect Pose through the front door, leaving the lights off as I went. I immediately got an alert on my phone that the door was open and that motion was detected, which reinforced the idea that the cameras were indeed working. I shut down the system, and then made my way to the back. There, I grabbed the broom I'd nearly bludgeoned Tyra with earlier, and then I unlocked the back door.

"Here goes nothing," I muttered, and then I pushed open the door in one quick, fluid motion.

There was a gasp, and then a shape moved in the too-dark alley. I reared back, ready to strike, when the shape spoke in a voice I recognized.

"Ash?"

"Topher?"

Thoroughly confused, I flipped on the light, which cascaded out into the alleyway, revealing Topher Newman, holding his phone up like a weapon, while wearing yet another '80s band T-shirt; this time Poison. Was he old enough to like bands like that? They were dated, even for me.

"What are you doing here?" I asked him, ushering him inside, though I kept hold of the broom, just in case.

"I got a text," he said. "It said to meet here."

"A text from whom?"

He swallowed, tugged at the neck of his tee. His eyes roved all around, as if he expected someone to leap out at us at any moment.

"I don't know. I didn't have them in my contacts, but they said it was important." He paused. "It wasn't you?"

"No," I said, a sense of dread growing. I closed the door and double-checked to make sure the lock engaged. "Can I see the text?"

"Yeah." Topher tapped on his phone's screen. He frowned, repeated the tapping. "Wait."

"What's wrong?"

"The text. It's gone." He turned his phone toward me, but since I never saw the text in the first place, I had to take his word for it.

"Okay," I said, anxiety through the roof. "Run me through it again. You got a text telling you to meet someone here? When was this?"

"About an hour ago. I was at home, listening to *1984*, when I got it. It only said to meet out back of A Purrfect Pose in an hour."

"And you just decided to come?"

Topher reddened. "I thought it might be from you."

There was a moment when I wondered why that mattered, before an idea hit me. I decided not to pursue the matter any further.

I paced away from him, mind racing. Through the cat room door, I heard a meow as the cats began to realize they weren't alone. Until I was certain a killer wasn't lying in wait somewhere nearby, I didn't want to let them out.

"You don't think it was from him, do you?" Topher was following me. "The killer, I mean."

"I don't know." But it was likely. Hunter had gotten a mysterious text that caused him to get involved with Jonas Valentine. The text hadn't vanished like Topher's, but that meant little. The killer could be learning. They could have realized their mistake with Hunter and decided on advanced tactics.

Which meant the killer might be technologically savvy.

That would mean they wouldn't necessarily need the security system password to disable the cameras. What if they had some sort of device that could shut them down? All they'd need to know was that the cameras were there, right?

Of course, I knew no one who had that kind of knowledge. I wasn't even sure it was possible outside the movies.

"Did you see anyone outside when you arrived?" I asked Topher.

He shook his head. "You're the first person I've seen since I got here."

Did that mean I got here first? Or was the killer out there somewhere, watching us?

I found my eyes drifting toward the cameras. Could he be watching us, even now?

Stop it, Ash. I was thoroughly creeping myself out.

A knock on the front door startled a yelp from me, which in turn, caused Topher to nearly bolt. I grabbed him by the arm, stopping him, and raised a finger to my lips. He nodded in understanding.

"Wait here," I whispered when the knock came again. "I'll see who it is."

And then I crept down the hall, into the main room, to do just that.

Through the plate glass windows, I could see Jordan Allen Leslie pacing on the sidewalk. A stuffed squirrel was in his hand. Breathing a sigh of relief, I hurried to the door and opened it.

"Did you find them?" he asked.

"I did. It's a student of mine."

Jordan frowned as he looked past me. "A student? At this hour?"

"He got a text message, asking him to come," I said. "You didn't happen to see anyone else out here tonight, did you?"

Across the square, a couple walked hand in hand down the sidewalk in the direction of The Hop. Jordan turned toward them and then gave me a flat, pointed look.

"Point taken. Anyone who didn't belong, I mean?"

"Just the person I called you about. I swear, this whole murder thing has me jumping at shadows. Why would a student of yours be here this late when they know you aren't open? A text? I don't think I'd respond to such a thing, not with what happened."

No, neither did I. Then again, I'd headed straight over when Jordan had called, so I suppose that wasn't entirely true.

"He thought it was from me," I said, not quite sure why I felt the need to defend Topher, but I did. "If you see anyone else in the next few minutes, please let me know."

"The next few minutes? I don't think so. I'm not sticking around here this late." Jordan waved a hand in a warding-off gesture. "I'm going back home to Ginger and staying inside where it's safe. I suggest you do the same thing."

And then he turned and walked briskly away.

Once he was gone, I closed the door, locked it, and then returned to the back, where I found Topher peeking out of my office.

"Who was it?" he asked.

"The dog groomer. He's the one who called me, telling me you were here."

Topher frowned at that, stepped out of my office. "Why would someone invite me here and then not show up?" he asked.

I put an arm around him and led him out of the back, into the front of A Purrfect Pose where it felt, I don't know, safer. Strange thought considering Jonas's body had been left there.

"I wish I knew," I said. "But if you get any more texts from someone you don't know, you should contact the police right away."

His nod was a little too fast. "You're right. It was stupid coming here." He glanced behind him, down the hallway. "Do the police have anything yet?"

"What do you mean?"

"Like, a clue. Was there something left here that would point to who killed Professor Valentine?"

I thought of the photo I'd found, of the knife that had come from the Valentine home, and then decided it best not to worry him. He was already shaken up enough as it was.

And considering Fay Valentine, a woman he liked and respected, might be involved, I wanted to be doubly cautious.

"As far as I know, nothing was found," I said, hoping the lie wouldn't come back and bite me on the butt. "The police are on the case, so I'm sure they'll figure out who did it soon enough."

"But why would the murderer contact me?" he asked. "I don't know anything!"

I wished I could have said something reassuring, something that would ease his mind and allow him to sleep easy, but what could I say? Someone *had* sent him a text, just like they had Hunter. Was it a setup? An attempt at another murder?

A prank?

It made me wonder if Topher Newman knew something, something that had the killer worried. He knew Professor Valentine. Both of them, in fact. If Fay killed her husband, perhaps she was afraid he'd seen or heard something.

I had no idea how to ask him about it, so I did the next best thing.

"Go home," I told him. "Lock your doors, call someone to come stay with you if it helps. Chad, maybe. And, in the morning, you should call the police, tell them everything you know about Professor Valentine." I paused, unsure if I should add the next bit or not, but decided to do it anyway. "And Fay."

Topher frowned. "Fay had nothing to do with it," he said before shaking his head. "But you're right. I shouldn't have come. I'll be more careful." He started for the door, and then said over his shoulder before he left, "You should too."

That was advice he needn't have given, but I appreciated it nonetheless.

Alone, I took a few moments to check on the cats, and then made sure A Purrfect Pose was locked up tight. It wasn't until I was almost to my car that a new thought hit me.

Topher had been lured here through text message, just as Hunter had been to the pickup at the college.

How did the killer lure Jonas Valentine to his death?

A text made sense. It also might explain why Jonas had brought a knife. Strange, cryptic texts had a tendency to make people paranoid. It would make sense if he'd decided to protect himself.

Sure, Topher's text had vanished, but Hunter's hadn't the last time I'd spoken to him. Perhaps Jonas's text—if he'd indeed gotten one—was still there, on his phone, waiting to be found. A text would lead to a number, which would lead to a name.

And hopefully, a killer.

CHAPTER 17

I had big plans for Tuesday. I was going to find Hunter and make him tell me everything he knew. About Jonas Valentine. About the money he borrowed. Everything. And then I was going to convince him to go to the police. He was going to take the photo and the package of pills with him. He was going to show Chief Higgins the text he'd received. I'd be at his side the entire way.

Once I was done with that, and the killer was identified, I planned on spending the rest of the day at A Purrfect Pose getting the studio ready to resume classes—and to spend a few quality hours with the cats.

I could visualize it so clearly, I was smiling by the time I'd showered and was dressed for the day.

And then someone knocked at my door.

"I don't appreciate what you did by ambushing me in front of a prospective renter," Ian Banks said as he stomped inside. "But I'm here now and I'm going to get this done and out of the way. No complaints."

I opened my mouth to do just that, but at his glare, I closed it and motioned for him to proceed.

I figured he'd be there for an hour, maybe two.

It took him eight.

"What's wrong with it?" I asked him after hour three. He'd already come and gone twice, claiming he needed to grab something from his office, but I never saw what it was he'd needed, only that it ate another fifteen minutes of his time with each visit.

"It sticks," Ian snapped. "Leave me be so I can deal with it."

Hour four was met with a cracking sound as he tore the doorframe apart. Then he left again, leaving me with a gaping hole that allowed anyone who walked by to peer inside my apartment. I had to keep Luna locked up in my bedroom so she couldn't wander out into the hall.

Thankfully, only Pavan and Seo-Jun passed on their way upstairs before Ian returned with fresh wood, some paint, and a box of nails.

From that point on, I hid in my bedroom with Luna. Between the pounding and cursing, I wanted nothing to do with what was happening to my door. I spent much of my time online, looking for some sign of Hunter, a post on social media, an email I missed, but there was nothing. A text to Alexi told me she'd likewise come up empty.

So, I called Olivia.

"Hi, A—what in the world is that racket?"

"Sorry." I just about had to shout it. "Ian's fixing my door."

"It sounds like your apartment is falling in."

A loud curse came from the living room. It was followed by a moment of silence.

"I have a question for you," I said quickly while there was a break in the noise. "A student of mine showed up at A Purr-fect Pose last night. He'd gotten a text from someone, asking him to meet them there. He didn't know who it was from, and later, when I asked to see the text, it was missing."

A beat, then, "Was there a question in there somewhere?"

"Jonas Valentine's phone. Did he have a text from someone asking him to meet them at A Purrfect Pose on the night of the murder?"

Olivia sighed. "I couldn't tell you—"

"I'm not asking for confidential info," I said. "I was just thinking that if there was a text, then maybe it'll lead to the killer. Hunter got one too, remember? From the VH person?"

"I know, Ash. I can't tell you if he had a text because we don't have his phone. It wasn't at the scene."

"Oh." I frowned. "Where is it then?"

"Beats me. I'll check with Dan and see if he asked the widow for it. I'm guessing he did, but it can't hurt to double-check."

"Thanks," I said. "It might not amount to anything, but I do hope it helps."

"Me too, Ash. Me too."

I hung up just as the hammering began once again.

A few hours later, the noise stopped and didn't immediately start up again. I rose from my bed and peeked out of my bedroom. Ian was repainting the doorframe, glowering at it like it had personally attacked him. When he noticed me, he motioned me over.

"The wood had swelled," he explained. "I thought I could shave it down, but it was too old and started splintering, so I replaced it. The door opens and closes without sticking now." He wiped sweat from his face, shook it off his hand. "If Mr. Fitzgerald comes around asking about me, please let him know what I did for you."

I chose not to point out that it was part of his job to fix things like a sticking door. Instead, I smiled, thanked Ian, and let him finish his painting.

By the time he was gone, it was too late to get anything done. I opened and closed my door a few times to make sure it did indeed work properly now. Leon Fitzgerald didn't come to my door asking about Ian, or anything else for that matter. Edna stopped by at one point and we gossiped for a good half an hour before I settled in to eat dinner. Alone. Like always.

While I was eating, I got a message from Kiersten at the shelter. She'd been to A Purrfect Pose and had taken care of the cats for me—I'd texted her during the construction. She also told me Lulu's application had been approved and that she could pick up her new feline companion whenever she wanted.

A quick call to Lulu set up an appointment for Wednesday morning, which had me up bright and early, and looking forward to what I hoped would be a good first half of my day.

The second half I wasn't so sure about. That dinner with Dad was looking mighty ominous at this point, but at least I could ask him about Hunter while I was there.

Lulu was waiting for me outside the front doors of A Purrfect Pose, practically dancing from foot to foot. As soon as she saw me walking toward her, she erupted into a huge smile, arms going wide as she rushed over to me.

"I'm so excited," she said, wrapping me in a hug. "I haven't told Cal yet, but that's okay. He won't say no."

I sucked in a deep breath when she released me. She'd just about squeezed the life out of me. "How is Cal doing?"

"Oh, he's fine. A slight sprain. He was limping around by the evening without trouble, and walking normally this morning. I think he just wanted to check out my friends without seeming like he was doing it."

"Seems like a painful way to do it."

Lulu laughed. "Wouldn't surprise me if he'd tried to sneak a peek through the window and hurt his knee that way. Not that he doesn't trust me, but he's kind of shy, you know?"

If she said so. "Let's go in and get your cat."

Since Higgins had given me permission to open again, we went in through the front door. A rush of emotion washed over me as we stepped inside. No, I wasn't holding a class today, but I soon would. And no, Jonas's killer hadn't been apprehended as of yet, and Hunter was still missing, but I was starting to feel as if the worst was finally behind me.

"I can't wait until Friday," Lulu said, rubbing her hands together. When I'd called her about her application's approval, I'd told her the good news. "I've been trying to keep active, but this is so much easier, you know? I think it's the social aspect. It makes you want to try harder, to, I don't know, look good in front of everyone else."

Through the glass, the cats perked up as we approached. Two ran to the window and placed their paws on it, meowing. A handful of others, including Lulu's new pet, rushed the door.

"There he is!" she said as soon as the door was open. The little gray kitten made straight for her, as if he knew he was going home with her today. "Oh no! I left the carrier in my car down the street. I should have brought it in with me. I was just so excited, I completely forgot."

"It's all right. If you want to get it, I have a few things to take care of in the office, so you won't be making me wait."

"If you're sure . . . ?" At my nod, she grinned. "I'll be right back." She started for the door, and then realized she was still holding her kitten. She kissed him atop the head, returned him to the cat room, and then bustled out the door for her carrier.

The first thing I did when she was gone was write out a note for anyone who walked by that we'd be opening again on Friday. I planned on contacting everyone personally, but wanted to let the world know too. Not that most people would care, but I was just so darn happy about it.

Once that was done, I began cleaning up the mess the police had left in my office. I opened the top drawer to my desk to dump a few stray pencils inside, and found myself staring at a folded sheet of paper.

The password.

I picked up the page, turned it over in my hands a few times, and then opened and closed it like I thought it might tell me something. There was nothing to see but the password, written in my own hand. I frowned at it, and then, since it no longer worked, I tossed it into the trash.

Hunter was back here alone. He could have snooped around in my desk while I was dealing with Jordan Leslie and Olivia before he'd taken off. I hated to think it, but rifling through my desk was exactly the sort of thing Hunter would do.

Lulu returned a few minutes later, a brand-new cat carrier in hand. It still had the tag hanging from the handle, but she didn't seem to care. She was all smiles as she urged the gray kitten into the carrier, and then spent the next couple of minutes cooing at him through the metal bars.

"Here," I said, handing her a small plastic bag. "There are treats and toys inside."

She took it with a grin. "This is so exciting. I can't wait to get him home."

"You're going to be a great pet mom," I told her.

"I hope so." Lulu turned to face the empty front room. "You know, I hate to say it, but I think everything is going to turn out for the best. That maybe what's happened isn't such a bad thing."

"What do you mean?"

"That whole murder business." She shuddered. "It's terrible, and I hate that someone died, but he wasn't a nice man."

"That's what I've heard," I said. "Did he do or say something to you?"

"Me?" Lulu shook her head. "No. But that last day we held class here, I saw him say something rather nasty to his wife,

Fay. She's such a nice lady, and doesn't deserve to be verbally berated like that."

"When was this?" I asked. "I never saw him say anything to her." If I had, I would have stepped in.

"You missed it. You were outside dealing with J. Allen at the time. I'm not sure what they were arguing about, but whatever it was, it upset Fay pretty badly and she ended up going into the back for a little while to get away from him." A stricken look passed across Lulu's face then. "I should have gone back to check on her, but I wasn't sure it was my place."

"Fay went into the back?" I asked. I could feel the blood draining from my face, and hoped that Lulu couldn't see it.

Thankfully, she was too busy peering in at her gray kitten to notice. "She did. She came back out just before you returned, looking just as rattled as when she'd left, if not more so."

When Lulu left a short time later, I found myself standing alone in A Purrfect Pose, wondering whether Fay Valentine had been the one snooping around in my office, not Hunter. She might have gone in there to get away from Jonas, opened the drawer, just to have something to do with her hands, and then . . . what? She saw the password and concocted a plan to murder her husband and leave him here?

It made some semblance of sense. Sure, if she was the one who'd taken the photo of Jonas with Hunter, then she'd already had a plan before finding the password. Maybe it wasn't for murder, but blackmail. She could have been planning on divorcing him and wanted to make sure he left her everything in the split. One way to do that would be to threaten to ruin his name, his career.

There were still a lot of holes in my theory, of course. She was supposedly with her mother on the night of the murder. How would she have known to contact Hunter? Why here? I couldn't imagine that finding the password was all it took.

I spent the next few hours thinking about it as I picked up after the police and set everything to rights. I let the cats roam freely as I worked, which meant I spent more time shooing cats off papers than picking said papers up. The work was slow, but I couldn't say it wasn't enjoyable.

When I was finished, the studio looked like it had pre–murder investigation. I had just enough time to walk home for a shower before I would need to head over to Dad's for dinner.

And what was I going to do about Fay Valentine?

It looked like I'd just have to wait and see.

Wayne Daniels—Dad—lived at the edge of Cardinal Lake, the town, not the actual lake, in a small housing development of similarly built houses. Every property had one small tree in the front yard on the right side, near the sidewalk. Every lawn was mowed by a professional, so they were all the exact same height. Same siding. Same driveway. Same two-car garage. Same, well, everything.

When he and Mom had divorced, she'd taken the house and he'd moved here. Every time I'd visited him since, I had to check the address a dozen times to make sure I had the right house. At night, when it was dark and the streetlights turned on, I found the whole housing development to be a little creepy thanks to the sameness. It was like something out of a horror movie.

I approached the front door, dread churning a hole in my gut. Every step dragged, and I could *feel* an invisible weight pressing down on me. Something felt off; something more than usual.

When I knocked and the door opened, I knew why.

"Ash, don't be mad," Kara said before I could react. "I made Wayne let me stay. It's not his fault."

My first instinct was to turn and walk away. No shouting.

No getting mad or frustrated or any of the other emotions that swirled through me upon seeing my former best friend, current step— . . . Nope, I couldn't even think it.

"Ash," Dad said, moving to stand behind Kara. "Please, come in."

They both stepped aside. I braced myself with the thought that it was only one dinner, one night. If it went poorly, I didn't have to come back again. I could always call Dad, meet with him in public every once in a while, and call it good.

No, it wasn't a perfect solution. But I was here. It would have to do.

I entered the house.

Dad led the way into the dining room. Decorations were sparse, but that had always been Dad's way. He liked his possessions to be functional, and knickknacks were anything but. That didn't mean the place was boring, but it wasn't visually stunning, either.

"Let me get you something to drink," he said.

"Water is fine," I said before he could decide to bring me a beer. "Thank you."

"Yeah. Sure." His smile was uncertain as he headed for the kitchen.

"Ash . . ." Kara sat down in the chair across from me. She looked the same as she always had. Dark brown hair that curled naturally inward at her chin. Brown eyes. A build that was solid, but not in an unhealthy way. "Can we talk?"

Bottles clinked in the kitchen. I could see Dad's shadow, and realized that he was giving us this time on purpose. My water was likely going to take as long to retrieve as I was willing to let Kara talk. I could smell something good coming from the kitchen, and decided letting her have her say was worth it for the meal afterward.

"I want to be friends," Kara said at my nod. "I hate that we stopped. I never wanted that."

"Neither did I," I said.

"I understand why it happened," she said. "This is . . . weird."

I laughed. "You don't say."

That brought a smile to Kara's face, and already, I could feel the tension cracking. "I swear, I never considered Wayne as anything more than your dad right up until, well, I did. It wasn't until he split with Cecilia that it happened. It was sudden."

"You're telling me," I said. "Everything's fine, and then one day, I look over and you're making googly eyes at him."

Kara winced. "I didn't want to hurt you. Neither of us did." She glanced toward the kitchen. Dad's shadow hadn't moved. "I don't want you calling me 'Mom' or anything like that either. It would be too weird for the both of us."

She could say that again. "Look, I . . ." I trailed off and studied Kara's face. There was pain there, pain I'd caused by all but abandoning her when she fell for Dad. Was I a bad person for that? I mean, sure, it was a strange situation.

But I'm a Branson. My situation was always strange.

And just like that, I realized that I could do this. Yes, there would be tough times. Yes, I would find myself wondering how it was even possible that my best friend had ended up with my dad. There'd always be that faint sense of betrayal, like she'd only stayed friends with me for as long as she had because of him.

But I knew that wasn't true. Kara had always been honest with me. She made him happy. Was that really such a bad thing?

"Truce?" I asked, reaching a hand across the table.

Kara's eyes filled with tears as she took my hand. "Truce."

If there hadn't been a table in front of us, we would have hugged, but I was afraid to stand. I was shaky, and still not quite sure I was doing the right thing by accepting the situation. Only time would tell if I was making a mistake.

Dad appeared, blinking rapidly. He handed me my water,

and then sat. "I wasn't sure what you wanted to eat, so I made pot roast. It used to be your favorite."

"It still is," I said.

He smiled and took Kara's hand. I had a moment where the old urge to flee from the sight tried to overtake me, but it calmed and I was able to sit there without cringing too hard.

"How have you been, Ash?" Dad asked. "How's your mother?"

"She's good," I said. "She's not a fan of my studio, but I think she'll get over it."

He chuckled. "I'm not surprised. She doesn't like it when things don't go her way."

The next thirty minutes were spent in casual conversation where we avoided any topic that might cause tension—other than talk of Cecilia Branson, of course. Dad served the pot roast, of which I ate about two helpings too many. I was just settling in, feeling as if I was finally at home, when I asked, "Have you talked to Hunter lately?"

Dad and Kara shared a look. "I can't say that I have," Dad said. Kara shook her head. "Why?"

"Have you heard about what happened at my studio?"

"The murder?" Kara asked, hugging herself. "I saw it on the news."

"Hunter is involved in that?" Dad asked. "I thought it was a random killing?"

Oh, how I wished that was the case. "The victim was posed inside the studio," I said. "And Hunter knew him." I briefly explained the connection. "Now, Hunter's missing, and I'm worried he's going to do something stupid."

Neither Kara nor Dad insulted me by saying, "He wouldn't do that." We all knew that Hunter practically lived on the wrong side of right.

"Let me try him," Dad said, rising. "I haven't talked to him in a few weeks." He pulled his phone from his pocket, dialed.

"Are you sure Hunter knew the guy?" Kara asked as Dad put in the call.

"I saw the picture myself."

"No answer," Dad said. "Should we go look for him? I know a few places where he likes to stay."

"I've checked them," I said. "He's not there, and no one's seen him."

"There is one—" Dad started, but he cut off when my phone rang.

For a crazy instant, I thought it would be Hunter. It *was* a sibling, just the wrong one.

"Hey, Alexi," I said, holding up a finger to Dad and Kara as I answered. "I'm at Dad's."

"Wow. How's that going?"

"Better than expected." Across the table, Kara smiled. "What's up?"

"I'd tell you not to worry about it since you're with Dad, but I don't think I can."

Uh-oh. I didn't like the sound of that. I stood and paced away from the table. "What's going on?"

"It's Hunter," Alexi said. There was a long pause, and I feared the next words out of her mouth would be something along the lines of "They found his body," or "He's been arrested."

Instead, she said the one thing I didn't expect.

"He's here."

"Here? As in, at your house?" I asked.

"Yep. Evan and the kids don't know it. I've got him stashed away in the garage and he's just about leaping from his skin. I'm not sure how long I can keep him here."

"I'll be right over," I said, clicking off. I turned to Dad and Kara. "I'm sorry, I've got to go."

"No, go on." Dad approached, hesitated, and then gave me one of those awkward hugs where only his hands touched my back and the rest of his body avoided any and all contact. "It was nice to see you. I'm so very glad you came."

"Me too," I said. And much to my surprise, I found it to be true.

"Come back anytime," Kara said, following me to the door. "And maybe we can get coffee?"

I smiled. "Of course." And then I hugged her. "I'll call you soon."

And then I was out the door, speeding my way to my sister's.

CHAPTER 18

It took ten minutes to drive to Alexi's, but it felt like an hour. Darkness had fallen, which made me start thinking about movies I'd seen where the killer decides to make their move in the middle of the night, right when things seem to be going the hero's way.

Not that I viewed myself as the hero or anything, but I couldn't help but worry.

I pulled into the driveway and jumped out the moment I was parked. The garage door was down, so I went for the front door, which opened as soon as I reached it.

Before I could speak, Alexi, looking grim, shook her head. From behind her, a familiar voice squealed.

"Auntie Ash!"

"Lily Rose!"

I accepted the hug from the enthusiastic five-year-old. Standing next to Evan in the dining room was Lily Rose's six-year-old brother, Philip, who was trying to act like he was much more mature than his sister and didn't need a hug. It took all of two seconds before he broke and rushed over to throw his arms around me.

"Hey, Ash," Evan said with a smile. "Come to babysit while your sister and I get in some quiet time alone?"

"You wish," Alexi said, closing the door as I waddled in, a child attached to each hip.

"A man can dream." Evan ran a hand over his buzzed short dark hair. He was tall, with a facial structure that looked like nothing more than a skull with dark skin pulled taut across it. It was as if Olivia had gotten all the weight, leaving nothing for her older brother.

"Auntie Ash, I've been working on my yoga," Lily Rose said. She extracted herself from me and then did something that might have been a yoga pose if it had involved a lot less swaying and resetting. And a form that stayed consistent.

"That's very good," I said. "Has your brother been helping?"

Philip crossed his arms. "I don't do yogi."

"It's *yoga!* With an -uh!" Lily Rose stomped a foot. "Don't you know anything?"

"I know more than you. You're just a baby."

"Am not! Mom!"

"Okay you two, time to go to bed." Alexi looked to a clearly amused Evan for help.

"But Aunt Ash is here!" Philip whined. "Can't we stay up?"

"Aunt Ash and I need to talk," Alexi said. "She promises to come over in a day or two and spend time with the both of you."

"Of course I will," I said. "We can work on our yoga."

"Yay!" Lily Rose beamed as she sprinted up the stairs to her bedroom. A belated "Good night, Mom!" filtered down the stairs.

Philip pouted a moment longer, and then gave me a quick hug before running up the stairs after his sister.

"The fun never ends," Evan said with a laugh. "I'll read the kids a story to give you two a few peaceful moments." He paused at the bottom of the stairs, his expression going serious. "I hope everything works out with Hunter." And then he was gone, up to read stories to his children.

As soon as they were gone, I turned to Alexi. "Is he still in the garage?"

"I wish." She frowned up the stairs a moment before facing me. "As soon as I got off the phone with you, he bolted."

"He what?" I wasn't surprised. Frustrated, yes, but not surprised.

"I should have gone upstairs and grabbed a pair of handcuffs. I knew the moment he got here he wasn't going to stay."

The question "Why would you have handcuffs?" formed on my lips, but I wisely didn't ask. I really, really didn't want to know.

A pair of squeals, followed by mad laughter came from upstairs. Both Alexi and I moved into the living room. I doubted the kids could have heard us, but I wanted to be safe. I didn't want them to think badly of their Uncle Hunter.

"Tell me what happened," I said.

Alexi waited a long moment, likely to make sure one of the kids didn't come tearing down the stairs, before she spoke. "So, Evan and I were eating dinner and the kids were making art with theirs."

"Anything good?"

"The food or the art?"

I laughed. "Either."

"Evan cooked, so the food was fantastic. I'm not so sure about the art." The light banter seemed to calm Alexi and as she spoke, the tension bled from her voice. "I heard something outside and went out to check."

"And there was Hunter."

"There was Hunter. He was pacing back and forth, acting freaked, so I took him into the garage to cool him down. He babbled a bit about feeling watched, that Higgins was out to get him. He insisted he needed to take care of things before anyone finds out, but he wouldn't tell me what things he needed to deal with, or what he was afraid people would discover."

"Sounds like he's gotten worse since I last saw him," I said.

"It was rough," Alexi admitted. "Once I got him to settle down, I went inside, told Evan that I found a rat in the garage—"

"Nice." I couldn't help but smile. Evan Chase, a man brave enough to marry a Branson, was deathly afraid of rodents. There was a good chance he wouldn't set foot in the garage for the next week.

"—and then I called you," Alexi continued. "When I went back, Hunter was strangely calm. He said he'd figured out what he needed to do. He told me not to worry, that he'll take care of everything, and then, against my protests, he left."

"Do you know where he went?"

"No clue. I had to go back in and assure Evan that I was wrong and it wasn't a rat, but a baby rabbit, which had run away when I shooed it out the door. Then you got here, and here we are."

Here we were, right back to where we'd started.

"What are we going to do?" I asked. "What does Hunter think *he's* going to do?"

"Whatever it is, it didn't sound good," Alexi said. "I got the impression he thinks he's making some sort of grand sacrifice by doing this on his own."

I didn't like the phrasing and paced away from Alexi so I didn't lose it. A sacrifice implied someone might not be coming back from it in one piece, and I desperately didn't want that someone to be my brother. Heck, anyone for that matter. One death was more than enough.

"We should call Olivia," I said. "Or Chief Higgins. *Somebody.*"

"I know," Alexi said. "But I don't know what to tell them.

That Hunter was here and that he's gone again? That he left, telling me nothing about where he was going or what he was going to do?"

"It will put them on alert," I said. "Maybe they'll spot him and stop him before he does something stupid."

"Maybe." Alexi didn't sound convinced. "I've got a bad feeling about this, Ash. I don't know what to do."

"Neither do I." I stepped forward and got my third Branson-Chase family hug of the night. Fourth, if you counted Dad. "Should we call him?"

"Can't hurt to try."

I waited while Alexi pulled out her cell. I could just barely hear the ring through the speaker, followed by the mechanical voice telling her that she'd reached Hunter's voicemail.

"Didn't think that would work," she said, clicking off and angrily shoving the phone back into her pocket. "Hunter can be such a jerk sometimes."

"What did he do now?" Evan asked, appearing at the stairs. "Did I miss something?"

Alexi and I shared a brief look. I heard her voice as clear as day in my head say, *Don't worry him,* before she spoke out loud.

"We can't reach him. He's been ignoring our calls."

Evan joined us in the living room. "Anything I can do to help?"

"No, you've done enough." Alexi rested a hand on his arm. "I might call Olivia, just to fill her in and see if she's learned anything new."

"If she had, she would have told me," Evan said. At his wife's pout, he added, "But it doesn't hurt to ask."

"Thank you," she said, blowing him a kiss.

"Anything for you, darling." He made his own kissy face.

I mock gagged before checking my Fitbit. "I'd better get

going," I said, noting the time. "I don't want to keep the two of you away from whatever it is you are planning to do once I'm gone."

"I'll check to make sure the kids are actually in bed," Evan said with a laugh. "You be safe, all right, Ash?"

"I will."

He leaned forward and kissed me on the cheek before he vanished up the stairs. The middle one squeaked, and a heart-beat later, there was a rustle upstairs that sounded a lot like a couple of kids scrambling for their beds.

"Get some sleep," Alexi said when he was gone. "I'll call Olivia, let her know what's happening. There's nothing else we can do tonight."

"I'll try," I said, hugging her. "Thank you."

"We're both going to have to kick Hunter's butt when this is over."

"You bring the steel-toed boots."

"The *pointed* steel-toed boots."

I just hoped that by morning, Hunter would still have a butt for us to kick.

"Ash! I know you're in there!"

The voice echoed down the stairs of my apartment complex, reached me as I checked my mailbox in the lobby and found it empty. Incessant pounding followed a moment later.

I'd just entered the building and I was already considering turning around and walking out. I could drive back over to Alexi's and sleep on her couch. Or I could camp out in my car until my unhappy guest left, which, by the sound of it, might not happen for a while.

But no, that wouldn't accomplish anything other than to make my neighbors annoyed with me.

With a sigh, I ascended the stairs, dreading what was to

come. When I reached my floor, I took a deep, calming breath, plastered on a strained smile, and then walked into the fire.

"Hi, Ginny," I said, noting Edna standing at her door with a frown on her face. "What brings you over at this hour?"

Ginny spun, eyes startled and wide. "Ash?" The surprise faded as she slammed her fists onto her hips. "Where have you been?"

I didn't know how it was her business, but I was playing nice here, so I answered. "I had dinner with my dad and Kara. You remember her, don't you?"

Ginny had always liked Kara, so I hoped bringing her up would ease some of the tension.

It didn't.

"I do. And I doubt you were at dinner this late."

"No, I went to Alexi's afterward." I couldn't hold the smile any longer. My shoulders sagged as I approached the door. "I'm pretty tired, Ginny. Is there something you needed?"

"Pretty tired? Is that what you have to say to me? After what you've done?" Her tone rose in pitch with every word.

I unlocked my door, stepped inside my apartment. I didn't need this tonight, but at the same time, I couldn't leave Ginny standing there, clearly upset by something she thought I did. Not if I wanted to be friends with Drew. It was best to nip this in the bud now.

"Do you want to come in for a minute?" I asked, eyes flickering over to Edna. She had that look on her face that told me that she and Pavan were going to have an interesting conversation about me in the morning. "To talk."

Ginny tapped her foot, arms crossed, as she considered it. Out here, she had an audience. Sometimes, with her, that was what mattered.

"Please," I said, stepping aside, giving her space to enter. "Let's sort this out." Whatever *this* was.

Ginny shot Edna a look, and then heaved an overly dramatic sigh. "I suppose we should." She entered the apartment as if she'd been the one to suggest it.

Once Ginny was inside, I closed the door, once more inordinately ecstatic that it actually *did* close.

"Okay," I said, turning to face Ginny. "What's this about?"

"What do you think?" she asked, adopting her favorite crossed-arms stance. "It's about you and Drew."

I blinked at her. Didn't we just do this the other day? "There *is* no me and Drew."

"You say that, but you don't mean it."

"No, Ginny, I do mean it. We're just friends."

"Do friends *embrace* like lovers in the middle of town where everyone can see?"

Ah. Now I understood. It took all my willpower not to heave a heavy sigh and just walk away.

"I was upset, Ginny. Hunter is in trouble. You've probably heard about the murder at A Purrfect Pose. Hunter is involved in that. I needed to talk to a friend so I didn't go crazy."

"You have other friends!" She stomped a foot. "Why does it have to be Drew?"

I closed my eyes. I wasn't angry with Ginny for being jealous here. In some ways, I understood her. She was afraid of losing him, and despite my insistence that I wasn't interested in him in that way anymore, I was the biggest threat to their relationship.

"I called Drew because he's been my friend since we were little," I said. "Our relationship afterward had nothing to do with it. I needed someone I could trust, someone who has been there for me all my life. And when I started to panic, he hugged me to keep me from falling apart. There was nothing more to it than that."

"But—"

"No, Ginny. There are no 'buts' here. I needed a friend and Drew answered the call. He even met the guy I'm seeing." Or *was* seeing, considering I hadn't heard from Walker since he'd walked in on the hug between Drew and me at The Hop. "Drew really does care about you and I'm okay with that. You should be too."

Ginny looked as if she wanted to stay angry with me. Every muscle in her body appeared taut, ready to snap, and that included her jaw muscles. She stared at me, seemingly building up that anger before she suddenly dropped down onto my couch, face buried in her hands.

"I'm sorry, Ash." Her voice was muffled by her palms. "I heard about you hugging him and after what . . . and we . . ." She made a frustrated sound.

I crossed the room and sat down beside her. Gently, I rested a hand on her back. "I get it, Ginny, I do. You don't want to lose him. You hear stories, think the worst. It's natural, especially if you're scared." Then, as kindly as I could, I asked, "Did you ask Drew about it?"

"No." Quiet. Sullen.

"He would have told you the same thing I'm telling you now. You have nothing to worry about. Drew and I are over. We're both good with how things are now. Neither of us are looking back."

Ginny nodded into her hands, refused to look up. "I know. It's just . . . You took him from me when you started dating in school. I waited years for him to notice me. And when he finally did, I felt like I was his second choice. You'll always be his first, Ash. And, no offense, but it burns me to know it."

"It's not a competition," I said, trying, and failing, to keep the frustration out of my voice. "There are no firsts and seconds here. Drew cares for you now just as much as he did for me back then." And then, to appease her, "Maybe more so."

"Do you think?" She looked at me askance.

"I do. Talk to Drew about it." I stood, hoping Ginny would do the same, but halfway up, a thought hit me, and I all but forgot about her.

Where's Luna?

She wasn't on her perch by the window. She hadn't come to investigate when I'd let Ginny in, nor when we'd sat down to talk, as was her habit. She hadn't snuck past me, out of the apartment, when I'd entered.

Ginny was saying something, but the words were gibberish to my ears. I spun away from her and went for the hall. When I'd left, Luna had been snoozing on her perch, content as could be, yet I was questioning myself. Had I locked her in the bathroom after my shower? I didn't remember closing the door, yet, there it was, closed.

As I reached it, a faint meow came from the other side. When I opened the door, Luna darted out of the bathroom at a hundred miles an hour, and ran straight for her litter box.

My heart was thumping in my ears. Luna was safe, but I *knew* I hadn't closed her in the bathroom. I'd looked right at her when I'd left, had said goodbye.

So then, *how did she get in there?*

"Ash?" Ginny asked as I returned to the living room. "Are you all right? You look like you've seen a ghost. Hey!" She stumbled as I put a hand on her back and guided her toward the door. "What's going on."

"I'm sorry," I said, eyes roving the apartment, looking for something missing or out of place. "You've got to go." I opened the door and all but pushed her out the door. I was going to pay for that later, but right then I was on high alert and having her there was a risk.

Ginny said something else. I missed it thanks to the sound of the door closing in her face.

I was seeing it now. A book I'd been reading was sitting

askew on the table. Box flaps that were normally tucked and closed were hanging open. A drawer wasn't quite closed in the kitchen. The flowers Walker had given me were gone. No, I could see the stems poking out of the sink where they'd been dumped.

Someone had been here.

I paused by Luna to pet her. She was now at her water dish, drinking. Someone had been here and they'd locked her up before going through my things. Was it to get her out of the way? Was it to keep her safe while they searched? Or in case I came home and we fought?

I slid a knife from the knife block and turned back to the hall. My bedroom door was open, but someone could still be in there. Ginny had acted like she thought I was inside. Was that because she was stubborn?

Or because she'd heard someone?

I walked slowly toward the hall, knife held in a sweaty grip. I kept thinking that I should call the police from the safety of Edna's apartment, that I was taking too big a risk investigating myself.

But this was *my* apartment, just like A Purrfect Pose was *my* studio. In each case, someone had invaded the space, left me feeling dirty. And that someone could very well have been the *same* someone. A killer.

Which is why you shouldn't be doing this on your own, dingbat.

I ignored the voice in my head as I reached the bedroom. I held my breath, counted silently to three, and then I leapt through, knife held above my head, ready to strike.

No one was there.

The same went for the rest of the apartment. I checked, and rechecked, every corner, closet, and drawer. Things were out of place, and all my boxes had been opened and riffled through. The intruder hadn't thrown things willy-nilly around the room, thankfully, but it was clear they'd been searching my place.

But for what?

Edna.

I rushed to the door and burst out into the hallway, thinking to bang on Edna's door like Ginny had been mine, but Edna was still standing outside her apartment, the frown still on her face. When she saw me come barreling out of my apartment, knife clutched in my hand, she gasped and stepped back into her own apartment, hand on the door as if to close it.

"Wait!" I shouted. "Edna. Hold on." I hid the knife behind my back, though she'd already seen it. "I have a question for you. It's important."

"Is it about that woman who just left here in a huff?" she asked.

"No." Or I didn't think it was. I couldn't imagine Ginny breaking in, going through my things, and then leaving, just so she could beat on the door afterward. "Did you see anyone else here this evening while I was gone?"

Edna's nod was slow, thoughtful. "I dare say I did. Didn't you know?"

I shook my head.

"They had to have shown up about five minutes after you left earlier this evening. I told them they'd just missed you, and he said that it was okay, that they'd leave you a note." She paused. "There wasn't a note?"

I noted she used the word "he" and ignored her question. "It was a man who came here?" A man like Walker Hawk, perhaps? It would explain why the flowers had been dumped out. He was mad at me for the lunch date I'd had with Drew.

But why go through all my boxes?

"It was," Edna said. "You really didn't know they were coming?"

"No, I didn't. Do you know who it was?" I asked. "Was it the guy who picked me up the other day?"

"No, it wasn't him," Edna said. "This young man had a key and I'd never met him before."

"He had a key?" I asked. My heart was thumping in my ears so loudly, I almost didn't hear what Edna said next.

"He did," she said with a nod. "And when I asked him who he was, he told me that he was your brother."

CHAPTER 19

Needless to say, I didn't sleep all that much that night.

Every sound had me shooting bolt upright in bed, listening to make sure it wasn't someone trying to get in. I'd once more blocked off the door with boxes of kitchen supplies, but those could be pushed aside if the invader was determined enough.

By morning, I was grumpy, worn out, and fully expecting the day to start with a disaster.

But when I checked my phone, there were no texts from Alexi telling me that Hunter had been arrested for whatever it was he had planned. A quick perusal of the local news sites told me the same thing.

It looked like one crisis had been averted.

For now.

Luna was flopping around the apartment, acting the part of a starving kitty, when I dragged myself out of bed, so I fed her before I showered. The grogginess slowly fled, which caused my brain to start working semi-properly again.

Why had Hunter been here? What could he possibly have been looking for? He'd taken the photograph already. Had he left something else here? Something like the package of pills? Why dump out Walker's flowers? Why bother opening all my boxes? If he'd left something here, he would know where to find it.

How did he get a key?

As I crunched on my morning cereal, a creeping suspicion started working its way through me. By the time I'd rinsed out my bowl, I was positive I was right.

I picked up my phone, anger simmering just beneath the surface, and put in a call.

"What is it, Ash? I already fixed your door."

"Ian, did you give someone a key to my apartment?"

The pregnant pause that followed told me I'd guessed right.

"Ian!" If steam could have shot out of my ears, it would have. "Why would you do something like that?"

"Hey! The guy said it was your birthday and that he wanted to leave you a surprise present. What did you expect me to do? I thought you'd be happy!"

"You thought that I'd be happy that you gave a stranger a key to my apartment?"

"He said he was your brother."

"And if he wasn't?"

Another long pause gave me time to think of all the horrible things that could have happened. What if I'd come home while whoever had been here was still here? What if they'd decided to wait for me? What if they planted evidence to frame me? What if . . .

"Look, Ash," Ian said, doing his best to sound diplomatic, but I could hear the chagrin in his voice. "I'll be there in fifteen minutes with a brand-new lock for your door, okay? There's no need for this to escalate."

I was shaking so badly by then, I couldn't respond in any way other than to hang up.

Someone had been in my apartment. I would put money on it that the someone *wasn't* Hunter. He wouldn't have gone through my things, my boxes, which had included personal items Hunter would never want to touch or look at, even accidentally. Edna didn't know Hunter by sight. She didn't know his voice. Anyone could have said they were my brother and she, like Ian, wouldn't be the wiser.

I sat down at the table and tried to calm myself. I should have called Ian last night when Edna first mentioned someone had gotten in with a key. I should have made him change the locks right then and there. If it had been the killer, they could have come back at any point in the night, and, despite my precautions, they could have gotten in.

A whole new bout of anxiety swept through me. Had they come back?

I'd heard sounds in the night, like always. It was an apartment complex, so there were people moving around all the time. Could one of the clicks I'd heard in the night been my lock? Had a killer tried to get in?

I rose and checked the door. It was still locked, so if someone *had* tried to get in while I'd slept, they'd relocked the door after they realized they couldn't get past the boxes.

Ian arrived a few minutes later, a shiny new doorknob and lock in hand. He got to work without comment. I stood by, steaming, trying to come up with something to say that wouldn't end up getting me evicted. I failed, so I remained silent.

Once he was finished, Ian handed over the key. "I'm going to go ahead and cut your next month's rent in half." He wouldn't meet my eye as he spoke. "Make that the next two months." A hesitation. "Three. Three should do it."

"I . . ." Was still so mad, I left it at that.

Ian scurried out a moment later, his proverbial tail tucked between his legs. A new lock was nice and all, but it wouldn't help much when I lay down at night. It would take weeks, possibly months, before I felt secure in my apartment again.

I considered my next move. Priority one: find Hunter. I dialed his number, got voicemail, and hung up. Predictable. That meant I'd need to drive around, hitting up all his old haunts and coming up with new ones in which he might have tucked himself away.

Unfortunately, I had no idea where to start.

So, I moved on to priority two.

I called Fay Valentine.

"Hi, Fay, it's Ash," I said when she answered. "I have a question for you." When she didn't respond, I plowed ahead. "You wouldn't happen to know where Jonas's phone might be, would you?"

"His phone?" She sounded tired, as if she'd had as long as a night as I'd had.

"His cell." I was about to explain my theory that the killer had lured him to A Purrfect Pose through text, but caught myself. If Fay was the killer, then she already knew that, and letting her know that I suspected would be bad. "It wasn't at the scene and I was curious if he left it at the house."

"I don't know." She sighed. "I can look for it, I suppose."

"Thanks," I said. "I'll let you get back to your morning."

She clicked off without saying goodbye.

Something was off. She'd sounded tired, yes, but there was something else in her voice, something . . . secretive? I wasn't sure that was the right word, but it had me worried.

If Fay found Jonas's phone, nothing would stop her from accessing it and deleting evidence; if there was any to find. The same went for her own phone. If she suspected I was onto her—and if she had something to do with her husband's death—she could dispose of any texts, emails, or photos that would prove her guilt. And that didn't just mean a text to a co-conspirator. A bloody glove. An agenda where she'd written, *Kill Jonas.* Anything.

I needed to be there if and when she found the phone.

I grabbed my keys and purse, and after a moment's hesitation, a knife from the block. I wrapped the blade in a hand towel, carefully slid it into my purse, handle up so I could easily reach it, and then headed for my car.

Of course, fate wasn't done punching me in the gut quite yet.

"Ash, I'm glad I caught you."

Walker Hawk was just about to open the door to my building as I stepped outside. The sky was bright blue, void of clouds, with just a hint of a cool breeze to keep the warmth from becoming overwhelming. It was a fantastic day, yet I knew I wouldn't be able to shake the metaphorical storm cloud that had begun gathering over my head the moment I'd woken.

"Hi, Walker." I left it at that. I could already tell by his expression that this wasn't going to be a happy conversation.

He shoved his hands into his pockets and glanced up at the sky. If I'd been in a better mood, I might have snapped a photo. He looked, more than ever, like a cover model. The pose. The outfit. The sight was nearly enough to melt away the frustrations of the morning.

"I'm not sure how to say this," he said, not meeting my eye. "I came here with this big old speech in my head, but now that I'm here, it feels wrong to have rehearsed it."

"Just say it," I said. "I've messed up and—"

"No!" He reached out and rested a hand on my shoulder briefly before dropping it. "No, you haven't messed up. But I guess after everything, I've sort of realized that this—that we— wouldn't work out. You're great and all, and I . . ." He scuffed his boot on the sidewalk. "I guess I—"

"You don't have to explain," I said through the lump that had grown in my throat. "I understand."

"I'm leaving Cardinal Lake." He blurted it out like it burned his tongue. "If I planned on staying, I'd probably give this thing we had a shot, but I'm not, and I wouldn't feel right asking you to come with me when I don't even know where I'm going yet and you have your life and business here."

"You're leaving?" All the negativity of the day had me thinking that it was my fault, that I'd driven him clear out of town by . . . what? Hugging Drew? I was being stupid, and I knew it.

"I am," Walker said. "I have a job lined up. Wasn't sure I was going to take it, but the more I thought about it, the more I realized that I want to go. Coming here was a mistake. Not entirely a bad one." He smiled at me. "But a mistake nonetheless."

A wild thought shot through my head then. Walker was leaving after a man was murdered, so therefore, he must have killed him and was fleeing town.

But that didn't feel right. Nothing in his demeanor made me think he was running away. And why do it days after the murder when he could have run the night of? He seemed genuine. And yeah, he could be putting me on, but I didn't think so.

"It's all right, Walker," I said. "I understand. I really do."

He nodded, looked down at his boots. "I'm sorry, Ash. I really do like you. I wish things could be different, but . . ."

"But they aren't."

"But they aren't."

Walker's gaze found my own. There was a moment where I considered what it would be like to just up and leave Cardinal Lake, leave the Branson name behind, and throw caution to the wind and see where it took me.

And then the moment passed.

"Goodbye, Walker," I said.

"Goodbye, Ash." He leaned forward, kissed me on the cheek, and then he walked away.

I let him go, feeling as if I was doing the right thing. Yes, I felt I'd missed an opportunity, but hey, there'd be others, right? For a first fling after Drew, it hadn't been so bad, despite consisting of a single, solitary date.

I gave Walker time to drive off into the sunset before I made for my own car. I was already dialing Alexi before I was behind the wheel.

"Walker's gone," I said when she answered.

"Like, the killer got him?"

I laughed, surprising myself. "No. He's leaving town. A job, I guess."

"He's the guy you were seeing, right?"

"He was."

"I'm sorry, Ash. That sucks."

"It does. And, I guess it doesn't. I'm okay." And I was. Much to my surprise, that mental storm cloud was breaking up. "Is there any news on the Hunter front?"

"Nothing on this end. You?"

"Not a thing."

"Damn. I'll keep looking."

"Me too. Then we can have a nice long chat about him and other recent unpleasantries I've had to deal with." Like Ian Banks. Alexi was going to flip when she heard that he'd handed out a key to my apartment.

"Keep me posted?"

"Of course."

We clicked off. I did a quick search, found the address I was looking for, and then, determined to take care of this thing once and for all, I was on the way.

The Valentine house was a modest white two-story with a black tile roof, a two-car garage, and a small unattractive yard. I got the feeling that neither Jonas nor Fay were very much into landscaping—or spending much time at home, for that matter. A car was parked outside the garage, sitting slightly askew. I pulled in behind it and headed for the door.

I wasn't sure what I was going to say when Fay answered the door. "Did you steal my security password and then lure your husband through text to A Purrfect Pose where you killed him?" didn't seem like the best opening salvo, but it was the only thing that I could think of.

But I was going to have to do something. I was tired. Tired

of being afraid. Tired of wondering where Hunter might be. If Fay Valentine had killed Jonas, and I could prove it, Hunter would no longer be in danger. I wasn't even sure he was at risk now. Fay wasn't a serial killer. She was a scorned, abused woman, who'd done what she thought she needed to do in order to escape the man who'd hurt her.

Or so I hoped.

I checked my purse to make sure the knife was still there. As footfalls approached from the other side of the door, I took a deep breath and readied myself to confront Fay.

Fate, however, once again decided to step in and complicate things.

The door swung open, but it wasn't Fay Valentine who answered. It was Topher Newman in a rumpled Van Halen tee.

"Ms. Branson! Err, Ash." He looked startled, but quickly recovered. He looked chipper, if not confused. "What are you doing here?"

"I could ask you the same question," I said. It came out snarkier than I'd intended, but I'd had a day.

Topher's face flushed. "I came over to try to convince Professor Valentine to stay at the college and not leave town. She didn't want to get into it, so we've been talking about music instead."

"Music?"

"Yeah. Van Halen. Bands like that. She likes Sammy Hagar, but I prefer the David Lee Roth era. You know, songs like 'Jump.'" I half expected him to give me a Diamond Dave leap, but Topher remained grounded.

"Fay's home, then?" I asked. And with Topher here, I doubted she'd gone in search of Jonas's missing cellphone. *A blessing in disguise?*

"Yeah." Topher cleared his throat. "I can take you back to her, if you want?"

"Yes, thank you."

Topher stepped aside, fingering his shirt, which was old and worn, with a small tear at the lower back. It looked as if someone had been wearing the shirt since the eighties when the David Lee Roth–fronted era of Van Halen was originally active.

I entered, catching a whiff of Topher as I passed. He smelled strongly of lilac soap, which threw me for a loop. Had he showered just before coming over?

"Have you had any luck convincing Fay to stay?" I asked him as he closed the door behind me.

"I'm not sure," he said. "Like I said, we didn't talk about it much. I get the feeling she's reconsidering. I hope she does. We really do love her at CLU."

A stack of books sat on a table near the door. Dust had settled atop them, telling me they'd been there a long time. I imagined Fay hauling them from the college, depositing them on the table, just before getting into it with Jonas. There, they remained, forgotten, even now.

Topher's phone buzzed. He tugged it from his front pocket, and then came to an abrupt stop as soon as he checked the screen. I caught a glimpse of the words "Lovers' Perch" before he closed the text.

"Sorry, Ash, I've got to go."

"A friend?" I asked, meaning more. Every town seemed to have a place like Lovers' Perch. It was a small clearing on an overlook that gave a clear view of the lake over the tops of the trees. It was the kind of place you went to when you wanted to be alone, even if "alone" was a relative term. There were always multiple cars with steamed-up windows parked along the overlook. They were usually occupied by overly hormonal teens.

Drew and I had spent far more time there than I'd ever admit. Normally, the place was empty at this time of morning, but not always. I'm not saying how I knew that.

Topher flashed me a hesitant smile. "Yeah, something like

that." His phone started playing a song—his ringtone, I assumed. All I heard before he declined the call was a somewhat familiar tapping that sounded kind of like a motorcycle starting up, or maybe a bunch of pencils being drummed on pads of paper. I couldn't quite place the tune. "Fay's on the back deck, through there." He pointed.

"Thanks, Topher. I'll tell her you're leaving." I paused, smiled. "But I won't say where you're going."

"Uh, thanks." And then he was speed-walking to the door.

I walked the short distance through the kitchen, to the back deck where Fay was reclining with a mug of what I assumed was coffee in hand. She was staring off in the distance, clearly lost in her own thoughts. She didn't glance back when I opened the sliding door. She didn't speak. She continued to stare, the coffee held under her chin, seemingly, like the books on the table by the door, forgotten.

"Fay?" I asked. "It's Ash."

She jumped ever so slightly, causing her coffee to slosh in her mug, but not spill over. She set it down on the table in front of her. "Ash?" She glanced back, a brief flare of panic passing over her before vanishing. "You called earlier. I'm sorry I haven't gotten the chance to look for Jonas's phone. Topher is here."

"I saw him when I came in." I took in her robe, the way it was pulled tightly around her throat. A sneaking suspicion started in the back of my mind, one I steadfastly ignored. "He had to leave."

"I see." She turned back to the trees at the back of her property. "I suppose it was time he went."

I eased down into a chair next to her. "Was he here long?"

She didn't answer. She just kept staring, hand going to her robe, up near her throat.

"Are you all right?" I asked her.

Fay took a deep breath, nostrils flaring as she did, and when she let it out, her entire body sagged. "Am I? I don't know. I suppose I'm . . . confused? Is that the right word?"

"Confused about what?"

Fay lifted her hand to touch her lips. She was still staring off into the distance, as if searching for answers in the sway of the branches.

"Fay?" I asked. I was starting to grow alarmed. "Did something happen?"

"Jonas . . ." She blinked, shook her head. "I was so lonely. And he was here, and . . ."

"Jonas was here? When?" Even as I asked it, I realized my mistake.

"No. Topher. I . . ." She cleared her throat, straightened. "Jonas is gone. I have nothing to be ashamed of." She glanced at me out of the corner of her eye, as if checking to see if I was judging her.

Was I? On one hand, Jonas had died only a few days ago. Fay could very well be his killer. And if what I was interpreting from her demeanor, from Topher's scent, was correct, she hadn't wasted time in moving on.

But looking at her, I thought I understood. Killer or not, she was conflicted, scared.

Alone.

"It has to be hard," I said, not sure what else to say.

"It is. Jonas and I were married for so long. And while things had been tough as of late, we were still together. Now I . . . I have no one. I'm not sure what to do with myself."

"I understand," I said, and I meant it. Though, now wasn't the time to get into my feelings about Drew and Walker and the looming *aloneness* that awaited me.

"I thought I was steadfast. When Jonas was alive, I was. Even when things were bad, I was loyal to him." She sniffed, wiped at her eye. "When Topher approached me at A Purrfect Pose—"

"Wait, he approached you?"

She nodded. "On that horrible Friday morning. Jonas said some rather unflattering things to me and I'd gone to the back to catch my breath. Topher was there. He pulled me into the office and told me . . . Well, what he told me is none of your business. Just know, I turned him down."

A memory reared back and slapped me upside the head. "Topher asked to go to the restroom," I blurted, more for my benefit than Fay's.

But Topher didn't go to the restroom.

He went into the office.

"When he showed up here late last night, I suppose my guard was down. He seemed upset, worried. He kept saying he'd lost something, but couldn't find it. I was trying to calm him down and the next thing I knew . . ." She put a hand to her forehead. "God, what was I thinking?"

I was on my feet and didn't remember rising.

It was Topher.

He'd asked to go to the restroom. He went into my office instead. He found the password. He had a crush on Fay Valentine. She turned him down, probably by invoking her husband's name.

"Ash?" Fay's concerned voice seemed to come from far away. "I didn't mean to unload on you like that. It's embarrassing, and I suppose I needed to say it out loud to make sense of it."

I barely heard her.

Topher needed to get rid of Jonas so Fay would consider him as a proper suitor. How could he do that? Jonas is selling stimulants to his students, something Topher knew. He decides to blackmail him. He contacts Hunter. How? Why him? No clue, but he does. Hunter picks up the package at the college. Topher takes the photo from the safety of the brush, just off the walking trail. And like me, he tears a hole in his shirt on the thorns there.

The *Van Halen* shirt.

VH. The name of the person who'd texted Hunter.

"I've got to go," I said, nearly stumbling over my own two feet as I turned for the door.

The tapping drumbeat I recognized on Topher's phone. I knew that song, thanks to Dad, who used to listen to it in the car to annoy Mom. It was almost too on point to be real. I mean, "Hot for Teacher"? Really?

By the time I was through the house and in the driveway, I was running. Topher Newman had killed Jonas Valentine. He'd used Hunter to set him up. Hunter had his number, thanks to that anonymous "VH" message.

The text Topher had received when I'd arrived. Lovers' Perch. Hunter told Alexi that he was going to take care of the problem himself.

My brother was about to come face-to-face with a killer who was close to having everything he wanted. Hunter was the final loose end, and he'd just served himself up on a silver platter.

CHAPTER 20

The phone rang in my ear before it was answered with a blast of sound and Olivia's overstressed voice.

"Ash? I can't talk right now. There's been—"

"Olivia!" I cut her off, eyes riveted to the road in front of me. "I know where Hunter is. He's with the killer."

"What? Slow down. What's going on now?"

In the background of the call, a siren rose and faded away. I could vaguely hear shouts and more oncoming sirens. Wherever she was, something was going on.

"Topher Newman killed Jonas Valentine. He set Hunter up and now Hunter is meeting with him. Alone, Olivia. Send everyone!"

"Back. Up." Olivia sounded distant, despite her harsh, commanding tone, before she was back with a faint rustle. "Ash, where are you? Please tell me you're not going to wherever this meeting is taking place."

"It's at Lovers' Perch." As requested, I didn't tell her I was headed there, which I, of course, was.

"Ash, you—" Another siren rose and then it cut off with a screeching of tires on pavement. More shouts followed. Olivia spoke quickly once it died down. "Listen very carefully, Ash.

There's been a car accident at the square. The entire force is here managing the situation. No one can help you right now."

Frustration had me squeezing my phone to keep from throwing it through the windshield. "Hunter is in danger!"

"I know," Olivia said. "I'm going to talk to Chief Higgins as soon as I hang up here. There's a good chance he'll let me go, but it is going to take time. It's a mess here, Ash. Everyone is okay, but traffic is backed up as far as I can see. I'm not sure how long it will be before any of us can get out of here. At this rate, I might have to walk."

More protests were on my lips, but I didn't utter them. There wasn't anything Olivia could do, trapped as she was. It appeared as if I was on my own.

"Sit tight, Ash. *Do not* go and try to play the hero."

"I won't."

I clicked off and continued on my way to do just that.

There was no way I was going to leave Hunter to fend for himself. He had to know he'd contacted a murderer, or at least someone connected to the murder. But would Hunter prepare for it properly? Knowing him, he'd just try to hand over the package of pills and hope to still get paid.

But Topher didn't care about the pills, and he likely didn't have the promised ten grand. He'd wanted to get rid of Jonas Valentine, which he did, and now Hunter was a liability. A loose end that needed to be snipped.

And with Hunter out of the way, what proof did we have that Topher was involved in Jonas's death?

My next call went to Alexi.

"I know where Hunter is," I said before she could so much as say "Hello."

"Great." A pause. "Where?"

"Lovers' Perch. I'm headed there now. He's with Jonas's killer."

"What? Ash—"

"If you're going to tell me not to go rushing in like a fool, Olivia already beat you to it." A rudimentary sign made by a high schooler was hammered to a tree. It proclaimed Lovers' Perch to be just ahead.

"Do you at least have something to defend yourself?"

I glanced at my purse. The knife handle could just barely be seen poking from the top.

"I do." If Topher had a gun, I was cooked, but I had no other choice. "All right, I'm here. I've got to go."

"I'll be there in—"

I didn't hear how long it would take Alexi to join me since I'd already clicked off.

Topher's car was parked ahead. I couldn't see anyone inside, or anywhere within view. A dented metal barrier kept cars from overshooting the parking spaces and flying down the hill. A path led off to the right to a more private, treed location, for those who preferred the open air to the confines of their vehicle.

I parked behind Topher's car and removed the knife from my purse. I weighed it in my hand, unable to imagine a situation where I actually *stabbed* someone, and then I climbed out. A quick look around, and then I was headed for the path deeper into the woods.

It didn't take long before I heard voices ahead. The trees here were thick and the path wound haphazardly through them, so it was hard to tell what was being said or where exactly they were coming from. I did recognize Hunter's voice, followed by Topher's. They were muffled, but the tone told me that things were escalating.

I ran the rest of the way to the small clearing in which they stood.

Hunter stood near the railing at the private overlook. A backpack dangled from one hand. He was holding his other hand out, palm outward, in a warding-off gesture. A pair of wooden benches stood between him and Topher, who had a sturdy-looking stick in his hands.

"Just take it and go," Hunter was saying, holding the backpack up. "It's all here."

Topher stepped around the first worn bench that had given many lovers more than their fair share of splinters over the years. "Are you trying to give me drugs?" he asked. "To force them on me?"

"You're the one who told me to get them for you!" Hunter's eyes found me as I burst into the clearing. They widened briefly before he turned his complete focus onto Topher, who had his back to me and hadn't heard me approach. "I don't even need the money. Just take it."

Topher's grip tightened on the stick. He gave it a practice swing and then spun it like a baseball bat. He took another step forward, putting him nearly within striking distance of Hunter, with the single bench between them.

"I don't care what you did, or to who, all right?" Hunter said, voice rising in pitch. "I just want it to end, man."

"What *I* did?" I could hear the smile in Topher's voice. "I don't think anyone's going to see it that way. You're the one who met with the guy, took his pills. But instead of selling them like you were supposed to, you kept them. Professor Valentine got angry. When he confronted you, you killed him."

"That's not true and you know it." Hunter offered the backpack again, but it was clear Topher had no intention of taking it.

I crept forward, making sure to keep out of Topher's line of sight. It was sunny, and while there were a lot of trees bordering the small clearing, they were far enough away that I'd have nowhere to hide if he were to glance back.

"True or not, that's what the police will determine." Topher eased forward, causing Hunter to take a step back, putting him alarmingly close to the railing, which was only waist high. A good push and he'd go tumbling down the hillside.

"Yeah? And what are you going to tell them about me?" Hunter asked.

"That's easy. I found a photograph of you and Professor Valentine. When you found out about it, you contacted me and I tried to give it to you, but you attacked me instead. I was forced to defend myself with whatever I could find." He hefted the stick. "Where is the photograph by the way?"

"I have it," Hunter said. I thought he was going to tell Topher that he'd put it somewhere safe, that if something were to happen to him, the real story would come out and he'd never get away with either murder.

But Hunter being Hunter, he said, "It's in the backpack with everything else."

I wanted to scream at him. If that was true, he was giving everything away. His leverage. The evidence. Once the backpack was in Topher's hands, he could do whatever he pleased, and who would say otherwise?

I would.

My hand trembled on the knife. Despite the fact that Topher had my brother's back to the void, I still wasn't sure I could use the knife on him. I wasn't a killer. I didn't even like to kill flies or spiders in my apartment.

"Set it down," Topher said, nodding toward the backpack. "Then step back against the rail, hands raised and empty."

Hunter eased the backpack down and then raised both hands as he stepped back. He was sweating and I could tell through the tension in his shoulders that he desperately wanted to look my way. I was his last hope.

Topher heaved a sigh. "Kick it over here."

Hunter did as he was told.

Stick held at the ready, Topher unzipped the backpack, glanced inside. I was getting closer, but not close enough. I could rush him, but if he heard me too early, he'd have time to react. His stick had a much longer reach than my knife. And while I'd have Hunter's help, he didn't have a weapon. There were no stray sticks or rocks near enough for him to reach.

"I just want to say that there's nothing personal here," Topher said, zipping the backpack back up. "Professor Valentine wouldn't go away on his own and I needed to find a way to get rid of him. You were a convenient scapegoat, easy to manipulate. For what it's worth, I'm sorry."

I hefted my knife, took a step forward. One more step and I could . . . well, I wasn't sure what I'd do. But I'd be close enough that Topher would have to take me and my knife seriously.

"This was all for Fay," Topher said. "We're going to have a happy life. Unfortunately, you won't be around for the wedding."

Hunter's eyes widened. "You don't have to—"

My phone went off.

Everything that followed seemed to happen all at once.

Topher spun around, his mouth forming a perfect O as he raised his stick. I rushed forward, still not sure what I was going to do, but needing to do *something.* Hunter likewise ran at Topher, but before he could leap upon him, he tripped over the backpack and went sprawling into the dirt with an "Oof!" that echoed off the trees.

I screamed. Topher swung.

And like a thing out of a movie, I, mid-stride, bent backward to avoid the blow from the stick. It wasn't a *Matrix*-like move exactly—I landed on my rear—but it sure felt like it as the stick whizzed past my face. It just barely missed my nose.

The missed swing put Topher off-balance like a batter trying to hit well outside the strike zone. He staggered, and nearly fell, putting his face about waist high in front of me.

I scrambled to my feet and then lifted my right knee like I

was doing the standing one knee to chest pose. In my head, George's voice corrected with *tadasana pavanmuktasana* as my knee connected to Topher's face on the rise. I smacked him on the back of the head with the hilt of my knife for good measure.

Topher dropped, body going limp. His stick bounced away, out of his reach, leaving him defenseless.

Not wanting to take a chance that this was a ruse of some kind, I leapt atop Topher's back and locked my knees against his sides. He groaned, but didn't otherwise make a move.

The faint sound of a siren approached, telling me Olivia, or one of the other officers, had gotten free of the square. Behind me, Hunter rose to his feet.

"Nice moves," he said. "You'll have to show me how to do that sometime."

"Come to class," I told him.

And then I settled in atop Topher's back to wait for the police to finally arrive.

"Mr. Newman confessed to everything," Olivia said before taking a large gulp of freshly squeezed lemonade. "Right down to the murder of Professor Valentine. He took one look at Chief Higgins and caved."

"I don't blame him," I said. "Chief Higgins is scary."

Olivia laughed. "He's a big teddy bear once you get to know him." She leaned forward and winked. "A teddy bear with claws."

A bunch of us were gathered in my apartment two days after Topher was arrested. My legs were burning from my yoga sessions earlier in the day, but I was feeling good. Great, even.

"Why did he leave Jonas at A Purrfect Pose?" I asked. "To frame me?"

Olivia shrugged. "I suppose he wanted Hunter to take the

fall. Since Hunter's your brother, he figured we'd make the connection."

"That doesn't make much sense," Sierra said with a shake of her head. "Hunter would never do something that would hurt Ash. And he wouldn't know a yoga pose, even if it slapped him upside the head."

"Or crashed into his nose," I added with a smile. My lower thigh still hurt from where it had met Topher's face.

Olivia spread her hands and shrugged. "Who knows why he thought what he did? Killers aren't known for their sharp minds." She paused. "Well, not all of them are. I'm pretty sure he was making it up as he went." She looked at me. "Chief Higgins still isn't happy with you, by the way."

"Even though I caught the bad guy?" I asked.

"You could have been hurt, Ash."

"I know." I looked around my apartment, which was crowded. Aaron and Henna were snuggled up close to one another on my couch, petting Luna, who was soaking in all the attention she could. Bri was talking to Kiersten, while Evan and Alexi stood protectively next to Hunter, who had the same chagrined look on his face that he'd had when the police had arrived to take Topher into custody.

Life was moving forward and everything was slowly getting back to normal. A Purrfect Pose was open again. CLU was looking for a new English instructor since Fay Valentine was leaving town. The science spot had already been filled, but I didn't know by whom. Walker Hawk was gone. Mom was still harping on me to come back to work at Branson Designs.

And Hunter . . .

He must have felt my attention on him because he glanced over my way, and then he strode across the room to join us.

"Hey, Sis," he said as Olivia and Sierra casually stepped away.

"Hey, Br—" I made a face. "Nope, not calling you 'Bro.' "

"It doesn't sound right coming from you."

"No, it does not."

"So . . ." He rubbed at the back of his head. "I should probably explain why I needed the money."

"Yes, you should."

He cleared his throat, made a show about how uncomfortable it made him to talk about it, and then he said it in a rush.

"I'm having a baby."

I stared at him, my mind supplying a pregnant Hunter and not quite figuring out how to make it compute. "Eh?"

He laughed. "I just found out about it a few months ago. And we're keeping it hush-hush, which is why I haven't told anyone. I wanted the money so I could make sure the kid's cared for."

"Hunter . . . I . . ." I shook my head. "I didn't even know you were dating anyone."

His face flushed red and he became very, very nervous. "Yeah, well, everyone's going to know soon enough."

I didn't like his tone one bit. "Care to explain?" I asked him.

"It's Lita."

I just stared at him. I had no idea who he was talking about.

"Lita Higgins."

All the air was sucked from the room. "Higgins? As in . . . ?"

"Chief Higgins's daughter," Hunter said. "We met when I was being held for something stupid a couple years back. We got to talking, and have been secretly seeing each other ever since."

Chief Higgins's *daughter?* I didn't even know he had a daughter.

And Hunter, my brother, had gotten her pregnant.

Oh boy. There's no way that was going to end well.

"Does Mom know?" I somehow managed to choke out through my shock.

"Yeah. It's why she gave me the money in the first place. I asked Dad, but he didn't have anything to give."

Mom knew. She'd looked me in the eye and hadn't said a word. A part of me was proud of her loyalty to a son I thought she was on the verge of disowning. She'd made it sound that way, anyway.

And Dad? It made sense that Hunter would have gone to him first. And hadn't Mom said something about Dad not having the money? It was staring me in the face the whole time.

Before I could come up with anything else to say, Sierra appeared. She threw an arm across my shoulder, grinned like a fool at my fool of a brother.

"Hey, Hunter. Staying out of trouble?"

He smiled, shot me a wink. "Oh, the trouble's just begun." And then he walked away.

"What was that all about?" Sierra asked.

I couldn't answer her. The moment Chief Dan Higgins learned about his daughter. With Hunter. A baby . . .

It looked like there might be another murder taking place in Cardinal Lake in the very near future.

"We should get started, Ash," Alexi said, joining us with Evan at her side. "The babysitter's only going to be able to watch the kids for another two hours."

I shook off my concern about Hunter. For now.

Besides, we weren't there to dwell on troubles. We were there to celebrate.

And to unpack.

"Okay, everyone!" I said, clapping my hands together and drawing every eye in the room. "Thank you for coming to my unpacking party."

A cheer went around the room.

I walked over to the nearest box and popped it open. A small part of my life lay inside, packed not so neatly away. On top was a simple thing, a photograph of my family, back before

Mom and Dad had split. Hunter, Alexi, and I were grinning stupidly into the camera. If I recalled correctly, Hunter had muttered something that had caused Alexi and me to nearly burst into laughter, and Mom to start to scowl and lean away from Dad just as the cameraman snapped the photo.

It was the perfect representation of our family, fractured or not.

I picked it up, held it high.

And then, with a grin a mile wide, I said, "It's time I turned this place into my home."

Visit our website at
KensingtonBooks.com
to sign up for our newsletters, read
more from your favorite authors, see
books by series, view reading group
guides, and more!

BOOK CLUB
BETWEEN THE CHAPTERS

Become a Part of Our
Between the Chapters Book Club
Community and Join the Conversation

Betweenthechapters.net